SIX-SIDED CRAP SHOOT

NASH RUNNING BEAR MYSTERY
BOOK SIX

BAER CHARLTON

Cover design by Roslyn McFarland, Far Lands Publishing

Sketch artist Kelly Eamon

Rogena Mitchell-Jones, Literary Editor
RMJ Manuscript Service, www.rogenamitchell.com

Published by Mordant Media, Portland, Oregon

ISBN: 978-1-949316-42-1 (Print)
ISBN: 978-1-949316-43-8 (eBook)

10 9 8 7 6 5 4 3 2 1

CONTENTS

Powder

OK

Diego Ignacio Constantino y Espinoza glanced at the ticket on the order wheel with a bittersweet tug. Judith's two on the over-easy eggs looked more like his first girlfriend's printed signature —Zoe.

At thirty-two, with more heroin injection tracks in her arms than she had veins, she was at the end of the street trash cycle. But she was more exotic than pathetic to a sixteen-year-old runaway from East Los Angeles. As his surrogate mother and lover, she had steered him away from injecting hard drugs. But the rest of the street had taken hold.

As he reached up with his tattooed left hand, movement across the street caught his eye. In the tiny town of Big Pine, a clean black SUV stands out as being a tourist or worse. The three men standing at the open back were the latter. Dice had seen the scene a hundred times before. Gang bangers and harder, passing out guns for a hit. There were no masks to hide their identities. This would not be a quiet robbery. This was a hit. A straight-up killing—with no witnesses.

He scanned the small restaurant. The four men huddled in the corner booth had come in over twenty minutes before. He had never seen them before. They still hadn't ordered more than coffee.

Dice rewound his memory tape. He recalled two of the four mysterious figures carrying large, heavy, black gym bags. It didn't raise any red flags at the time. As he thought about it more, he remembered there wasn't a gym in Big Pine. And the one in Bishop had been closed for six months. Something wasn't adding up.

The only other customer was the older lady in the first booth. Cricket Street always came in when her Social Security check arrived. She deposited it at the bank. Then she came into the restaurant. Her order never varied: tea, a side of two eggs over-easy, and dry wheat toast cremated around the edges. She said it reminded her of her late father's devil-may-care attitude toward life. She had worked for Inyo County, but he had been an undercover cop for Los Angeles.

Dice began slapping the small chrome bell with his steel spatula. "Judith, Mary, for the last fucking time, your orders are up. Come get them now before I throw them out."

The blond and the brunette slid up to the counter from both sides. "I don't have an order—"

Dice growled quietly. "Shut up. Both of you. Grab Cricket and drag her into the back with you. And you had better be there in four seconds. No excuses."

Mary opened her mouth.

"Now." He held up his oversized French knife. At six and a half feet tall, Dice favored a sixteen-inch blade instead of the standard ten.

He stood with the thick door to the cooler cracked open. As the girls burst through the door with the woman, he waved the knife at the opening.

"But I don't want to…"

Dice waved his knife in the air like it was his hand as he opened the door wider. Judith's eyes were enormous as the bell over the front door tinkled. He held his knife and finger to his lips. Slipping the knife into its holster on his hip, he reached for the top rack next to the door and grabbed the ratty old jacket. Shoving it into Judith's hands, he leaned in and warned them quietly. "Put this on Cricket so she doesn't freeze. Don't make a sound. And don't come out for at least ten or fifteen minutes. No matter what you hear."

Mary pointed toward the front. Dice shook his head. "I've got it. Not a sound, and stay in here."

The voices out front in the restaurant were getting louder as he closed the thick, insulated door. Bolting out the back door, he hustled to where he had parked his truck in the small alley, as his right hand found the functions on his watch. His old habit of timing actions pushed the button for the timer.

Reaching behind the seat of the older truck, he pulled out the .223 hunting rifle. He could drop a deer with a clean headshot, but the Marine Corps had trained him with worse to be more accurate. At least more accurate than he had learned on the mean streets of East Los Angeles as a young gang banger.

He pulled out the clip and checked. It was full. Pulling the bolt, he checked for the shell in the pipe. Reaching under the seat, he grabbed the extra clip.

At the end of the building, he turned toward the main street and the side window that looked into the restaurant. Stopping at the edge of the window, he pulled his knife from the sheath hanging from his belt. He slowly pushed the tip of the knifepoint across the lower corner of the window. Raising the knife, he could see the gunmen reflected in the mirror finish.

He flinched away as the window exploded from the gunfire. Sheathing his knife, he raised the rifle and waited. Counting five shotgun blasts. He waited for the two louder assault rifles to clear their clips. There were only a few small-gun gunshots from the four in the booth.

He heard a clip bounce metallically off the floor. Rolling along the wall to the edge of the blown-out window, he kept his body behind the window jamb and wall. The shotgunner was feeding more shells into his pump. The taller blond was fumbling with a fresh clip for his weapon.

Dice aimed his rifle at the head of the man, still standing with his rifle on his shoulder. He squeezed the trigger, and the man's blue eyes turned into one blue, and the other darkened—into blood. The man crumpled to the floor as the other two jerked at the sound of another gun.

Dice shifted his sights to the other rifleman's mouth, opening in surprise. Dice's shot severed his neck through the short goatee with a single shot. The body is still folding as Dice gives the shotgunner a center eye.

Leaning over the jagged edges of glass rimming the blown-out window, he scanned the four men in the booth. He guessed they were ground meat before the shotgun had destroyed the window. With the back of his knuckles, he felt the large bags. The forms inside moved distinctively. "Money." He looked across the street and snorted softly. He had seen it before in Los Angeles. The drug seller had thought about the large bags of money. And then decided to kill the golden goose and worry about finding a new one later.

From the size of the bags, Dice figured he could live comfortably in Mexico for many years, but without looking over his shoulder at every noise and shadow.

Looking behind, he found and picked up his three shells. From experience, he knew the hollow-point bullets would never be traceable. Carefully stepping out of the shattered glass gravel, he scanned for any sign he had been there. Two more tourist cars drove past. They were oblivious to anything but the music on their radios, the long miles driven, and more to come.

He walked back to his truck. Stowing the rifle, he dropped the three shells into his bag of other shells to be reloaded. He flipped his wrist. The counter on his watch clicked through the forty-seventh second. Climbing in, he drove the truck and parked it two blocks into the residential neighborhood. It would escape any police investigation.

Dice checked himself in the mirror on the back of the office door. He smirked at the small sign printed on the mirror, extolling *Presentation is Everything.*

Resetting his watch, he opened the cold room door to a tiny squeak from one waitress. Cricket sat quietly, wearing the jacket like a shawl.

The older woman glanced at the two waitresses. "We heard a bunch of gunshots."

Dice smiled at the unflappable nature of a woman who had seen everything and probably taken part in half of it. "You three can come out now. But you need to stay here in the back. I need to call the sheriff."

Judith examined him up and down. "Are you okay?"

He nodded. "Yeah. I was watching through the pass-through in case they might come back here."

She smirked. "And what would you have done? Cook them a bad burger?"

He slid the knife halfway out of its sheath.

She snorted. "Yeah. Big man with the knife. What happened out there?"

He tilted his head forward. "They shot each other."

2

GRAB A CAR

NASH LEANED her right hip against the ticket counter. Her voice
was soft and lowered so only the ticket agent could hear. The super-
visor, walking behind her, never flinched. "And we both have
weapons."

The ticket agent froze. Her eyes grew as the blood left her face.
Her mouth still trapped the tiny pink tip of her tongue as she raised
her face. It stopped at the thin wallets held at the edge of the high
counter.

Muna rolled along the edge of the counter. "Usually, we let
Magic Rick warn you guys, but we finished early and drove straight
over. According to the app on my phone, there were still a few seats
left on our two first-class flights." Her eyes circled in a roll and
came to a landing with the agent in the center. "Is there a
problem?"

The woman hummed. "I'm more used to federal employees
taking the super saver seats near the back."

Muna looked at Nash. "What was the air marshal saying about
getting stuck in a window seat with a woman and three babies in
row thirty-two?"

Nash shrugged. "I stopped listening after the part of the drunk breaking the flight attendant's jaw with another guy's head."

The ticket agent rolled her eyes. "Never happened. That was on Spirit, and they never get marshals. Let me see those flights again." She looked at the paper and then glanced back up at Muna. "And if you're going to spin a yarn, get the facts straight. They don't have thirty-two. Their rows stop at thirty. They have the extra bulkhead for the third bathroom because it's a shit show." She continued typing in the destinations.

Nash shrugged. "Don't forget the dog."

The ticket agent looked up and leaned forward to look at Powder. "She rides in the front. I'll see if we can find a companion seat for you."

Nash straightened as she fished the phone out of her pocket. She glanced at the caller as she thumbed the green icon. "Deputy director. We're just trying to find seats on planes."

"Yeah. Probably not so much."

Nash frowned. "What's up?"

The phone muffled from rubbing his shirt. "Thanks Millie. Tell him I'll call in the morning when I know more." The sound cleared. "Sorry about that. Do you remember where we stayed while probing the bombing range?"

Nash's eyes narrowed as her face turned to disgust. "Olancha. Yeah... why?"

"I think this is about fifty miles north of there and four hundred times nicer."

"Where?"

He noisily shuffled some paper near the phone. Nash could tell he was enjoying himself. The KABAR knife had stuck in his craw or funny bone. She wasn't sure which. "Ah... here it is. Big Pine."

"What are we looking at?"

Muna frowned and held her palm out to stop the ticketing agent.

"Seven dead. There is north of a few million dollars and a ton of brass on the floor. The LEO wants an expert to look at it. They're holding the crime scene."

Nash mouthed the word, *fuck*. "Have they moved the bodies?"

Tony shuffled the papers together and tapped them straight on the top of the desk. Nash could tell he had shifted to his speakerphone. "Evidently, the first on the scene had just enough time to count bodies and make it back out the front door so as not to soil the scene."

Nash looked at the ticketing agent and rolled her eyes as her head vibrated. "So, I have to step over someone's vomit to get to my crime scene. And we're catching this because…?"

The deputy director paused the tapping of papers. "Did I mention there was a boatload of brass and shotgun shells?"

Nash picked up her Go-bag and nodded away from the ticket counter. "So they suspect it was a professional hit. Jesus, Tony, this is California. They grow those right next to the cauliflower and lettuce. Accessories are on aisles ten and fourteen."

"Professional hit squad who got whacked themselves. It's less than twenty miles from the state line. And two large bags of what they believe is cash."

Nash nodded at the sign, pointing toward the car rentals. "What? No reservation to throw in there, Tony?"

Even through the growl, she could hear the smirk. He had done his research. "Paiute reservation is seventeen miles away in Bishop. The temperature won't drop below forty tonight. You might want a faster car. If you can find one."

Nash thumbed the red icon as she pointed the phone at the green sign. Muna smirked with understanding.

Muna flashed her badge. "Where are you hiding a Hell Cat in white, please?"

The man could have passed for central casting's number-one pick for Ichabod Crane. His bony fingers paused on the keyboard as his eyes slowed at the identification and badge, and then he took in the two women. "We don't. Your type never brings them back in rentable condition."

Nash leaned in. "If you check with San Francisco, they can confirm I returned a red one. We had it detailed and clean, ready for frontline exposure."

He held her stare through several heartbeats. With his left hand, he reached out and picked up his phone, pushing the side button. "This is Jonathan at LAX. Did you guys ever have a Hell Cat in red?" His nod was spare. "Yeah, those are only on the exotic lot... but you rented it to an FBI agent?" He hummed through another explanation. "What condition upon return?" His one eyebrow was a perfect imitation of Mister Spock. He hung up.

He looked at Nash. "I apologize for being skeptical. We hear horror stories about some of our cars. Vegas gets cars back with dead bodies in the trunk or bullet holes in the trunks and windows. They had one a while back; it ended up in a war zone movie. Even the engine was driven to hell. Some people have no respect."

Nash nodded as her eyes drooped in commiseration. She pointed at Muna. "Well, she's an excellent driver. No speeding tickets or even a jay-walking ticket to her name. We just need a solid car with a solid engine. It doesn't have to be a Hemi."

His eyebrow seemed to be pinned to his upper brow. "And the white?"

Muna cleared her throat. "The most common fleet color. A gray or tan would also work. They're the least noticeable. On second thought, the gray or tan would be better."

His scrutiny shifted to the shorter agent. His fingers typed and then paused. "I have a Chrysler three hundred. Silver gray. It's got four thousand miles on it, so it's broken in." He glanced at Nash. "It's a five-point-seven-liter engine. Will that work? They have large gas tanks, so if you keep your foot out of it, they're good for about four hundred miles."

Muna handed him her ID and credit card. "I think we have a frequent flyer number as well."

He gave her a hard look.

Nash pushed the green icon on her phone.

"Travel. This is… Oh, hello, Super Agent. What can I do for you tonight?"

"Evening, Mister Magic. I'm glad you're in late."

"Just flogging the Hawaii stuff. What's up?"

"We're at LAX. We're trying to rent a car."

"Pass the phone over to them. I've got you covered."

The man looked at the phone skeptically. "Hello?"

The agent listened and then typed in a few keystrokes. "Oh yes. I see it here now. Yes, sir. A pleasure doing business with you. When are you coming down to see your son again?" He smiled. "Great. We'll see you then, Rick." He hung up the phone and handed it back to Nash. "Next time, Agent. Lead with the big gun."

Nash smiled. One never knows who knows whom.

The man picked up his walkie-talkie as the printer ground out the paperwork. "Jose, please bring up the Chrysler three hundred number one-seven-three-four. Make sure the windows are clean and park it at the curb."

The radio crackled. "K."

Nash side-eyed the paperwork. "Don't you need my driver's license number as well?"

He hung his head at her. "It was in there the moment I put her information in. We're used to you tag-teaming our cars. Magic Rick just helped justify the request for horsepower. And a better rate. Just keep it in California, and don't pull a Colorado with it. It's a lovely car. Even if Rick vouches for you."

Nash didn't even glance at the speedometer when Muna was driving. She rested her head against the cool glass and drifted in and out. Even Powder opted for the backseat and spread out.

Muna nosed the car up behind what looked like it could be a federal unit, except it was a black Suburban instead of an Explorer.

This close to the border, the Nevada plate was meaningless. "Either they called in another crew, or it's a tourist."

Nash rolled her head and looked out the front window. She blinked. "Private. Wrong plates for a federal unit. Even the undercover doesn't use the commercial format. See any LEOs?"

Muna pointed to the other side of the restaurant. The tan nose of a sheriff's cruiser was the only part lit by the light from the streetlight. Nash guessed the officer went lights-out right after they rolled up the sidewalks in a small town. She shrugged her face as she rolled her eyes. "Let's break out the Vicks and work the crime scene."

Nash frowned. "You up for this?"

The smaller woman smirked. "What, you never pulled an all-nighter after a long day?"

Nash pulled her door handle. "Just checking."

Muna pushed her door open. "I've got your back, Senior Agent. Let's see how messy the children were."

They popped the trunk while Powder found some grass. Pulling the crime scene bag open, Nash bent into the trunk. "Let's see what Los Angeles gave us and never expected to get back." She pulled out two boxes of gloves and checked the sizes. One large and one small. "Ah… they remembered. I'm touched."

Muna pulled the other bag open. Evidence bags were on top, covered by a full strap of yellow evidence teepees. She laid them out in the trunk. She scanned the lights, dusting powder kits, and other gear most missed when they built their kits. Smiling, she pulled out the small envelope and straightened her back. Sliding the card out, she recognized the handwriting of the squint in the labs. She handed the card to Nash.

Nash stood to get the light on the card. "What's this?" Opening the card, she read. "Kick ass, you two. We WIFLEs need to stick together. Sigourney." She looked at Muna. "Was she the one in the autopsy?"

Muna nodded. "She started before you were born. She

mentioned the year she started in the autopsy. I didn't say anything —it was before my parents got married."

Nash smiled as she handed the card back. "Save this. As Mina would say, she deserves a gushy bouquet."

Muna washed her hand over her crime scene kit. "And about twenty pounds of dark chocolate."

Movement caught Muna's eye.

Nash followed her look across the street. The deputy still rubbed his eyes and face as he crossed the four empty lanes.

The deputy's rumbling voice was what Nash's father used to call deep water. "Are you two the FBI agents I'm supposed to wait for?"

Nash nodded. "Any coffee around here?"

The man chuckled. "I'll buy it if you fly it. The restaurant is closed. But Bishop is only fifteen up the road. Jacks is twenty-four-seven and has better coffee than anything we have at the sub-station. But if you're going, I'll want some breakfast, too."

Muna looked at Nash. "They'd probably have it ready and packed when I get there." She turned back to the deputy. "What do you want to order?"

"Cowpuncher. Full stack of pancakes, three eggs, bacon, and sausage."

Nash growled. "It'll be cold and hard as Uncle's heart when she gets it back here."

The man smirked. "It's not your usual crime scene. We can still get at and use the microwave in the kitchen and the other end of the waitress station."

Nash thought for a moment. "Call them. Order four of them and as much coffee as possible in hot carafes. I read the preliminary report. We can bring more food later, but coffee will be critical."

Nash frowned as she looked at Muna. "What about the pork?"

Muna shrugged and pointed at Powder. "She gets extra rations."

The deputy chuckled. "The cook might be Norm. He's Jewish. He'll know what to swap for the pig. How do you like your eggs?"

"Anyway, they can't fly away. The place was Jack's?"

"Halfway through town. On the left. You can't miss it."

Nash closed the trunk. "We'll be back shortly."

The man smiled as he pointed across the street. "You can park next to my cruiser when you get back. I'll pull down the tape over the entrance."

3

WALK US THROUGH

THE THREE SAT LOOKING at the dark parking lot and the back of the two cars. Most of the food was good, even after the microwave. The eggs were standard rubber. Jacks had understood the assignment and packed an insulated pressure coffee urn with two gallons of coffee.

Nash swallowed and wiped the napkin at her mouth. "You weren't the first on the scene…"

Deputy Johnson's voice was like the smooth sand at the bottom of a deep well. It took time for the sound to rattle up the pipe, but it oozed gently and was comforting when it got out. "Watkins was. He's on the day shift. We don't get this kind of stuff up here. Mostly some pot or drugs. There will be a fistfight or three at the start of the fishing season, but we usually babysit the area. Independence gets most people trapped on the side of Mount Whitney or the occasional shot hunter. But we're not the big city. It's why I moved here after I got back from touring the sandcastles. With my aversion to loud noises, I wanted peace and quiet."

Muna looked through the top of her eyes as she bit the end of the toast. Chewing, she pointed her thumb toward the other end of the restaurant. "Did you look over the quiet bloodbath, Vern?"

His chuckle came from deep down the well in his chest. "I did. I used my Boy Scout binoculars from over here while there was still light. After this mess, my therapist at the VA will enjoy full employment again."

Nash pushed the last of her eggs and bacon over to Powder. "What's your take on the firefight?"

"The two guns I could see in the booth were nines. A couple of holes start below the table and splinter the top. I'm guessing there will be some skid marks as well. But looking at the three over here, they were standing. And even in this dawn light, I can see they wore vests. But the bleed-out is from the heads. But then, I only looked from here. I wanted to leave your scene pristine." He smirked at Nash.

Her quick laugh was all breath. "You didn't want to risk blowback for shitting on my crime scene." Her side-pulled smirk matched his. "Which service?"

"ANG." He turned to Muna, frowned, and smiled at her half-cocked head. "Air National Guard for the civilians. It's like the military, except for all the walking and naps. And despite what the bubble heads try to tell you, in the sand, nobody had better food." His smile grew to match hers. He could tell she was a quick study to take in information. "I started with comms or communications. Commonly thought of as radio, but we could also direct helicopters, sorties, or just be ordering pizza takeout."

Nash's snickered softly. She looked over at Muna. "Ordering a takeout pizza is calling in a drone or air strike on a residential location. Usually, you hoped, was lit up by a targeting laser." She turned back to the man, pushing away half his breakfast as he sipped more coffee. "And they moved you into..."

His eyes rolled to one side, and his eyelids eased down and opened. "It was like someone called a comms convention. There were six grunts for every job. So I found myself some entertainment. The base commander found me stripping down some hanger queens and asked if I enjoyed wrenching. I looked him in the eye and told him I hate the smell of oil and burned grease or getting dirty."

Nash barked a laugh.

"Yeah. His Class-A inspection went from my solid black hands up my black arms and smeared my chest and face." He rolled his eyes. "He pointed at my red, blistered bare feet and told me I had to wear Jesus slippers until I got the fungus under control."

Nash smirked as she leaned back with her mug near her mouth. "Damnedest nasty stuff. Rarely cures until you hit stateside."

Vern wagged his brush-cut head. "Nope. The real deal. It took coming home and about a month of nightly soaks in the alkaline hot springs up Bishop's way to almost cure. A buddy wanted me to hunt with him up in the Mono Craters. We camped on the backside of Mono Lake. I knew I wasn't cured when I first stepped into the water. But the next night, it didn't burn so much. On the third night, we went swimming. That night, we found every scratch, bruise, abrasion, or insult our skin had ever collected. But by the end of the five days, we had a winter's worth of deer meat, a year of jerky, and no more sand rot."

Muna smirked at the commonality the man and Nash shared between the military and the hunting. "Did you go back?"

"To the sand?" He shook his head. "I was done." He glanced at Powder's intense stare. The tongue slipped out and wiped her upper lip. He pushed his plate over to her.

"No. The lake."

He chuckled. "Sure. Anytime we need meat. I only have deer and coyote in my freezer."

Nash rolled her eyes with a yawning smile. "Coy what?"

His smile pursed. "The Fish and Game call them Tule Elk. The ranchers around here call them an expensive pest. A herd can wipe out a couple of acres of young alfalfa in a single night. Taking a few of them a year doesn't affect a herd of a few thousand, but it can feed many people who can't afford much more than mac and cheese. We spread it around where we know it will help."

They sipped on their coffee as the warm pink of the sky turned more yellow.

Nash put down her empty mug as she looked at the other end of the restaurant. "A couple of shots through the table... I'm guessing with maybe matching holes in the ceiling?" Her eyes danced around the table, looking for an answer. "Under the table at the short distance might have gotten some leg, and then upper shot when they fell..."

He softly rocked. "How much did you see in the sand?"

"More than my share. Why?"

He pushed his chin down the restaurant. "Take a look. Dead while they were falling, or dead when they dropped?"

Nash looked at the three mounds on the floor. They weren't spread out like they were reaching. They puddled like dropped damp towels in the bathroom. Her eyes stepped from spot to spot and back. The one black form in the booth with the pistol still hanging from the finger. The other form, half coming from the bench like a waterfall onto the floor. A glint of steel caught in his crotch. And back to the three large rag piles on the floor.

Her eyes narrowed as she looked at the deputy. "I don't think it's all here."

Half of his forehead raised as he nodded a twitch. "My guess is only about ninety percent of it." He pointed at the scene. "I'm out on my speculative limb here. But I think the window blew out with the first rounds of the shotgun. The long guns are most likely full auto, judging by the random spread of holes. The defenders didn't have time to get their pistols above the table. They were expecting buyers instead of an ambush. Everything is a hot mess, and then someone's clip is empty. Maybe the shotgun is first, or maybe second. But he's reloading, and I'm betting it's a pump, not a clip... And then Mister Final drops the three. Bing, bang, bong."

Muna squints one eye. "Where's Mister Final, and what's he shooting?"

Vern points at the window. "He's on the other side of the

window. They cleared the glass for him, so it doesn't matter if what he's shooting is small and quiet. It just needs to be accurate." His mouth screws up as he thinks. "A low velocity like a 30-30 still has enough punch to cause a lot of damage and leave the skull. An AR-15 is small but also fast and powerful. It'll whip through a head and still leave the guy time to finish his thought. A .22 long-rifle would work if the shooter were exceptionally good. But the least off, and it's just a facial crash. But they dropped these. So I will guess either a Tokarev TT or the Makarov PP if it's a pistol or a .223 for a rifle."

Muna wiggled on the bench as she leaned into the discussion. "Let's stick with the Russians. TT or PP and why?"

His eyes opened wider. "Hmm, a shooter." His smile widened. "The TT has a bit more stopping power, and if you're shooting from across the street, it has more accuracy. But the bullet would still exit the skull. The PP is lighter, smaller, easier to conceal, but still with the stopping power of the British PPK or our .380." His head rocked back and forth. "So, I'd go with the PP. It's quieter as well."

Nash glanced out the window at the full morning light. "Ready to string some tape?"

Vern smiled at the clean plates in front of Powder. "I've got about a thousand yards of fresh tape. And your dog needs some lawn." He pointed over his shoulder and across the parking lot. "Nobody will mow the edging over this way in the next decade."

Nash looked at Powder as Muna slid out of the booth. "Did you hear the man? The potty is over there. But I'll be over here, but I don't want you near the broken glass."

Powder glanced up and gave her a nose and a tiny tongue on the chin.

Nash started sliding out. "We're good."

Vern snorted a soft laugh as he slid out. "I wish my kids had been that easy."

They stood in the doorway, watching Powder go to where she knew the accepted toilet was. Nash turned. "How old?"

"The twenty-five-year-old boy is just finishing his master's down in Irvine. And the girl is just wrapping up her extra credits at a tiny college over the hills in Deep Springs."

Nash smiled at knowing about the most obscure college in the United States. "My wife is a Springer. Fine college."

His eyes opened tall. "Does she run the universe?"

Muna stepped out behind them. "Pretty much."

They turned.

Muna burped a happy harrumph. "Well, at least the Washington D.C. part of the universe. What's your Anteater do?"

His right eyebrow ticked the last notch higher. "If you say you graduated from Irvine, I'm going to stop right here."

Muna leaned her head with a smirk. "We know people."

"He's an electrical engineering geek."

Nash pursed her lips. "Computers or green energy?"

Vern's eyes narrowed. "I think both. He was the lead builder for the solar racer they ran all the way across—"

Nash and Muna chorused. "Australia."

Nash closed her eyes, tilted her head back, and pointed at Muna. "And they came in…?"

Muna squinted one eye. "I want to say first… but I'm going to go with second. There was a problem with a back axle or something."

Vern laughed. "What's the sex ratio of the team, and how many collective toes do they have?"

Muna giggled. "The team is skewed female, and Baby is missing her two pinkies."

His face fell open. "How…?"

Nash pushed his mouth closed. "Like we said. We know people. And if he's friends with Baby, she's probably already assessed him about going to work for the company she works for."

"He said something about dredging rivers and bays or something."

Nash nodded. "Best playdate he could ever spend his life at. We're going to get our gear."

Powder stopped and looked both ways down the empty highway before tagging along behind the women. Vern studied the two long black braids, white shirts, and black leather pants. Only the nature of the boots was different. He guessed military and non-military.

4

SORTING THE EXPECTED

THE TRUNK WAS STILL cool as Nash reached in. But as she touched the crime scene bag, her hands and forearms warmed as if from a fireplace. She paused, expecting a vision to continue. But it was only the warm flush in her hands.

"Nash?"

"I'm good. Just..." She grabbed the handles and pulled the bags from the well. "Curious. My hands and arms got warm when I touched the bags. It's gone now, but it felt like it was going to..."

Muna tilted her head. "A vision?"

"Yeah. But it was just the physical flush." She closed the trunk. Looking across the main street, she snorted softly at Powder sitting at the back doors of a black SUV. It made little sense. The early morning had no warming heat. They watched Powder as they returned to the restaurant and the waiting deputy.

The deputy bobbed his chin out. "Is she going to just sit in the sun all day?"

Nash glanced back and called. "Goofball. Not every black SUV is a drug dealer..."

Muna stared at her and then peered back at the interior crime scene. "Unless they are..."

They turned toward the deputy as a battered truck turned out of the side street and headed south. "Recognize the truck?"

He shook his head as he raised his radio to his mouth. He peeked at his watch. "Too early." Returning the radio to his hip, he drew out his cell phone. He peered north as the phone rang. "Hey, George? Vern." He drew the upper lip and a thin blond mustache through his teeth. "I'm in Big Pine. I need a Slim Jim to have some doors popped on a Chevy SUV." He swung to face south. "Okay. Thanks. I'm at the restaurant. You won't miss the yellow tape."

Nash studied him as he hung up. "You don't carry lock-out gear in your cruiser?"

He winced. "Maybe. But them getting here from Bishop is usually faster than me trying to open a convertible with the top down. Besides, he gets a forty-five-buck bump at the end of the month."

Muna nodded. "Play to your strengths and spread it around." She glanced over her shoulder. "Should I call the boys?"

"Let's see what we've got first." Nash snapped open her bag and tugged out the large gloves. "I'll start at the end of the building. Help Vern run the tape out before the citizens poke their noses where they don't belong. And then take photos." She looked at the deputy. "Did you guys do any photos yet?"

"The medical examiner is up in the backcountry with a doe tag, hoping it's not a bust for the fourth time. The photographer just started their three weeks of school photos. He can't get away unless it's during an evening..." The deputy's voice trailed off with the litany of fighting crime in the country on a borrowed shoestring.

Nash snapped the wrist of the blue glove. "Let me guess. The forensics team is out inoculating a herd of cows and will be available right after church."

Vern's voice dropped a register as his shoulders slumped. "Sounds like you've been here before."

Nash waved her finger back and forth along the street. "This?

This is the town I grew up in—only a third the size and half as many dogs. Let me see what I can do."

She pulled her phone out and searched for the number. "Maggie, please. Special Agent Nash Running Bear calling." She mirrored a half smile at Muna as she watched the thin smile grow with recognition. "Hey, Maggie. Do you know where Big Pine is in the Owens Valley?"

As she listened, she frowned. She lowered the phone and squinted at the deputy. "You have fishing here?" At the man's smile, she raised the phone. "Yeah Mags. He said to bring your fishing guns as well. And can you drag an experienced photographer as well?" Her eyes closed as she nodded. "Seven that we can see so far. If you can catch a chopper, I'm sure we can get it covered. If not by your DD, I'll strong-arm mine. This is a complicated scene, and I need the best for it. Thanks. I'll call Washington now."

Muna held her hands up. "And...?"

Nash looked at them and then around. "Where's the crime tape?"

Muna growled as Nash poked the number for the deputy director.

"Yeah, Nash?"

"I need a KABAR prober or a huge solid."

The deputy director viewed the blinking button on his desk phone. "You called on my cell phone, so I'm guessing it's the solid you really want."

"I need the team out of Los Angeles to come do the forensics and photo work. There's a lot here. And I don't think it's what looks so obvious on the surface."

"Okay..."

"I need them now. As in helicopter now."

He glanced up as his secretary stepped into the doorway. "Done. You're covered. Call me at dawn tomorrow and fill me in."

The phone snicked a metal finish in her ear.

Nash redialed the previous number. "Tell Maggie she has clearance for any helicopter she needs to get here ASAP. I don't care if it has a bunny on the side. Just get it and get here. Thanks." She stowed the phone and bent to play with Powder's ear. "Why don't you take a nap? I need to go play in the broken glass."

The text ringtone vibrated her pocket. She pulled it out and frowned at the number and text.

"Cavalry at Reno. On the way."

Nash frowned as she slipped the riddle back into her pocket. *Why would the boys be on their way? And where are they going?*

She stood at the end of the building. The shattered glass made an arch pattern. Most of the pellets of tempered glass reached nine or ten feet. The shape of the scatter sloped back to the sides of the window. At the edges, the glass pellets were as much inside as out.

If the shotgun was an automatic, it could have been the double hump she had seen years ago in another case. The second spray of tiny lead pellets and their air movement had pushed the falling rain of glass fragments in a second direction. But this single hump pattern confirmed the deputy's assessment of a pump shotgun. The second fired shell was too slow to distort the fall of the rain of glass.

Nash studied the small parking lot and then the next side of the street. Across the street was another parking lot for what looked like a hardware store. The solid brick wall seemed pecked at by decades of heat and storms. A few pellets of lead, or even the substantial bullets of whatever the other two were shooting, weren't worth searching for. She turned back to scanning the scatter.

Standing at the glass field's peak, she peered into the restaurant. She could barely see the three bodies on the floor. Standing, they would have been easier targets. But she still thought she was in the wrong location.

Before studying house-to-house tactics at Quantico, she cleared houses, hovels, and buildings in the sandbox. The drill instructor's hard-bitten voice on the tiny island in San Diego had gone a long way toward her bringing her team home. Tactical vests look sexy until they aren't enough.

Nash shifted to her left and closer to the wall instead of the open window. Six feet from the wall, she squatted. The shatter was uniform across the first three feet of the pattern. Pulling out her tiny Mag Light, she shined it along the left edge of the pattern. About two feet out from the wall, a slight white swirl appeared among the sparkling pellets. The swirl was where heavy shoes or boots had pivoted—grinding the pellets to smaller dust. Only one footprint. The right. The shooter stood protected behind the wall and then stepped out, turned, and fired.

She drew out her phone and tried to take a photo. It didn't show right, even when zooming in and holding out her arms. The vibration startled her, and she dropped the phone. It landed outside the pattern. *Shit.*

She tried to thumb the phone open, but the glass wouldn't read the gloves. *Shit.* She bit her left index finger and tore the end of the glove off.

She glared at the senseless number. "Running Bear."

"We're at the truck stop in Minden. Is Muna with you?"

"Who the hell is this?"

She could almost feel the blush through the phone. "Um... Felix?"

Nash groaned and reached out to rest her left hand on the building. The heel of her hand pushed on the window trim. "What are you guys up to?"

"Um... you'd have to talk to Uncle about that. He rattled our cage at two this morning and said we had fifteen minutes to get the bus on the road."

Her finger hovered over the wood, poised to tap in impatience. Her eyelids drifted closed. "And the toy box?"

"Fully loaded and loaded for... um... bear?"

And there it is... Her finger dropped to the wood of the window trim. The contact was complete.

The window shattered as the rumbling blast from a shotgun roared through the room. A steady rain of bullets followed, two coming from automatic rifles and another from a closer handgun.

Thud! A bullet tore its way through the metal frame of the large window, sending a shudder through Nash's body, making her heart slow. It was her training—remaining unwavering when your body desperately craves to run or fight. She waited while counting until she heard the distinct sound of a metal clip dropping onto the hard linoleum floor and bouncing away. Then, the other automatic stopped firing.

Peeking over the edge of what had been a large window, Nash sighted through the open sites of her varmint rifle at the man feeding shells into his shotgun. His eye disappeared just before he folded like empty laundry. Moving right, she aimed an automatic rifle and fired. A dot appeared through the chin and throat. Shifting to the last man standing, the hole pierced through his neck. Gurgles escaped from his grasping hand as he dropped.

Focusing on the probing hand, she saw a similar color between it and her as it blindly felt with the back of two knuckles for something in the large bag. Money. As it rolled over to withdraw, she saw the heavy tattooing.

"Nash?"

"Did we lose you?"

"Hey Indian? Are you there?"

Nash twitched, and she examined her finger—now raised from the sun-battered wood. "Yeah. Yeah, Uncle. I'm here."

"I thought you had hung up on the kid. What did you need?"

She withdrew her gloved hand from the window frame, staring at the one naked finger. "Need? I didn't call you. Felix called me. What are you boys up to?"

"You called about one o'clock this morning. Woke me up. Thomas heard the phone ring across the pasture. You said to get the boys and the toy box and to head for Bishop. What are you doing?"

Nash shook her head. "No phone call. I slept the whole way. Muna drove. We left L.A. at about nine. She was hell-bent to get here as soon as possible."

"That's a lot of hurry-up just to get to last night's stick game."

She could feel the old man's stare through the phone and four hundred miles away. "Maybe. But we didn't want the local flies to shit on our seven bodies and four million dollars."

The whistle was low and long. "You sure pull the doozies. So why are we coming?"

"I keep… just a minute." She held the phone out in front of her and washed the conversation away. She tapped the green button to call up her phone app. She selected the past calls. There was a six-hour gap from when she left Los Angeles and arrived in Big Pine.

She cycled back to Uncle. "Just like I said. The last call last night was nine forty-eight in Los Angeles. The next call was at four fifteen this morning. No calls to you. What did you hear me tell you?"

The quietness felt heavier than a death sentence. Nash knew they were both beginning to realize what type of call it had been.

But what did Thomas hear?

Uncle's voice sounded like a low rumbling from the innermost depths of his soul, almost inaudible. "We're coming. Watch your backside, Indian."

5

HELICOPTERS AND OTHER FLYING OBJECTS

THE TRUCK PULLED UP, and Vern walked out to grab the bags. No money, no chatting, just a delivery.

The three had dug into the stew. It felt good in the light chill of the day. Nash guessed it wouldn't get much above fifty-eight by two o'clock before it started colder. They had shut off the gas. Nobody was cooking, and the crime scene didn't need to be heated.

Nash froze with a spoon of stew in her mouth. She frowned and looked around.

Muna closed one eye as she looked at Nash. "The buzzing sound?"

"Yeah..."

The three stood as Nash's pocket vibrated. She glanced at the caller. "What's up Alex?"

"Uncle's parking. We're about a block away in a school parking lot. Felix already has a mapper working on the south side of the restaurant. Please don't shoot it. It's powder blue with tiny red blinking lights. As we get stable, I'll take over the mapper, and he'll bring in some gnats to map the interior."

Nash slid out of the booth and stepped over to look down the length of the restaurant. She spotted the blue drone. She watched as it drifted back and forth across the glass debris field. "The mapping is…?"

Felix's younger voice cut in. "It's 3-D mapping. Once we have it all, we can call it holographically or on the computer. If we need to, we can convert the file to an STL file, and Muna can print it out on one of her 3-D printers." She could hear him grunting and then the bus door opening. "I'm bringing my new little drones. So we can map anything in a building."

Nash's phone vibrated in her hand. She glanced at the new caller. "Gotta go, Felix." She poked the screen and heard the roar of a helicopter. "Maggie?"

The voice was almost strident. "Nash. The pilot says we're at the south end of Big Pine. What are we looking for?"

"Same as always, Maggie. Yellow tape. It's an inside and outside job. Come up the Main Street." She turned to see Vern pointing at the field across the small side street. "Watch for me in the street. You're going to park just past the restaurant." The roar stopped, and Nash headed for the door. She glanced back at Muna. "Have Felix—"

"Oof." The young man with cases in his hands stumbled back.

Nash smiled and steadied him. "Sorry. I didn't see you. I've gotta go direct traffic. Get set up, but don't start until I'm back. Muna can help."

She looked down the main street as she pushed through the glass door. The distinct shape of a Blackhawk was patiently flying about a hundred feet above the street. She held her hand out at the small, white sedan, hesitating to drive into the helicopter's path. The man's window lowered.

Nash smiled. "Go ahead. He's going to be landing over here. They're friendlies."

The man glanced at the restaurant strung with yellow crime tape. "I wasn't sure…" He rolled his window up as he picked up speed.

Nash waved at the Air Force Pave Hawk. Her two arms were

straight up in a touchdown configuration. Then, her right arm dropped to indicate the field of broken asphalt with the half-burned-out building sitting at the back. She guessed at a used car lot at one time. Probably the roaring nineties before the recession.

The chopper nosed up and swung the tail around. There was no wind, so the pilot was setting down for ease of dismounting the forensic team. Nash crossed her arms as the helicopter settled for the pilot to shut down. A white hand appeared in front of his dark face shield. The engines cycled into silence, and just the swoosh of the blades disturbed the air.

The woman slid out of the side door and turned to hand her helmet back. Pulling two black cases, she turned and hunched over as she strode out under the swinging blades.

Nash stuck her hand out. "Welcome to Big Pine, Maggie. Let me take a case."

She handed over the smaller one. "Thanks, Nash. Don't drop it. It's the most important one."

Nash frowned at the battered olive-drab metal case. It looked like someone had kicked the case out of more helicopter doors than Nash had been as a SEAL. "Fingerprinting?"

The woman smiled. "Fishing tackle."

Nash laughs. "You might want to talk to Deputy Vern Johnson. The only fishing is the Owens River. He mentioned Nightcrawlers, some weight, and treble hooks if you're keeping the fish."

Maggie smiled. "The only things I fish for are perps." She pointed at the battered case. "It was my father's fingerprint dusting kit. He gave it to me when I graduated from Quantico. With a lifetime membership of WIFLE from my mother. She was Capital Police for seventeen years before they transferred to San Diego."

As they entered the restaurant, a cluster of tiny drones hovered in the air over the counter. Maggie raised an eyebrow at Nash. Nash smirked. "Boys and their toys, meet Felix." She pointed at the young man beside Muna, sitting in the last booth near the bathrooms. The ubiquitous laptops were open in front of them.

Maggie leaned closer. "There's a young girl there, too."

"That's Muna."

Maggie teased. "Thee Muna? Where are the pork rinds?"

Muna glanced up. She raised her right hand in the Vulcan salute. "Live long."

Maggie giggled at someone knowing her secret love. She responded with the Klingon saying, "Today is a good day to die."

Felix looked up and then leaned back in the booth. "I'm just calibrating the swarm before we task them to mapping. I noticed they shot through the table. You want the 3-D of the underside as well, right?"

Nash nodded. "How long will it take to map the interior so they can get to work?"

He leaned forward and started typing. "I'll send them as a rotating swarm. It's risky, but they should have the crime scene half of the restaurant done in an hour. They can start on the outside. Alex already called back the Falcon, and it's rendering the glass now on Muna's mainframe. It took so long because of the refractive nature of the glass pellets. But it'll be reproducible within a thousandth of a percent."

Nash snorted softly. "I expect nothing less." She watched the other end of the restaurant as the swarm of tiny drones took their various positions above the bodies. "Where's—?"

The deep voice was more like tumbling rocks in a small stream. "I see the calvary has arrived."

Nash and Maggie turned toward the two men in the doorway.

"Well, as I live and breathe. What are you doing in the Southlands, Uncle?"

Nash squinted one eye. "You know each other?"

Uncle stepped in for a hug. "Of course we do. I got the second dance at her wedding."

Maggie hugged and then pushed him back but held his shoulders as she looked at Nash. "I married DEA. My husband likes to think he can hunt. But he never brings anything back we can't buy at the market. I figure he just goes up to sit and drink whatever they drink up in the hills."

Nash growled. "Have you ever had iced Squaw Tea?"

"Only when we make sun tea with a lot of mint and some packets of the other stuff. If there isn't some caffeine, why drink it?" She frowned at Uncle. "What are you doing here?"

He jerked his thumb over his shoulder at the deputy crossing the street toward the tow truck. "I think I'm here for what they find."

Maggie studied the large black SUV. "Not your usual tourist wagon."

Nash shook her head. "Chevy. Not the usual federal fleet, either."

"The Hoss Cartwright in the tow truck?"

Nash grinned. "To pop the locks, the deputy can't."

Maggie crossed her arms as she ground around to look squarely at Nash. "I thought all cops knew how to…?"

Nash closed her eyes and pushed her chin toward the two men across the street. "Some kind of rural jurisdiction dispute. If the chain of custody isn't broken, I don't get into pissing matches on the back of the barn. Their playground, their rules. I just want the job done."

The large Chevy driver's door swung open. The tow truck driver adjusted his ten-gallon cowboy hat, leaned in, and tapped a button with something. Every eye watched as they walked to the back doors and opened them.

The cowboy stepped back as he held up his hands. Vern nodded to Uncle.

Uncle pulled on the blue gloves as he walked across the street. Three cars slowed and stopped as he glared at them. He didn't look like law enforcement, but they had seen the mass of yellow tape, the sheriff's deputy, and the hulking helicopter in the empty field of a parking lot. Blue gloves are blue gloves.

Nash stepped out of the restaurant's glass door as the rest of

Maggie's crew waddled up with black cases sporting various stickers on them.

The tall blond in the dark blue LAPD windbreaker gently put his cases down. He glanced at the men standing around the black SUV and then at Maggie. "Part of the crime scene?"

The older Indian with the twin braids past his chest stepped back. He looked across the street. He pointed at Nash. Then, putting the edge of his open hand against his mouth, he moved it forward, pointing with his entire hand. He held up his hands to show the size of a medium dog, and then his left hand was two fingers. His right hand worked like a small bird picking at the other hand's fingers. Finally, he grabbed the two fingers and brought his hands down.

Maggie groaned. "Tell me you understand his sign language."

Nash harrumphed. "Easy. Old Indian say that when three white men go hunting other evil white men, they haul a metric butt-load of very nasty drugs. Schedule two. Probably fentanyl. Maybe three million dollars' worth. Or forty-million street value."

The older woman narrowed her eyes. "I call bullshit. He didn't say all that…"

Nash waved her finger at Uncle. "He's not tall."

"What's his height got to do with it?"

"Old Indians use shorthand." Nash flipped her head as she pulled the two blue gloves out of her back pocket. "Let's go see if I'm right."

Maggie pulled on her gloves and looked back at the short, black-haired woman. "Bring your case for outside dusting. Andy, fire up your camera." She caught up with Nash at the center of the high-way. "How did he guess three million dollars' worth?"

Nash tossed her head back at the restaurant and looked over her orange aviator glasses. "There are two large ballistic bags with the bodies. They're full of straps. Maybe footballs, but at least straps. My dog triggered on the SUV. I wasn't thinking drugs until Uncle called."

Uncle pointed into the back luggage area. Along with more weapons were two smaller bags. The size was more the size someone would go to the gym with.

Nash looked at them. "Care to guess?"

Uncle hung his hands on his hips. "From what you said about the bags in the kill zone, two things fit the price of those little bags. Coke or fentanyl. Coke in blocks of powder or blue vacuum-packed pills. Or gold."

Nash weighed the guess. "Dinner?"

Uncle growled. "Nah." He flicked his hand at the deputy. "Vern's got elk steaks for dinner. But I'm going with a half-and-half."

"How do you figure?"

He flicked his hand in the air, motioning to the restaurant's parking lot across the street. "Look at the silver Chrysler in the lot next to your rental. It's got Nevada plates. But it has a Reno license plate bracket—you know, like a city who wants to get wild yet still get some sleep occasionally."

Nash frowned and leaned sideways to see the license on the SUV.

Maggie took one step back. "Orange Chevrolet."

Nash side-eyed Uncle. "Let's open them up."

Uncle held out his hand. "I'm old and don't have a respirator. And it's your crime scene."

Nash squinted at Maggie. "How much Narcan do you carry?"

The woman pulled a nasal injector out of her back pocket.

Nash's growl was more of a rumble. She held her breath. The zippers were industrial and hardly used. Silver showed through one zipper and blue through the other.

She stepped back. The four harmonized. "Fifty-fifty... Shit."

6

WHAT NOW

Twin snakes wound around her arms. The heads filled the back of the hands spread along the bar. The twitching muscles that would make most men proud rolled the tattoos. Other than snakes, a single mark on her arms was a small green thirteen on the web of her right hand. A small greenish-black tear dripped next to her right eye. Nowadays, it is more of a warning not to start something they couldn't finish. Her tear tattoo proved she had finished what she started long ago.

"What are you going to do now?"

Dice rolled the glass around in the wet ring on the bar. He shrugged. "I don't know."

The woman, known by many as Mama, sucked on her lower lip. With one last chew, she stood straight and snapped the damp towel onto her shoulder. "What were you thinking?"

He gently shook his head. "I wasn't. I saw the guys pulling out the weapons, and I was a fifteen-year-old peeper all over again. The girls are the only family I have now. I knew what was coming. They weren't bothering with masks to hide their identities. They were coming in to clean house."

Her breath slowed as she grabbed a glass from the rack and started polishing the clean. "So you went all marine on them. What did you tell the cops?"

"I told them I watched the two sets of guys kill each other. I was hiding in the cook's station, watching."

She turned and placed the beer glass in the freezer. "And they bought it?"

His voice was on the border of a whine. "It's a small town. Drunks or car wrecks are the worst they see. People getting shot are other drunk hunters tagging drunk hunters."

She scratched the short hair behind her ear. "But you went out to your truck, got a rifle, and went back in blasting… What did you think was going to happen?"

He furrowed his face at her. "That's not how it went down."

She shot more water into his glass. "Then what happened?"

"I made sure the girls and Cricket were safe and then went outside. I wasn't sure they would blow the window out, but big commercial glass is tempered. So even if I had to spend the first bullet shattering the glass, it would still only cost me the first second. But as I got to the window, the shotgun guy blew high and opened the window for me. Then, it was a matter of waiting to hear the first clip drop. The shooters were a team. Their shots were matched. When one dropped a clip, the other would be cleared as well. So when I heard the clip hit the floor, I already knew who would get what and in which progression. Same as in the Marine Corps. Take out the biggest or most imminent threat first and work your way down the chain. With three, it was about four heartbeats. Five tops."

Mama flipped the towel over her shoulder and leaned back against the stainless-steel back bar. Her right hand cupped the side of her left elbow as the left hand worked her neck. "Where's the rifle?"

"It's in the truck."

Her head worried into her left hand as she squeezed her neck. "What are you planning to do with it?"

He shook his head as he sipped on the water. Putting the glass back on the bar, he shrugged his right shoulder. "It's not like a hot seller on the street. It's just a varmint rifle. Probably worth more up in Ranch Country than in Boyle Heights. But I'm not sure I should dump it."

She ground her neck and head over her hand as she side-eyed him.

"Half of me keeps screaming about how I was protecting the girls, so I was in the right."

She took in a long, slow breath and blew it out slower. "But...?"

"I went outside to do the shooting. I wasn't defending the moment I stepped out the back door. It was hunting. It was exactly what the corps trained me to do. Be a hunter. A killer."

She snapped the towel out in the air to the right of her. "And you didn't miss a single appointment with the shrink at the VA. You have a track record of what they trained you to do. What were you thinking when it was happening?"

He hung his head and mumbled. She snapped the towel in the air above his head. He twitched, but his head rose as slow as his smile. "You know that doesn't work anymore."

Her smile was warm. "It's good to see you more relaxed. The country is doing you good." She floated the towel back over her shoulder. "So what was going through your head?"

"Counting. Just like when I was a peeper. Same as when I was clearing a hooch in the sandbox. I always counted."

"How long?"

He closed his eyes. "Six from the truck to the window. Two were on standby till the window blew. Three until I heard the clip hit the floor. Four to clear the three. Three to check the bags. Five to get back to the truck. Twenty-three round-trip. Twenty-eight heartbeats."

Mama frowned as she crossed her arms over her defined chest. "Bags. What bags?"

"Like gym bags, but larger. Too big to pass as carry-on."

"Black?" He nodded. "What was in them?"

"It felt like money."

She squinted. "Felt? You didn't check?"

He pulled on his left ear. "You know the bundles of money when it comes from a bank?"

She nodded. "Yeah. With the paper band on them."

"You only have to feel the shape once to know what it is. We're talking mucho dinero, ese. The kind of bag full you need to spend the rest of your life in Mexico." He held up his two fingers and walked them back and forth. "And there were two bags."

She whistled low. "That be some serious shit, pequeño."

He bobbed his head. "Serious."

She drew in a long breath through her nose. "Where are you staying?"

"Shorty's couch. His girlfriend went down to see her grand-mother in Baja for a month. I just need a few days to clear my head. They'll start looking for me with new questions in a few days."

"Are you going back?"

He furled his lips and winced. "I have a clean record since the corps. If I don't play clean, upstanding citizen, they will snoop around. They say my juvie record is sealed, but is it really?"

"Well, stop in before you go back up." She pushed her chin out. "How are you set for cash?"

He stood. "I have enough. Why? Do you need some?"

She smiled. "Pendejo."

He pointed his finger at her. "Keep hangin', Mama."

"Stay safe."

———

Nash sipped on her coffee as she watched the six tiny drones twitch and jerk over the bodies and under the table. She thought about the first body Oz had rigged at the Body Farm. The body was under a large beam. There were only about three inches of clearance under the beam to the body and the critical detail. The blood had oozed from a stab wound to the belly of the victim. But it was the thin monofilament fish line running from the bomb planted in the body to the beam above. If the body moved—everyone died. It wasn't the first no-win situation Nash had encountered. In the sandbox, she and her crew had come across plenty.

She rolled her head to watch Muna. The eyes were dancing back and forth between the two laptops. "Are they getting the underside of the table?"

Muna nodded quietly. "It lined up and shot the ballistic angles of the ones penetrating the top. There are three lodged in the wood but never breached. It got ballistic angles on those as well. The black-haired guy on the right was the most active shooter." She leaned over and studied the laptop in front of Felix. "It's mapping the shotgun blasts now. He'll get the ballistic lines for the ARs next."

Maggie muttered into her mug. "What the fuck am I doing here? The high school kid just knocked off three-quarters of my week's work."

Nash recognized the sentiment. She leaned her head so only Maggie could hear. "If you play nice with the kid, you might find out Homeland recruited him as he walked down from getting his high school diploma at fifteen. CIA and all the military intelligence officers were sitting in the front row. He didn't turn sixteen until late summer." She watched Maggie's eyes grow. "Yeah, he spends most of his time fending off boredom. Set up a lab in Irvine where he can teach, and I'm sure he would love to come down and bring any number of your teams up to speed."

"Why Irvine?"

Nash's smirk could get her twenty years for conspiracy. "He's sweet on another genius who has a multi-million-dollar business there. The place is crawling with what looks like a high school sleepover. And everyone can run circles around your brightest." She pointed at the tiny drones. "Those are the most boring of what he's invented since he was fifteen years old."

Maggie frowned. "Why is he working for Homeland?"

Nash peeked back at the two youngsters focused on the laptops. She turned back as her voice register lowered. "Same reason Muna is working for the FBI. It's a respectable job where they gain experience. I don't doubt that when Muna gets bored with her morning shooting range and the scope of her work for us, she'll jump ship and make real money. As for Felix, can you imagine him being snapped up by a Fortune 500 business? Picture the interview on Fifth Avenue." Her head vibrated. "When he jumps, it will be to someone who approached him on his turf."

The swarm of drones charged them and then jinked and landed on the table next to Felix. He never even looked at them. He knew they would do what they were supposed to do.

Nash looked back at Maggie. "They're perfectly lined up in two rows of three columns. Can your people do the same?"

Maggie glanced back and then sank deeper into the booth as she sipped her coffee. "I'd kill for someone like him."

"Set up the training center. Find your biggest nerds, and turn them loose with him. I'm sure he can do it for a week or two. From what he's alluded to, Homeland hasn't a clue where he is most of the time. They just deposit his checks, and he requisitions hardware. For a nineteen-year-old kid, it's heaven."

Maggie frowned and looked past Nash. "Wait. What? He's only nineteen?"

Nash shrugged. "He just got his weapons license about a month ago. I don't even think he's strapped. In fact, Muna said he was still waffling about what kind of side-arm he wanted to carry."

Maggie slumped. "Forget employee. I just want to adopt him."

"I think you'd have to stand in line. A certain blonde has her sights on him." Nash rolled her head back and faced the younger two. "Are you two finished with the crime scene?"

Felix peered up, blinking like he was just waking up. "Oh. Sorry. Yes, it's all theirs."

Nash turned back with a pursed smile. Nash gave her a pursed smile. "You have your release." Go forth and do what you do best."

The woman stood and glanced over at the other booth. "Yeah. I'm not so sure anymore."

7

BODY TEMPERATURE

UNCLE AND ALEX had moved the bus and toy box onto the empty lot next to the helicopter. The crew joined them for coffee and machaca burritos Uncle made from their stash of jerky.

"Oh no. We're old hands at this. We flew Running Bear and her boss into a bombing range down the valley about a year or more ago. Fun times. We wired them down and then parked on the highway while they probed their way through the unexploded bombs." The two women pilots chuckled.

Alex smirked. "She told her boss the only way she would take her dog into that kind of shit show was if he was strapped to her back. I don't know what the show was in D.C. at the time, but he was a trooper about the probing for bombs."

The rocks in Uncle's chest river rumbled as he laughed. "Her wife says he still hasn't gotten over his hot date with the KA-BAR knife. Obviously, the knife has become a running joke at the head office." He rolled his head over to Alex.

Alex held out his hand toward the pilots. "Go ahead. They won't be there."

Uncle pulled on one of his braids as he formed the story. "We were hunting last month, and my partner found a rock. It's flat on one side and will sit nicely on a desk."

Alex adjusted his sitting and leaned in. "We got a new laser cutter, and I wondered if it could slice a hole in the rock."

Felix and Muna walked up. They looked bored. Felix's eyes perked up. "Are you talking about the sword in the stone?"

The two pilots, Trouble and Cotton, looked up as they got the gist of the story. Cotton leaned back. "How's it look?"

Felix fished his phone out of his pocket. "A couple more passes, and the knife will sit deeper in the stone." He turned the phone around for them to see.

Muna giggled. "It gets better. My 3-D printer can spit out a nameplate matching the stone, and we'll epoxy it to the face."

Trouble barked a laugh. "What's it going to say?"

Uncle laughed. "Only thing it can say. *He who draws the sword from the stone is worthy as my wingman.*"

They all laughed. Cotton recovered first. "Who are you going to give it to?"

Alex shrugged. "We can't decide. We might have to send Uncle back up the mountain for a second rock."

Trouble looked at her copilot. "It would be perfect if it was the other half of the cleaved stone."

Cotton smirked and gently rocked her head. The two had been the first female team in Pave Hawks and had worked as a team ever since. "I ought to get one of those for your husband."

Trouble snorted. "He'd just give it to our daughter-in-law."

Cotton rocked. "How many countries now?"

Trouble smirked at the others. "They are serious motorcyclists. They have seven more mountain passes to cross and will technically have crossed the highest hundred. But it's in one go worldwide, which is their last big goal."

Felix smiled and sat. Two wheels were his love. "Where?"

Trouble frowned. "Around the world…"

"Equatorial is a significant difference from the forty-ninth parallel. Go the north route, and you will trim over ten thousand. But the equator has other problems with jungles and heat. But if you want the whole shebang, do a pole-to-pole-to-pole."

Trouble laughed. "For their honeymoon, they picked up BMWs at the north end of Norway and drove into the fall in North Africa. They finished in Durban. Two years later, they made their first go from the top of Canada, but Ralph ended up with a staph infection in Panama. They went back and did the entire run two years later."

Felix licked his lips. "What about the only continental circum-navigation?"

She smiled. "They're thinking about it and talking to backers. You?"

"I'm designing a frame for a BMW. Some basic areas are always broken during endurance trips. I want to limit those problems to the bare minimum. Airless tires are another area I'm experimenting with. I've got twenty thousand on my current motorcycle, but it's losing tread. I want one that will get a higher mileage, around thirty or thirty-five. Then I only need one set of spares."

Uncle coughed in his fist. "Circumnavigate…?"

Felix smiled. "Australia. It's the only continent you can circum-navigate by sailing or driving. Well, you could walk it… Some guy tried riding camels all the way around, but the southern edge killed his livestock and almost him."

Uncle nodded and pointed across the street. "What are the young'uns up to?"

Muna snorted through her clenched teeth. "You know, old school. They're reproducing what we already did in an hour. They're going to be at it past dark."

Trouble pulled her phone out of her breast pocket and checked the text. "They might want to hustle it up. Their meat wagon is about an hour down the road." She texted back and slipped it back into her pocket with a smile. "I bought Maggie some time. I told them to stop wherever they found food and have lunch. Because there's nothing here."

Alex laughed. "Oh, we have about a hundred pounds of jerky left."

Cotton vibrated her head with a sour look. "No. Just no. They're mud pounders. Don't share."

Uncle filled his mug and stood. "I don't even want to know what that means. I'm going to go check in on the young'uns."

KNOCKING ON THE OPEN DOOR WAS SOFT.

The woman looked up from the one of many folders on her desk. Her smile was soft and slow as she stood. Dice wrapped his arms around the woman as she folded herself into his chest. His breath was soft on her neck. "¿Que onda, Odie?"

She leaned back, still gripping his arms. Her head wagged tired. "Same ol', same ol'. Nothing changes. Peepers in and me out." She squeezed his biceps. "You're still working out, I see." Putting two fingers to his chin, she turned his head to look at his neck. "I approve of the new look." Turning, she pointed at the worn chair as she walked back around her desk to sit.

Dice turned and quietly closed the door before sitting.

Her eyebrows rose.

His nod was slight as his eyes slid shut and then opened. "I'm in trouble."

"How bad?"

He studied his former probation officer and the woman he felt had saved his life. He had never lied to her. She was his sister, mother, aunt, and nana when he had none. "I killed three vatos."

Her eyes danced over his face, trying to find some hint that what he was saying was only a joke. But, as hard as the stone of the building, his former life as a gang banger at ten, she knew it was the straight truth. She stood and paused as she picked up her coffee mug. "I need coffee for this. You?"

He shook his head. His body didn't need any more reason to vibrate.

The mug was half empty as she set it down. The small glass in front of him had only a finger left of water. His story was methodical and meticulously detailed. "Any idea who they might have been?"

His head stuttered as it shook. "The truck they drove was a Chevy Suburban. The plates were from Orange County. They looked white, but there were no blond surfers. But it was how they got out the guns and walked across the street—they were all business. No masks."

She rocked in her chair. "A hit."

"With no witnesses."

She sighed. "Did you get the numbers?"

He reached into his pocket and pulled out a restaurant ticket. I got both.

She held out her hand as he pushed the piece of paper across the desk. She studied the two numbers. "What's the Chrysler?"

"They were the buyers from Reno. Definitely white guys. Blond, and the only tattoo I saw was one had a neck tattoo. It's the double-headed eagle. It's the logo for Ruger or something, but it used to be one of the Nazi symbols. I remember seeing it in some of the old Nuremberg movies. They were carved pieces on top of standards or something."

She nodded as she dialed her desk phone. "Yeah. I know the ones you mean. The wings are spread—" She stopped and looked at the phone. "Manny. It's Odie Escobar over at probation. I need you to run a couple of license plates for me." She peered at the paper and read it. "Thanks, I'll wait here." She hung up.

Dice frowned. "Just like that? No questions?"

Her half smile came with a shrug. "Back when you were banging, and I was just starting, they questioned everything. Even if my mommy knew I was making phone calls on a real phone."

"Pendejos."

"Si. But it was the times, and I was just a girl with a piece of paper. Then, one day, one of my questions turned back to a tip. They busted four vanloads of grass and two hundred of black tar. They made a righteous bust and put away seventeen heavies. That was the day they knew the street went both ways. And they never questioned me again."

"They're still pendejos."

Her smile was warm for one of her best success stories. "Do you know where I called?"

"If they can run license numbers—"

She held up her hand. "Stop. Just stop. You're better than petty hatred. Who did you think would be able to run plates?"

"But..."

Her head shook. "You remember a scrawny kid? He had thick glasses and could barely see, anyway."

Dice frowned. "In Juvey?" She nodded. "They called him Four-eyes. What about him?"

She pointed at the phone. "He got surgery. Well, a couple of surgeries. He had some serious growth behind his eyes or something. He can't see much better, but he's good with computers. He's a clerk for the county. A few years back, they put him in charge of scanning all the old records into computers. They were thinking of going back to the nineteen seventies. Last I heard, he had all the records of all the Japanese internment done and was closing in on the nineteen twenties."

Dice's whistle was low. "Mucho trabajo."

"Si. A lot of work. And he makes it look easy, but I'm sure there are long nights and no weekends. But with him, it's more. Pueblo de Los Ángeles dates to the late seventeen hundreds. Whereas the state of California dates to eighteen forty-nine. The church and Californios kept meticulous records of births, weddings, deaths, and land."

Dice's eyebrows rose as he pointed at the phone. "And little Four-eyes wants to put everything into computers. ¿Por qué?"

She sipped on her coffee as she leaned back in her squeaking chair. "I know how hard it is to get information out of some of the public records and even in the research stacks at the library. Imagine if all those and the church's records were at the stroke of a keyboard." She winked. "And he's been taking classes at Cal State."

"What's he studying?"

She rolled forward as the phone rang. Her eyebrows bounced above her smile. "History and computer science." She picked up the phone. "Escobar." She wrote on the yellow pad. "And the Chrysler?"

Dice watched as the names flowed across the paper. One name and address led to another and another.

"Any deeper dive on the Chevy and Dorfman?" She nodded as she listened. "I'd appreciate it. Give them my number if they want to talk to me directly." She dropped the pen. "No. But all I can tell you right now is the driver, and two others were killed in a hit yesterday." She shook her head. "No. It was up in the Owens Valley. Something about a drug deal gone sideways. Oh, and before I forget. There was a kid a little older than you. They called him Dice. He had Roll Dice tattooed on his fingers. He says hi." She smiled. A hit. "I'll let him know. Thanks, Four-eyes. You're the best." She hung up and turned the yellow pad around.

Dice read the name of the Chevy. "Ouch."

She raised her one eyebrow. "You recognize Dorfman?"

He rocked softly. "When I was in Pendleton, he was a name used for heavyweight drugs. He was an enforcer or something for the Orange Mafia. And they had ties deep in Mexico."

"¿Ahora qué?"

"Now?" He grimaced, and his cheek and eye twitched as he scanned the desk. He looked up sadly. "I think I need to go talk to Flaco's widow."

"Flaco Romerez? He's up in Soledad."

A half smile tugged at his cheek. "So many skinny kids..." He shook his head. "Roman Falcon Franckowiak. A kid I was friends with in Pendelton. He could have played for any NFL team's front-line, but he hated sports. He loved the Marines as much as his wife. But he also loved getting high. The last time I talked to her, she had a one-year chip."

"And you're going to go see her... why?"

He turned at the door. "If I'm going to be a citizen, I've gotta go back up to Big Pine. I'm not innocent, but maybe if I can help, I might get some slack." He recognized the cluster of tiny wrinkles gathered at the woman's left eye. "She's still connected in certain ways. Not involved, but knows people, and they know her."

8

TATTOOS AND TABOOS

"ROLAND DORFMAN. He has more than a few vehicles in his name. He could start his own used car lot." Muna turned the laptop around.

Nash read the list as she shook her head. "He's a big player." She glanced at the other end of the restaurant. "I don't think he'd get this close to his dirt."

Muna pulled up the driver's license and a few images from the social media side of the internet. "A little too old and recognizable as well."

Nash looked at the picture of him holding a large silver trophy with sailboats in the background. "Almost looks downright respectable." Powder leaned into her leg. She glanced down. "We're going for a walk. I need some air. And a deputy."

Muna closed the laptop. "He's over with Uncle and the boys. They're talking elk meat versus jerky."

Nash swayed back with a soft snort. "Unless you have some good steaks or rump roasts, you're just talking jerky."

Muna raised an eyebrow. "I Googled Tule Elk. They have steaks, at least. But I wouldn't bet on the roasts."

Nash bounced her eyebrows at the doorway. "Jerky. Trust me."

As she neared the men gathered in front of the bus, Nash nodded at the deputy. "Got a minute, Vern?"

He looked around at the other men and bounced up. "Sure, Nash. What's up?"

Nash pointed at Powder, sniffing beyond the front of the bus. "I'm walking the dog."

He narrowed his right eye. "And a damn fine job of it, too." He kept studying her as she pointedly ignored him.

She raised her hand in front of his face. She ran her right index finger over the back of her left hand. "See this color?"

He cleared his throat, and the extra air rattled into his bottom cellar or a deeper mine. "About like a lot of our Paiutes around here. And your point...?"

She looked north across the sun bleach pastureland. "How many of these Paiutes do you know?"

"Here? A few dozen. In Bishop, a hundred or so."

She turned and raised her gold-tinted dark glasses to the top of her head. "How many do you think have gang tattoos on their hands?"

He raised his left hand and wiped it along the brush cut on the back of his head. The skin and hair made a soft hissing sound. "Define gang tattoos."

She closed her eyes and thought. "A small crucifix on the web of the right hand. Across the fingers were two *Ls*, an oh or zero, and an *R*. Some kind of shield with a rat or something. The wrist bones lead into other hand bones, but the other tattoos muddied the bones." She opened her eyes to see him smiling.

"Mexican. He got most of it in juvenile hall before he became a marine. He's the cook. And the fingers are ROLL. His left hand says DICE. Don't shoot dice with him. You're going to lose. Where did you see his tattoos?"

She bit her upper lip. "It doesn't matter. Where is he?"

"He's got a trailer out east off Bartell Road. Why?"

"He was here when the shooting went down. I want to talk to him."

Vern cocked his head. "Right. His shift was working with Mary and Judith. He hurried the girls and old Mrs. Street into the cooler to protect them."

"Where was he during the shooting?"

Vern grimaced. "I wasn't paying much attention when I read Watkin's report. He rambles a lot. He thinks he gets paid by the word in his reports."

Nash leaned in and growled. "He's not the only one who rambles in this town."

Vern's eyes opened at the teeth being so close. "In the cook's station. He was watching through the pass-through."

Nash eased back onto her hind foot. Her voice softened. "And he was told not to leave town?"

His lips wound into a soft snarl to match his shrug. "I suppose, but most people stay anyway. Where are they going to go?"

She lowered her dark glasses down to the end of her nose and looked over the top. "Because he had to come to work this morning..." She slowly pushed her glasses up to her face. "Let's go see what kind of citizen he was."

The houses and trailers lay scattered among the old trash, junk cars, and metal and wood constructions Nash couldn't discern. She thought about how small towns seem to all be planned with the same foolscap paper, broken pencils, and warped straightedges. No matter how it's laid out, the lines blur and flow into other parts.

They pulled into what might have been a gravel driveway, which was just a section of the yard without weeds, sagebrush, or tumbleweed sprouts. The single-wide trailer didn't give Nash much hope of having been one of Axel's projects. But the rust looked like the same intensity.

Nash sat, leaning her arm in the Chrysler window. Her eyes walked from one end to the other end of the trailer. "Is this reservation land?"

Vern pulled the handle on his door and swung it open. "Nah. The rez starts about a block away. This is just poor white trash and a few Mexicans over this south end."

She turned and studied the man. The mix of his town wasn't something to hide. It was just a fact. She pushed her door open. "What's he drive?"

"A truck." He stopped as his mouth and one eye screwed closed. His other eye looked at the sky. "I couldn't rightly tell you what kind or year. After about the nineties, they all just got to look the same. Mostly, it came down to a red one, a blue one, or basic ranch golden-brown rust." He swung his head down and around. "But his is brown. I think."

Nash looked over her finger, holding her sunglasses at the tip of her nose. "Definitely."

He waffled his hand in the air as he reached the side of the trailer. A carpeted pallet made the stoop. "There are a lot of trucks in the area." He pounded on the door with the flat of his hand.

A hundred feet away, the door of the next trailer swung open. The woman squeezed herself out of the narrow door. Nash wondered how the calf-length Mumu didn't rip or cause the woman any other embarrassment. The telltale signs of large pendulous breasts swinging over a baker's stomach were enough to make Nash shy her head and watch the deputy.

Vern nodded his head. "Myrtle."

The woman exposed all three of her upper teeth. "Vern."

He glanced back at Nash with his lips curled in a grimace. Nash guessed this sort of conversation made up a mass of his job. He looked back at the woman lighting a cigarette. "Any idea where I might find Dice?"

Her sucking on the cigarette was measured and slow. "I heard the elk were back up this way a couple of days ago."

He nodded his head up and let it gently settle back down. Slow and gentle so as not to spook the local wildlife. "Protected species. He'd only go hunting at night with a spotlight."

She sucked on the cigarette and thought. "Grady has a spotlight."

Vern glanced back at Nash. "Yup. He certainly do that." His eyes grew large and wild before he closed them and looked back at the large, barefooted woman.

The tip of the cigarette flared bright red as she sucked. Her chest expanded until the teats split and rolled to each side in hiding. "Well…"

Vern's lips didn't move. His smile froze, with a half-inch of space between the upper and lower. His voice was little more than a whisper. "Here comes all the wisdom she's had since we graduated from the third grade." He pointed at the sky.

She flicked the butt out into what would pass as her driveway or ashtray. "It being daylight and all…"

Vern strained forward. "Wait for it… she can do it…"

"Maybe when he left yesterday…"

Vern's soft rumble was as muted as his foot shifting on the gravel. "You can do it Myrtle… I know you can."

"He done throwed a bag in the truck. So maybe he went down to see his family in L.A."

Vern's head moved up as his mouth opened in an exaggerated ah-ha. "Well thanks, Myrtle. I never would have thought of that. Good to see you, dear. Say hi to Grady when you see him."

Her hand raised almost to her waist height as she carefully turned back to the open door.

Nash and Vern didn't need to watch how the trailer would suck the body back in or how she could force it through the narrow door. Some things you just never need to see in your life.

As they settled in the car, they watched the door gently make its way closed. "And you went to school with her…?"

"All the way to the sixth grade. That's when her 4-H lamb kicked her in the head. We never saw her at school again."

Nash squinted one eye. "A lamb?"

The blond brush-cut moved back and forth over his grimace.

"Her father didn't know anything about feeding sheep. Better alfalfa is about five percent protein. But he raised hunting dogs. Well, he called them hunting dogs. So he fed the lamb the same dog food as his pack of dogs. By the county fair time, the lamb was as big as his Pitbull Mastiffs and just as mean."

Nash snorted. "A mean sheep." She started the car and looked over at a deadpan face.

"The lamb was a ram and intact. It had spent the summer fighting with the dogs. So when she tried to clip around his oysters…"

"Ouch."

He rocked and jerked his thumb behind them. "We weren't close enough to see the hoof prints still indenting her face and fore-head." He looked over. "A hundred and sixty-eight pounds of ram can really fuck a sixth grader up."

Nash swung the car onto the street and pointed it back toward downtown. "So, do we know where his family is in the tiny town of Los Angeles?"

He looked out the open window. "My guess is East Los Angeles. I'll have to check, but if he was ever in the system, we should have somewhere to reach out or start looking." He turned back and squinted at the Paiute driving. "Your description of his hand was particularly detailed…"

She cocked her head. Her one eyelid, he could see, was flutter-ing. "And…?"

"It wasn't in the interview report. You'd have to deal with him a lot to know those tattoos."

She glanced over. "What are you saying, Vern?"

He looked out the window as the town slid by. "I think there's a story there. Like the tattoos on his neck have been disappearing for the last year or so."

Nash pushed her lower lip out and then peeked over at the deputy. "Sounds like he's trying to change his life." Fingering the turn signal, she nosed the large car onto the small side street and into the parking lot. "What did he have on his neck before it disappeared?"

"Crossed pistols behind gang letters, BH. I talked to the gang detail at LAPD. They kicked me over to the deputies because East Los Angeles is a section of an unincorporated county. She looked the tattoos up and said the BH could stand for Boyle Heights or Big Hazard. But both gangs were defunct."

Nash paused with her little finger on the door latch. "And the crossed pistols?"

"Both were revolvers. They showed he was a proven banger."

She watched one of the forensic team take a couple of cases across the street to the helicopter. "Is there a meaning behind revolvers versus automatics?"

Vern dipped his head. "Yup. Juvenile versus adult."

Shit. Nash looked over. "Sealed records."

"Yup."

9

BAGGED AND TAGGED

NASH STOPPED JUST inside the doorway. Vern bounced off her back. She glanced back. "Do I have to write you up for following too close?"

He looked at the sound of the large, long zipper at the other end of the restaurant. Three filled body bags lay in the middle of the floor. "Well, this escalated quickly."

Nash looked back with a smirk. "You need to go get some Vicks?"

His head vibrated. "I got Covid in June. I still can't smell skunk if it walked up and slapped me. My taste isn't much better. I'll cook the elk tonight, but I might as well have oatmeal."

Nash turned to face him. "Trust me. Those guys are getting ripe."

He chuckled and pointed toward the table they had used as a command center. "I figured." A short tripod stood on the table with a camera and microphone attached.

"Say hi, guys." The speaker was tiny and tinny.

Nash rolled her eyes. "Are you set up on the bus?"

Muna's voice was a stifled giggle. "We were outside, but it's getting chilly."

Nash snorted with a gaping mouth. "And closer to the pig rinds."

Vern frowned at Nash. "She told me she ate kosher."

Nash growled as she turned back to watch the wind-down of the crime scene. "She does. The pork rinds are more like you and my breathing. It's beyond snacking. And unless you eat ghost peppers regularly, don't try to sneak a bite."

Maggie came over. There were smears on her white Tyvek bunny suit. "I fed your mini-me all the information from their wallets. The three on this side—"

Nash nodded. "The whackers."

Maggie frowned. "The what?"

Vern chuckled. He had watched late-night television. He pointed at the body bags. "The whackers. The guys in the bags. Those in the booth were the whackees. They were expecting a drug deal. But they got a whack job instead." He shrugged. "Pulp Fiction stuff. You have the whackers and those they whack—the whackees."

The older agent cringed at Nash. "Where do you get these people?"

Nash fluttered her eyelids shut. "It's my superhuman talent. What did you fly over to get here?"

"Desert."

"How much civilization?"

The woman narrowed her eyes at the blond deputy. "Do the blown-down old shacks and tortoise bushes count as civilization?"

Nash poked her thumb in Vern's direction. "And that is the civilization producing people like Vern."

Vern held up his hands. "Oh, hell no. That be city shit. I grew up in Randsburg. There were only four and a half of us in the school."

Nash tilted her head and stared at him. "Half?"

He shrugged. "My sister. She's the broken crayon in the baking dish."

"I thought you grew up here with Myrtle?"

He smiled. Smacked his lips in boredom and nodded down the restaurant. "Any surprises?"

Maggie gave up and glanced back at the scene. "There are eighty-three shells at this end. Five are twelve gauge from the pump. The rest are from the two AR-15s. The three weren't professional hitmen by any stretch of the imagination. They were just close enough, so their fucked-up over-spray hit enough of the other four to make up for their incompetence. I'd say out of the five shotgun blasts, two hit their mark."

Vern waved his finger at the body as they slipped it into the next zipper bag. "And the moneymen?"

"Probably more dangerous on a golf course. The one with his back this way never even got his pistol out. It's still trapped under his gut. If you're going to plump up, pack your weapon where you can reach it." She pointed at the corner of the booth where the front and side windows met. "The corner man cleared the table with his weapon. I'm guessing his single shot is somewhere on the ceiling. We'll find it when I can set up the laser. But he's got five holes in him from face to groin. But he also caught some of the shotgun as well."

Nash touched her finger to Maggie's arm. "Before you go to the trouble of setting up lasers... check in with Felix. He can probably point exactly where the slugs are."

The woman winced carefully. "Those tiny drones...?"

Nash rocked her head. "Very effective. It's all mapped. I was serious when I told you to set up a place for him to teach a master class. He can also teach your people how to build them cheaper than buying them."

"Noted." She turned back. "The other two barely got more than knee-jerk responses off. Under the table and on the bench seat, there are seven shells. The corner guy was packing a revolver."

Nash's left cheek twitched. "Preliminary take?"

Maggie furrowed her brow, her eyes darting from side to side. "It's all gibberish, really. Those four dimwits showed up with a metric butt-load of cash to a shoot-out. And these three vatos from down south thought it was a spectacular idea to push a drug deal sideways, even though they didn't know spit about their weapons. Much less shoot."

Adjusting his stance, Vern rested his left hand on his hip to point with his right. "Let me get this straight." He washes his hand flat in the air toward the scene. "These guys killed those guys because they threw the kitchen sink at them. But those guys got lucky, and out of their seven shots, they somehow managed to kill these three."

Maggie stared forward, emotionless. "I don't think Reno killed anything but a long drive. The two slugs penetrating the table we found in the ceiling. But four skid marks remain on the underside, so it makes sense the slugs are hiding back here somewhere. No matter: both firearms were nine millimeters. The bullets would have been through-and-through at twelve feet regardless of where they struck…" Her eyes shifted from Vern to Nash and back again. "The whackers. The shots killing them entered their skulls and never came out. I'm guessing all lead, low velocity, and a small slug."

Nash's voice was nothing but breath. "Squirrel gun."

Vern rumbled. "Around here, it's more of a bunny, coyote, or poaching rifle."

Maggie pointed at Vern. "We'll know more when we get them back to the lab. But I doubt if we get more than a smashed splat of lead on the back of the skull. Twenty-two long-rifle or more of a two-twenty-three. Same kind of slug, just a little more pushin' in the cushin'."

DICE CHECKED THE ADDRESS. HE KNEW IT WOULD BE A bar, but the front of the building made little sense. What had been a stainless-steel passenger railroad car was now two halves to look like two cars. They joined at the door in the center. The building stretched across the extensive parking lot. In the windows of the railcars were black silhouette cut-outs of people at a party. The large sign above the rail cars read *Eat, Drink, and Be Mary*.

He gently closed the truck door and studied the four cars in the large parking lot they had striped for at least a hundred vehicles. *It must be a wild place on Saturday nights*.

The door pulled with a soft breath of air. Every light was on. Bright for bar hours, but typical for the morning when the cleaning and stocking happened.

The voice behind the bar was gravel and all business. "We're closed. So put your dick back in your pants and come back tonight."

He didn't see who was talking. "Hello?"

The woman rose from her bent-over position behind the bar. Dice had only seen muscles like hers on incarcerated dudes who spent their days lifting weights and reading magazines. Her spiky, chopped hair had bright green tips jutting out wildly. The tight black wife-beater T-shirt stressed her bulging white biceps. The firm silicone breasts poked hard from beneath. She exuded a dangerous aura with her combative stance and authoritarian bearing. This was no run-of-the-mill dyke—she was the one not to be messed with.

Oh, that kind of bar.

She squinted. "Who the fuck are you?"

"Dice. I'm looking for Patricia Franckowiak."

The bartender studied the man standing relaxed in the middle of the bar. "How long did you practice saying the last name?"

Dice recognized the challenge. *Are you one of us or one of them?* He felt the earth below his feet become solid. He smiled. "I think it became tattooed in my brain about the fourth time her husband and I got drunk together. Patricia—is a name I nailed the first time Flaco introduced us."

The bartender reached across the bar as her smile grew. "Pussy. I hear Flaco was a hell of a dude."

He shook. "In some ways, he was like a little brother. But in a bar fight, he was the big brother and would stop everything before it went too far."

Pussy turned her head toward the doorway at the end of the long bar. "Tricia. Your hug is here." She turned back with a serious look on her face. "You were here for a hug, not a hit... right?"

The blond turned the corner, lugging three cases of beer. At the sight of Dice, she stopped and gently placed the beer on the end of the bar. Her movement was cautious. "Tell me you are real?"

He dragged his fingertips down his sides. "Soy yo, baby girl."

She charged him with a squeal and jumped into his arms. Her tears flowed as her face was buried into his neck, and her legs crossed around his waist. They stood rocking in the middle of the room.

Pussy leaned forward with her elbow on the bar and her chin in her palm. "Wow. She never hugs me like that."

Dice turned them so he could see Pussy. "When Flaco was alive. She wouldn't give me the time of day. Only grief."

Tricia pushed back on his shoulders and looked at him. "You always were dating the skanks. I would have treated you better if you had some taste in women." She pulled his head into her chest. "Where the fuck have you been?" His response was muffled in her chest. "What, pequeño? I can't hear you?" She hugged his head tighter as she giggled.

He walked over to where he hoped the bar was. He lowered the woman onto the stool he found with his foot. She let go.

She gasped. "Gosh, damn it. I haven't seen you in... what?"

He looked at her. "You had just gotten your one-year chip."

She smirked and glanced back at Pussy. They recognized a challenge. She fished her keys out of her pocket and held the chip up.

Dice shook his head slowly. "Jeez. Five years. That was fast." He pointed at the chip. "And I'm proud of you." He waved his open hand around the bar. "But throwing beer...?"

She smiled as she pointed at Pussy. "Did you meet Pussy? She's my sponsor. We meet every day before work, and others join us after work." She cocked her head. "What about you?"

He shrugged. "I live in a tiny town where I'm the cook at a restaurant. I don't have anyone to drink with. So for me, it's not a problem. But drinking was never my drug of choice. Books were."

Pussy's question had a steel edge. "Then what are you doing here?"

He looked past her at Pussy.

Tricia grabbed his shirt at the throat and tugged his head around. "She. Is. My. Sponsor. She gets to hear everything. And I mean everything. So open the guts, vato."

He held his palms out as he sat on the edge of the next stool. "A couple of days ago, the shit hit the fan."

She studied his face. "How much manure?"

"A trainload. The whole train."

"¿Que?"

"Remember Dorfman?"

Pussy straightened. "The drug dealer? Yeah…"

Tricia pointed behind her at Pussy.

Dice nodded. "I don't think it was him, but three guys came into the restaurant and killed four others from Reno. The three were driving a black Suburban. It's registered to Dorfman." He fished the paper out of his pocket and showed her.

She handed the paper back. "That's a lot of information there. What are you, a private eye now?"

"No. I got this from my old PO. Before I return, I need to gather as much information as possible on the guys and what they were doing."

Tricia narrowed her one eye. "Why?"

He glanced at Pussy. "Because I killed them."

10

SORT TIME

MAGGIE PULLED herself out of the bunny suit. Pushing the legs down to her ankles, she did the forensic dance they all did. Scraping the last of the legs and booties off her feet with the other foot. She kicked the heap of white fabric onto the sidewalk.

Nash watched passively. "Those anger management classes are working wonders."

Maggie didn't look back but raised both hands and middle fingers. They held in the air for what Nash recognized as the slow ten-count.

As she turned, the woman looked closer to her nearing retirement than she had in the morning. The gray hair wasn't as neatly combed into the darker bun but hung out in wild wisps. Her face was clamped down in anger. "Fuck." She turned and kicked the white fabric heap again. "Fuck, fuck, fuck, and the horse who brought you." She stood with her hands on her hips, then her shoulders slumped. Her last *fuck* was soft.

She turned and studied Nash. Then she smiled.

Powder pushed her nose at Nash's butt cheek and then sat down, leaning into her leg.

Maggie squatted and held her hand out. "I sure hope this is her calling us to dinner."

Nash glanced across the street, the parking lot, and past the helicopter. The men were standing around the grill. She swung back. "It looks like the meat just hit the grill." Her eyes narrowed. "How much time do you need to unwind?"

The woman scratched at the back of her hair. "More than a long weekend on the Sea of Cortez."

"Fishing?"

Her head wagged. "My husband does the fishing. I just go for tequila, scotch, bourbon, or whatever is on the boat. I take nine-teenth-century bodice rippers. Then I read and drink my way away from all this shit."

Nash rested her hand on the smaller shoulder. "I have some hundred-year-old scotch hidden in the bus."

"Jesus. And you didn't lead with that? What kind of human are you?"

Nash grimaced as she watched the two men closing the back doors of the refrigerated truck. "I prefer to get the work done before I drink. Where are they taking them?"

Maggie thought a moment and shrugged her face. "Heck, Nash. You're the lead on this. I don't care. Either my lab or they can take them up to Mike and Oz." She peeked at the taller woman. "It really is your choice."

Nash stretched her neck as she watched the man walking their way. "It's much longer to take them to San Francisco. But what about jurisdiction?"

"Something like this? You're from D.C. Your West Coast base is San Francisco. I'm in Los Angeles." She waved her hand at the men standing around the grill. "Where are the boys from?"

Nash snorted. "DEA, ATF, and Homeland out of the north-eastern butt-scratch of California."

Maggie smiled as the man walked up. "You got it all, Fred?"

He held out his phone. "All I need is a signature and where I'm going."

Maggie pointed at Nash. "Her John Henry. Do you know where the lab is in San Francisco?"

He handed the phone to Nash. "Sure. I've delivered to Andy plenty. They have some new squints there, so everything north of Santa Ynes Valley and Fresno goes north." He glanced at his watch and shrugged at Nash. "Do they have a graveyard shift on the receiving dock? Or are they still in pandemic short staffing?"

Nash handed the phone back. "Security is pulling double duty. When do you expect to be there?"

He tilted his head. "We'll stop in Olancha for dinner. So, about two in the morning, probably. Definitely before three. We'll jump over from the ninety-nine and come up through Gilroy and San Jose. The pass will have trucks, but the midnight boys roll."

Nash nodded. "I'll let San Francisco know what's coming."

Maggie leaned to one side and scratched behind Powder's ear as they watched the truck pull out and turn south. Her head swiveled back and forth. "I always wonder if they ever sleep."

Nash chuckled as they started across the street. They could smell the barbecue. "Their door was open earlier. I peeked in. There's no sleeper, but it looked like a couple of sleeping bags stuffed under the passenger seat."

Nash shrugged at the hard look she got. "It's enough..."

Maggie snorted. "Which branch were you?"

Nash smiled. "Marines."

"Figures."

DICE SET THE BEER KEG DOWN AND CONNECTED THE hoses. Bending over, he pushed the two kegs back into the cabinet.

The falsetto voice gushed from the bar. "Hey Pussy. Who's the new eye candy?"

Pussy's gruff voice stopped the conversation from getting more out of hand. "You boys go play in the backroom and leave my new sub to do his job."

The three men, dressed in latex versions of LAPD uniforms, groaned and turned away from the bar. "Spoilsport. You never share."

"Don't make me cut you off again this week."

They waved their hands but giggled as they returned to the pool tables.

Dice drew his breath in through his nose. "Thanks."

Pussy leaned against the bar as she pulled the towel through her right hand. "Listen. This kind of... action isn't for even the closets or curious. This is serious, up-front, and out on the fringe territory. If you need a break or need to leave, there's no judging here."

"Where am I going to go?"

Pussy tossed her head. "Go get Tricia's nose out of the books. Hell, this place ran for decades with no books. The IRS is afraid to audit us for fear they'd have to come here to do it. Talk to her. It sounds like you two have a lot to catch up on and figure out where you're going from here. And if you want a sounding board, I have a close friend who used to be a detective here in the OC. He's good people to have on your side." She pushed his shoulder with a motherly smile. "Run along, vato."

Dice knocked softly on the office door.

"Yeah?"

He opened the door and stuck his shy smile in. "Pussy said I can't throw any more beer. And she said you can't crunch any more numbers."

Tricia dropped the pencil into the ledger and closed it. "She's right. I'm going blind with this shit." She stood. "Come on. I need some air."

She unlocked a door between the office and the kitchen area. She smiled as she held the door.

He frowned at the stairs.

"You'll see."

They walked out onto a patio. Tricia stopped at a heater and turned it on. She turned. "I'd turn on the fire pit, but it doesn't put out the heat like this does." She pulled a couple of chairs over. "Sit."

Dice gazed around. The hill behind didn't show any buildings looking down. The buildings to the side were dark. Businesses. He smiled as he sat. "Your own private park."

"Pussy's daughters figured it out. They fly for Disneyland. You know, the Tinkerbell thing on the wire at the end of the fireworks or something." She waved her hand at his blank stare. "Anyway, they climbed up here one day and figured out where to hide the stairs. Two weeks later, we had a front yard with a view." She held her hand out at the sea of twinkling city lights.

Dice furled his face. "Pussy...?"

Tricia shrugged. "Trans? Yeah..."

"Daughters?"

Tricia shook her head. "Not really hers, but also not adopted. Just family. The girls are cousins but look like identical twins. And they are always together. So it's a relationship that's beyond me. And it's none of my business. But you...?"

He sat back with his finger on his chest. "¿A mí?"

"Yeah, you. What do you mean you killed them?"

He took a deep breath and blew it out. One star blinked red as it moved across the night sky.

As he talked, she moved closer and held his hands. She could feel the vibration. She knew he had maybe talked about it to someone else, but he hadn't talked in a way to let it go. It had been the same way with her husband. She had just never realized how much they were alike.

She sighed. "You need to tell Pussy this again tonight when we close. She knows people."

He twitched his head. "She mentioned some guy who used to be a detective."

"Yeah. He was a surfing buddy of the original owner, Mary. You know the old poster on the wall in the office…?"

"The giant wave with the surfer going straight down the face? Yeah…"

"That was Mary." She held her hands as if she were holding two basketballs. "Muy cajónes."

He winced. "Fuck balls, the dude on the wave was straight-up loco. And he lived?"

She nodded. "Get Pussy to tell you the entire story. But, like I said, she knows people you can talk to. There are people who can help and won't judge."

"Just arrest me…"

She rolled her head. "Now who's judging?" She pointed down at the building. "A half dozen of those guys in the bar tonight are cops. On the weekend, you can have your pick from brass to grunt. So don't judge."

THE METAL FEET AND THE WHIRRING OF THE ONE BIONIC leg preceded Mike into the autopsy lab. "How late were you thinking of staying?"

Oz dropped his head from looking at the ceiling while his hand was inside the corpse. He glanced at Mike and closed one eye. His smile pulled back. "Got it." Pulling his hand out, he held up the four-inch sliver of wood. "Shattered on a large re-sawing machine. There's a reason they usually use bandsaws for re-sawing, but this was an old-school twenty-six-inch table saw rigged in a six-blade gangsaw. This chunk left the blade just inside the subsonic. It entered his pelvis, shearing his femoral artery, and then headed north. I thought I'd find it in the lung… but it fooled me. But when all else fails…"

Mike harrumphed. "Go for the throat."

Oz turned and dropped the large splinter in the pan. "Oh, right, you'd heard the lecture." He smiled. "What were you asking?"

"How late did you plan to stay?"

"Ah yes." He pulled his gloves off. "Why?"

Mike held out his phone. "We have seven bodies hitting our dock around two tomorrow morning."

Oz turned his head and peeked out the side of his eye. "That's pretty specific."

Mike spun on his mechanical and stepped out with his bionic leg. "Nash tends to get that way when she wants something."

"What does she want?"

Mike stopped at the door and turned as he held up his phone. "Find the killing bullets in the three brown guys. The white guys do later." He looked over. "It sounded like she needed to go eat or something."

Oz burbled a laugh. "That would explain any of her moods. At the farm or the Q, we couldn't trust her around any food. Once a marine, always a marine." He pointed at the office area. "Did Chips come to do backup?"

Mike glanced at the large, dark office area. "Why would she be here?"

Oz lowered his head and stared through his bushy eyebrows. "Because Muna is in the field with Nash."

Mike shrugged. "Just for a couple of more days. They were wrapped up on the other case and only did this one as a favor for the Los Angeles office..." He frowned. Turning, he called out. "Hey, Chips?"

"Go home. You have bodies first thing in the morning."

Mike turned with wide eyes to see Oz laughing. "See. I have a sixth sense about her."

Mike frowned. "Does she have a key?"

Oz barked a laugh. "Hell. I don't even have a key. What would it go to? The loading dock doors, which are almost always open, or maybe the elevator? What do your keys go to?"

Mike pointed at the one locked set of file drawers.

Oz guffawed. "You lock those? Why?"

"It's required… I think."

With her hands jammed into the FBI hoodie pocket and Hello Kitty pajama bottoms, the blond walked out of the dark. "What part of early morning did you two not understand? It's past your bedtime."

Oz smirked. "What about your bedtime?"

She bent and opened the refrigerator. Pulling out a giant pickle in plastic and a wrapped sub sandwich, she fluttered one eye. "My shift started on Samoa time. I'm running a tin dredge. I'll go to bed after I check your bodies in. There will be seven. Which drawers do you want them in?"

Oz waved his left hand. "The entire west side is empty. Can you move them yourself?"

She blew a sharp breath through her nose. "I'm not touching any dead bodies. I'm getting a couple of pencil necks from the first floor to do it. They need real-life experiences beyond reading reports and crunching data."

Mike pursed his mouth. The crunch of muscle around his eyes was pain. "When did you make friends on the first floor?"

She spun on her bare heel. "Since a couple of them found me out back and asked about gaming computers. A girl's gotta find her fun somewhere. Now go home or go to bed or something. Busy day tomorrow. Nash wants her numbers by noon."

Mike looked at Oz as they echoed. "Shit."

Oz turned and growled. "Muna better get back here soon."

11

WALK IN THE PARK

"WE CAN GO OVER and look right now."

Maggie gazed at the restaurant with all the lights on. And wrapped in crime tape.

Muna chuckled. "Trust me. The slugs are where we say they are. But it's also oh-dark-sleepy time." She rolled her head over to where Nash and Uncle were sitting with their heads leaning back to the side of the bus. Drool was peeking at the side of Nash's mouth. Uncle's mouth was the cracked cavity a grandpa gets in the recliner after a large Thanksgiving dinner. Neither was snoring. But both were oblivious to the world.

Maggie nodded. "Did she drive up?"

Muna patted her chest. "But I snuck a nap this afternoon."

Maggie glanced at the pilots. "Has anyone made sleeping arrangements?"

Trouble glanced at Cotton. "We were just going to pull out some pads and sleep in the Hawk."

The sheriff's car nosed cautiously into the old parking lot. Vern waved, and the driver veered toward the bus instead of the helicopter. "This will get it sorted." As the deputy eased out of the car and walked over, Vern introduced him. "This is Pepper. What have we got for them, Pepper?"

The man's voice was more of a squeak. "We've got three rooms over at Ferguson's. And I've got the guestroom, and you have a foldout, don't you?"

Felix harrumphed. "Done. We sleep six, and the sheriff isn't with us on this trip. So Nash and Muna get the grand suite in the back, and we guys just bunk in the front."

Maggie pointed at Trouble and Cotton. "You want a guestroom or foldout?"

They both snorted and shook their heads. *The devil you know…*

She looked up at the deputy. "Then it's just us three. Where's this Ferguson place?"

Vern pointed behind the restaurant. "See the yellow two-story?"

"Yeah."

"Home sweet home. They're nice people. Let them know there will be… um…" He looked around. "Five, eight, ten. Ten for breakfast. She usually serves breakfast at eight."

Felix frowned. "We can rustle up breakfast here."

Vern shrugged. "Your loss. She's known for her biscuits and sausage gra… vy." His voice trailed off as he noticed Muna's raised eyebrow. "Yeah, maybe that's the better idea."

Muna nodded. "Trust us. We're good. But thank you for the elk tonight. I don't know if it was halal, but it was tasty."

Vern stood as Nash and Uncle sat back up. "I left you some jerky as well. We'll see you folks in the morning."

Nash called at the man's back. "Thanks, Vern."

He waved his hand over his head as his stride ate up the asphalt of the lot.

Pepper shook his head slowly. "That man is an amazing force of nature. Vern took over the crime scene at two o'clock yesterday afternoon. He never complains." He turned back. "Watkins got sick and still won't come in."

Nash turned at the door of the bus as she pushed Uncle in. "It happens. Night."

————

ALEX POINTED THE LASER. MOVING THE DOT TO A DARK crease in the upholstered booth, he chuckled. "Of course. It's the old hide the bullet hole in the dark crease trick."

Maggie groaned as she studied the depth of the structure. "Shit."

Uncle chuckled and lightly grabbed her shoulders. Gently guiding her out of the way, he smiled. Turning, he grabbed the table and drew it out of the way. Pointing at the end of the booth, he nodded his head. "Give me a hand here, Felix."

The kid scanned where the two large booths came together. "With what?"

Uncle harrumphed a short bark of understanding. Stepping to the join, he thumbed the welt running down the center between the booths. "Watch and learn the magic of old-school deception, young one." He fed his hand down behind one side of the roll of welting. "They put the corner in last. So the welt is on it. They know it's in place when it hides the crack." He jerked with his body, and a crevasse appeared between the two booths as the corner booth shifted.

Felix stepped to the other end of the moving booth and pulled. The curved booth split in two. "Wha...?"

Uncle chuckled. "They must get this in and out of those doors. The door's opening is thirty-six inches wide but only seventy-six inches high. So the height to the top of the booth is only thirty. Just pull this one out about a foot more, then we'll tip it up on its back."

As the two lifted, the hollow nature of the booth became evident. "There wasn't anything to really stop the slug." Uncle pushed the now upended booth half out of the way and pointed at the hole in the wall. "Just open the wall. You'll find your slug flattened on the inside of the outside brick wall. I checked the outside of the wall this morning. Nothing made it through, and no bricks appeared moved. So, it's inside here."

Muna walked in with her laptop under her arm. Her smirk was on the left side of her face.

Nash looked over from the counter. "Is this the guessing game?"

Muna nodded as she took a stool and set the laptop on the counter. Maggie frowned as Uncle nudged his elbow into her arm. His rumble was half a chuckle. "You'll get the hang of it."

Nash leaned back with her right arm hooked around the back of the stool. "North or south?"

Muna stretched her neck as she twisted her head into the air. "Let's start with south."

Felix snorted. "I call shotgun."

Muna touched the tip of her nose.

Nash clinched her eyes closed as she tried to recall what the shooters looked like. "I'm calling thirty and less than five in the slammer."

Uncle harrumphed. "Forty, and he served the full five-to-seven." He turned to Maggie.

She narrowed her eyes. "I'm guessing the game is priors and time served?" They all nodded. Her head tilted to one side. "The big Orange…? I'm going with twenty-two and under six months in county."

They all turned to Felix. "If he's the biggest offender, I'm going with forty-two and…um… two years and seven months in county."

Maggie frowned. "Why the seven months?"

Uncle chuckled. "Because at two and seven, he's over the halfway mark to Nash's five. But his offenses are over her thirty and my forty."

Muna poked at the icon. The rap sheet came up. "We have a sealed juvenile record and forty-seven counts from traffic to trafficking." She held up her hand. "Three to five in county, and was out at the three because the jail was over the limit." She pointed at Felix. "We have a winner."

Felix held his arms in the air as he imitated the roar of a stadium crowd. "And the crowd goes nuts."

Muna shook her head. "Call it. North or south?"

"North. And it's the old school. The revolver dude."

Muna touched her nose. She looked at Maggie. "Care to lead off?"

The older agent glanced at the agent on his knees, tearing apart the wall. "Sure. Under ten and no time." She nodded at Uncle.

He wiped his cheek and mouth. "Seven and under a month."

Nash shook her head. "He's the top boy. So I'll go with twelve and a week." She hung her head back to look at Felix.

He paced for a few moments. "He's too clean. And he's careful. Five and time served."

Muna pulled up the record. She held up her fist and counted out with her fingers. "Reckless driving at one hundred plus in a school zone. Two, aggravated assault reduced to public drunkenness. Three, hitting his wife. They dropped charges. Four, hitting his wife, charges dropped." She flipped her thumb out. "Beating his wife in front of a teacher and their child's third-grade class. The school did not drop the charges, and the judge left it with the twenty-two days waiting for trial and two years of probation." She held up her hand for silence. "*And* they let him go from the Reno Police Department for conduct unbecoming an officer."

Maggie pointed at Muna. "And there is the old-school revolver. No chasing brass."

TRICIA PUT THE LARGE MUG OF COFFEE ON THE COFFEE table. "How did you sleep?"

Dice pushed on the couch. "It's more comfortable than sleeping in the truck. And I know. I've spent plenty of nights in that truck." He sat up and reached for the coffee. He smelled the aroma.

"Still four sugars and a dash of cream?"

He nodded as she sipped. "It works."

She studied his neck and the lack of tattoos around the collar of the T-shirt. "How much of the past are you going to erase?"

He dodged his head. "All of it eventually. But the laser is more expensive than the ink was."

She blinked a few times as her eyes slewed sideways. "Um... talk to Pussy. I think there's a surgeon down here somewhere who is doing the work for free. He's helping kids kick the gangs."

"It would go a long way in helping. When you get tagged, you're just proud to be a part of something. But later, it also marks you. I got into fights in the corps just because I was in another gang. They didn't see that we were in the same bigger gang. It was the same old turf war and mentality. It's why I got out of the gangs and left the corps. I grew up. I wanted more and better."

She took his little finger and held on to it. It was the same when she would talk to him in the corps. She wasn't holding his hand. She wasn't coming on to him. It was like a caring aunt or nana. She just wanted him to talk and be honest because she was listening to him. "So what does the new Dice want?"

He shook his head as his wan smile grew. "Same as the old Dice. It's why I kept Flaco out of trouble. Half of life is no longer an option if you get a record."

"And the other half?"

"I talked to an FBI guy when I was based in Pendleton. He said if I opted to do marine Intelligence, it would give me a way in. But I was already in sniper, so the other way was to keep clean and get on with a police department somewhere for about five years."

"So why cook?"

He pulled up the sleeve of his T-shirt. "I'm skillful enough to like it. But I'm also about a year away from getting all the gang markings off. They sealed my gang life with my peeper records. So, if all I have are some random tattoos…"

She slumped. "And then three guys with guns…"

The pain washed across his face. "Three guys with guns."

Her eyes were wet. "So what now?"

"I guess I'll talk to Pussy's friend and snoop around down here. I have a few people I can reach out to who were in the gangs… And… if I can return with information to trade, maybe they'll listen to my side."

Her head cocked to the side, a sly smile playing on her lips. "Information? What kind of information are we talking about exactly?"

Dice leaned in closer, my voice barely above a whisper. "The kind to bring down some powerful people. Like names, activities, connections."

She raised her eyebrow skeptically. "In a bumfuck east of nowhere town? That's quite the tall order."

"Who knows? Somehow, I don't see Deputy Watkins or Johnson doing much of the NCIS stuff you see on TV. I think they call someone else in. Like the FBI or LAPD or something."

She took his finger and held it. "Okay… but how do you find that kind of information?"

His mouth pulled back in an evil smirk. "You find people who hate them enough to make it happen."

"And you know those people?"

He shrugged. "Maybe. Years ago, I had a friend. Even as a peeper, his nickname was chopper. Mostly because he had a face like a bulldog, he could also make the sounds of cars and motorcycles. You name the bike, and he would make you believe there was one driving by."

She slumped her head to one side. "You know there are four million people in just the Orange County…"

He smiled. "But there is only one biker gang named the Aztecs."

12

STEP IN SHIT

THE BAR FRONT was like many others. The old brick wall could have been built a hundred years ago or just last month. Two top windows held the obligatory neon signs for the beers served. A sign over the door was hand-painted but blistered and chipping to oblivion. A rough pyramid on top of the sign could have been King Tut's, a child's pile on the beach, or something from Chichen Itza. The single word left no doubt—Aztecs.

Five choppers waiting at the curb weren't the beauty princesses of doctors, lawyers, and dentists playing wannabe tough guys. The worn black paint and rusting chrome spoke more than hinted at long miles on rugged stretches of highway.

Dice paused with his hand on the brass door pull. The large sign left no doubt about what kind of bar waited on the other side of the thick wood. *If you aren't an Aztec, turn your colors inside out or leave them on your bike.* The door sounded like a duck with diarrhea as he pulled it open. He glanced up and chuckled at the wooden duck call. The same call had been made at the door of a bar in El Sereno. Everyone went there on Sunday morning for Menudo. Some memories of East Los Angeles you carry with you—or you duplicate.

The dark interior slowly became lighter as Dice stood beside the closed door. A room with pool tables to the left, a dark corner next to the jukebox, and an L-shaped bar dead ahead and wrapping around on the right. Seven tables for four in the middle. The doorway at the extreme right would lead to the toilets and probably an office. Two bikers were shooting pool out of boredom. Three sat at the knee of the bar. The large guy behind the bar stretched the largest wife-beater stores probably sold. His blond locks made Fabio look like a beginner. The shoulders and arms squeezing out of the shirt looked like someone had molded them from the combination of Arnold, Jason Momoa, and the Rock.

The bartender flipped a large towel onto his shoulder as he studied Dice. "Are you going to pussy out and stand there or just run?"

Dice twitched and walked to the bar. Pulling a stool, he sat. "Sorry. I have a problem with dark spaces."

"Night blindness?"

He shook his head. "No. Just bombs and sappers."

The man leaned forward as he spread his arms and hands on the edge of the bar. "What can I get you?"

Dice looked at him. "A coke with no ice."

The man narrowed one eye. "The café down the street has just the thing for you."

"But does Chopper hang out there?"

The man straightened and towered over the seated Dice. His sausage-sized finger pointed at the front door. "The choppers are at the curb."

Dice's head rocked minutely. "I'm looking for Romeo Kwak. His friends used to call him Chopper. He could mimic any motorcycle on the street—but mine."

The voice was from the dark corner behind him. "That's because the pinche vato never rode a scooter. He always had a hard-on for pickups."

Dice drooped his head. "Some teat suckers never get it through their heads. You can't sleep on a chopper, it's hard to fuck on a chopper, and it attracts too much attention if you try. But when the chopper pukes and dies, there's only one person to call…"

"I'd rather call my mother than trust any jarhead near my scooter."

Dice smiled at the giant behind the bar. "Yeah, that's what she told me last night. Twice."

"Give the man a coke, Tiny. He doesn't drink. But he can bring me another beer."

Dice picked up the two drinks and turned. The man in the wheelchair rolled out of the shadow. Dice put the drinks on the table and leaned in for a hug. The count was many breaths. Some jagged.

"I heard a truck pull up outside."

"I parked down the block."

"Could still smell the extra tires."

Dice pointed at the chair. "You added a couple of training wheels."

Chopper rocked his head back. "There aren't enough people like you. Some drunk working on his fifth DUI decided he didn't like the streetlight and stoplight. We were at the last reach of the pole—across the street."

"We…?"

The left eye sparkled with wetness. "My wife caught the worst of it." He turned his head so the scars on his neck and face were obvious. "When the power still turned her to charcoal, she grabbed my face. I like to think she wanted me to think of her every morning when I look in the mirror."

Dice rocked softly. "And do you?"

"Every night if I sleep. When I yawn, or it gets cold. Yeah. She got the best of it." He pointed at Dice's neck. "You're cleaning off the BH?"

Dice put the coke down. "Pretty much all of it. It's a long process."

Chopper pulled up his shirt to show the lack of tattoos. "There's a doc over in Santa Ana who will knock you out and work on the whole enchilada each time. It's painful for a few days, but it works out if you have someone to rub the cream on your back."

"I heard, but I'll take it if you have a name and number. This shit ain't cheap."

Chopper sipped on the beer as he studied his old friend. "Most of a lifetime… and then you walk into my bar. ¿Que pasa, ese?"

"I need some help."

The beer paused halfway through the sip. Chopper put it down. This wasn't the old days of just bullshitting around a conversation. The man was going for the throat. "What kind of help? And why?"

Dice smiled and poked the air at his old friend. "See. Only you were ever smart enough to ask the why. And there is the problem. But it's my problem."

Chopper leaned in. "Sometimes, a problem is the village's problem, too."

Dice shook his head. "Not this time. This problem I created, and only I can pay for it or hopefully make it a non-issue. But that's what I need help with."

"Okay. Shoot."

"There's a guy here in the OC. When I was down at Camp Pendelton, everyone knew his name. He was heavyweight into drugs and the Mexican Mafia. I need as much information as I can scrape out of the streets on him and his organization."

Chopper took a deep breath and blinked. Picking up his beer, he sighed. "Dorfman."

Dice nodded. "Dorfman."

Chopper's pull on the bottle was small but slow. The return to the table was silent. "Before we go any further down this wild ride to crazy town, I need to know what shit you stepped into. Because if it ain't life or death. You need to leave and never come back."

Dice looked at his hands in his lap. The scars were from cooking. But the tattoos on the inside could never be removed. He looked up. "I capped three of his drug dealers."

"You capped them. Like you pulled beanies on their heads and kicked them down the road…?"

"I shot them."

"Dead."

"Sí, muerto."

"As in no bullshit. Dead."

Dice nodded his head at the wheelchair. "As dead as your wife."

Chopper took a deep breath and let it out with a long sigh. He turned his head and stared into the pool room. "Rusty? Chase? Could you two join us, please?"

The pool cue landed on the table among the balls. The two silently came and took seats. Redish curly hair marked the thin man. The hawk nose also marked him as being of eastern Mexican descent and maybe more Spanish in him. The other had the round moon-face of the western, or Baja, in lower California. Chopper confirmed the names.

"What you can't guess about this bar or the Aztecs is what we do. Most gangs are into drugs and girls and anything else to get money. And ten years ago, you'd be right. But now, Rusty here used to deal meth. But now, he's a nurse's aide and about to get his RN license. He works at the children's hospital and two of the county's emergency rooms. He sees firsthand what the new street drugs are doing to people. Even kids."

The man fished his keys out of his pocket and dropped them on the table. Among the four keys was an Al-Anon chip.

Dice smiled gently. "How long?"

"Eight years."

"Congratulations."

The other biker dropped his two keys and a chip. "Seven. Rusty saved my life."

Chopper pointed at Chase. "He's a social worker. He teaches inmates how to read."

The man shrugged. "Among other things. I help them start a

new life. But reading is critical. Seventy-eight percent of the incarcerated at the county level can't read at a fourth-grade level."

Chopper held the beer bottle out toward Dice. "Dice here stepped in some shit and needs our help."

Chase pushed his lower lip out with a shrug. "¿Que?"

"He killed three men who work for Dorfman."

The two harmonized. "Sheee…it."

Uncle stepped up behind Nash. They watched the dog probe each section of the pulled-out booths. The nose was never more than a hand's length from the upholstery. "What do you think, FBI?"

Nash looked back. "Drug buy gone wrong? Yeah. But not because it's how it's presented. I think there's a lot more here than meets the eye."

Uncle grumped. "Where's the other shooter?"

Nash bobbed her head. "You too?"

He scratched at the base of his right braid. "Alex has a few questions as well."

Nash narrowed her eyes. "What does mister ATF have questions about? It can't be about the steaks last night. I saw him take the second one."

"Steaks were fine. But Felix and Maggie found all the nine-millimeter slugs. The forty-four bulldog only got off two. One is in the ceiling, and the other skates along that wall and into this back here. We figured we'd let Maggie's kid figure this one out."

Nash waved her finger at the young forensic agent with his hands on his hips, looking at the skate mark on the brick wall. "He's getting there." The man turned and frowned at the narrow brick wall bracing the corner near the door.

Uncle rocked his head as he pulled the end of his braid. "But no holes in the three from downstate."

Nash bumped her one eyebrow. "No enormous holes in the bodies…"

The older man rolled his eyes as his upper teeth skated on his lower lip. "So you still think it was a smaller weapon? Twenty-two or something?"

Nash watched the forensic agent walk down and examine the narrow pillar of a brick wall. "I still want to talk to the cook."

"Found it!" The forensic squint turned with the same proud look on his face he probably had the first time he went to the bathroom by himself. Except this time, his pants weren't around his ankles.

Nash smiled at Uncle and oozed a voice most only used for their dog. "Who's a good boy?"

Powder rose from her bored state of lying by the booths she had cleared. She watched for Nash's finger and then walked the length of the restaurant as if she was eighty years old and it was the death walk to the gas chamber.

Nash rolled her eyes. "I need to go take my daughter for a walk. Maybe find a stick for her to fetch."

Uncle laughed. "She fetches now?"

Nash's eye steamed with sarcasm as she turned to follow her dog out the door. Both were more than over this crime scene.

13

ROLL AGAIN

PUSSY RUBBED down the bar where the three had just left. Looking up at the door, she smiled at the man filling most of it. "You know. When Tricia talks about her husband, and you walk through the door, in my mind..."

Dice smiled. "They used to call us the salt and pepper twins. We wore the same size uniform. But he was blond and white. We would swap shirts to mess with the drill instructors in boot camp. Nobody could pronounce Flaco's name; he was white, blond, so the Espinoza bent them beyond getting mad. But his shooting was for crap."

Pussy laughed. "My girls are up on the roof with Tricia and Pounds. Now they're a couple of twins who will mess up your mind."

He snorted softly. "Tricia warned me."

The two young girls lounged in the chairs, talking to Tricia and a man. If there was a uniform of white tennis shoes, black with red-skulls leggings, and a Ramon's World Tour T-shirt, they were wearing it. Twins except the red dyed hair and green dyed hair.

He laughed. "Everyone told me they were identical. I can tell them apart. It's easy if you're not color blind."

Their giggle was more of a musical tinkle as they stood. The right hands extended in unison as the left hands pulled the wigs off to reveal the short blond pixie cut. Their voices were in musical harmony. "Hi. We're Tink. We've heard so much about you, Dice."

Dice stood with his mouth open and his hand halfway toward theirs.

Tricia laughed. "Oh. Flaco would have given his paycheck to see your face."

Dice twitched and finished shaking the hands with a chagrined smile. He eyed Tricia. "I'd give my left nut to see Flaco's face right now. I just spent the day with another old friend."

The two Tinks pointed at the chair. "Sit. This is Frank Pounds. He doesn't shake, but we've known him to quiver a bit."

Frank leaned forward and shook. "Ignore them. They won't have sex with you, but they love to fuck with your mind."

Tricia wormed open the small ice chest and pulled out a coke. She passed Dice the can. "I kind of filled Frank in on the situation. He can ask for the details."

Dice frowned and glanced at the two girls.

Frank waved his hand in dismissal. "Don't worry about the tinker toys. They just look like little girls. But they've heard and seen worse. Trust me."

One girl waved her hand at Dice. "We're studying to be trauma nurses. But every week, we stare down a half-mile of three-eighths-inch steel cable. When we leap off, it's a sixteen-story drop. There is no braking system or net. It's all about gravity and us. As for shooting three guys to protect your waitresses and an old lady. Hell. We're in. In our book…" The other girl chimed in. "It puts you in standing with Frankie. That's hero shit."

Dice raised an eyebrow as he looked at the other man.

Frank shrugged. "It was all part of my job."

The chorus of Tink scoffed. "Yeah, as a retired surfer bum who plays with his coyotes."

"Coyotes? As in wild dogs?"

Tricia patted his hand. "Not so wild. They sleep with him and his girlfriend. But not in a kinky way." She glared at the two girls. "Or so I've been told."

Pounds growled. "Can we get back to the matter at hand?" He rolled his head toward Dice. "So, how can I help?"

Dice shrugged. "I reached out to an old friend I knew back in the gang days. He and his buddies used to be criminal types but have gone straight. But they have connections with other biker gangs and the street."

A smile tugged at Pound's cheek. "There's a biker club in the seedier part of Fullerton. They've been turning around a lot of kids in the area. One member was on my trauma team during my last surgery when they replaced my spine. I'd call Tinkerbell, but she won't be out of surgery until after nine."

Dice narrowed his eyes and pointed at the two girls, who giggled. "We're Tink. She's Tinkerbell, but we call her Belle. Yeah, she's kind of pretty."

Frank snickered. "Actually, her name is Pan. But her Russian name is closer to Tinkerbell."

Tricia snickers. "Don't even try to keep up, Dice. It's all confusing, but it makes sense. Like sleeping with wild dogs."

Dice leaned forward. "The nurse? Did he have curly reddish hair?"

The Tinks nodded. "He was an orderly or something who spent a lot of time in your room. He's Latino but with curly dark red hair. On a horse, it would be chestnut."

Dice held his thumb to his upper lip and curved his index finger to show the shape of a large, hooked nose.

The girls giggled and pointed. "That's him."

"Rusty."

Frank leaned his head back. "Your friend is an Aztec?"

Dice smiled toothily. "Si."

"You have respected friends. How are they going to help you?"

Dice hopped his chair a little closer to the heater. "The three guys who are my problem worked for a guy named Dorfman."

"Ouch." Frank groaned. "I didn't know that part. He's the original Teflon Boss. When I was a detective, we always had a half-dozen folders open on his operations. I couldn't prove it, but when I worked on Mary's murder and met them…" He pointed at the building and then at the girls. "We busted an operation bringing weed and fentanyl in with submarines. It was a highly sophisticated operation requiring a huge cash outlay to set it up. And it's just as expensive to keep it going. I'm pretty sure Dorfman backed it."

Dice frowned. "But you busted the operation…"

"We busted the people servicing the underwater drop stations and even captured two of their submarines. But that's like arresting two drunk jarheads and saying you busted the president's drunken crew. The little bees are never the queen bee. But now we know what we're looking for offshore, and the Coast Guard regularly trolls for any new structures."

"But you weren't going head-on at Dorfman. I mean, if I heard you right, you were investigating the original owner's murder."

Frank nodded. "But it was all connected. Mary had found something and had gone diving to investigate. His body turned up on the beach for his troubles—without his head. It was to send a message. But it also scared the hell out of a lot of the wealthy people. They live on the peninsula, where the money is simply supposed to meet the sea. Not dead bodies to upset their early morning stroll on the sand."

Dice started chuckling.

Tricia poked his arm. "What's so funny?"

He pointed at Frank. "The rich people pay to have clean beaches. They specifically buy houses there for the peace and quiet."

"Yeah?"

"I moved to Big Pine because it has a population of a few hundred people. The cops take the drunks home because the jail is thirty miles away. The deputies find out who stole the chicken and go get it back. Only big things are the tourists who drive stupidly and get in wrecks. Or the hunters who drink and shoot another hunter. But it's rare. I moved there because it was quiet. So I could cook, clean the tattoos off, and then find a law enforcement job somewhere." He pointed at Pounds. "They got a dead body without a head, and I got three jerks doing a whack job in my restaurant."

Frank sat up. His eyes bounced from the floor to the girls, then to the city, and back to Dice. "Where's Big Pine, again?"

Dice waved over his shoulder in the night air. "About three hundred up highway three-ninety-five. It's in the Owens Valley. The next town is Bishop. Why?"

Frank fished his phone out of his pocket and pushed a number and then the speaker icon. He sat back.

The little girl's voice was laughing. "Hey, my toes are itching. When are we going to have a girls' night out on the roof?"

He smiled and glanced at his toes, showing out from the tips of his huaraches. "Soon, Ming, soon. But first, where's Chips?"

"Up north. She's filling in for Muna. They're up in the high desert on a murder or something. Why?"

"I need some information. Thanks. I'll call in a couple of days. My toes grossed Pan and the dog out this morning."

"Are you sure it was your toes or your shirt?"

He looked down at the T-shirt he was wearing. "Nope. The toes. I'm wearing the Beach Boys at Crystal Cove today."

"Yeah, yeah, yeah. I've heard that one before. Go talk to Chips. But keep it short. She's about to go on shift with a tin dredge in New Zealand."

"Got it. Night, cutie pie." He cut the connection before he got grief for playing Daddy.

He scrolled for the number and poked the green icon.

The young woman's voice was edgy. "This better be good. I go live in seven minutes in New Zealand."

"Short. Where's Muna and Nash?"

He could hear her looking at old school Post-it Notes. He started humming the theme song for Jeopardy.

"You're off-key. They're in Big Pine, California. Seven bodies. Gangland whack job. I signed the bodies into here at two-fourteen this morning. Mike and Oz finished at six-twelve this evening. Anything else you need?"

Pounds glanced at Dice. "There were four who got heavily shot up. But the other three? How were they killed?"

He could hear her humming as she scanned a report—probably on one of her screens. "Single shot to the head of each. One got it through the right eye. One through the jaw and throat where the slug merged with the spine, and the other between the eyes."

"And the bullet in each was...?"

She cleared her throat in irritation. "Why do I think you know this already?"

"Chips, what did Mike and Oz say?"

"Soft lead slug. Deformed beyond any kind of identification. I gotta go."

"Did they note a weight or size slug?"

"They only wrote two, two, and a three." The connection died.

Frank slipped his phone into his pocket. He smirked at Dice. "You want the good news or the okay news?"

Dice sighed. "The only good day was yesterday."

Frank smiled. "Oorah. The worst news is they've identified the slug as being from a two-twenty-three. The better news is, they're smashed all to hell. How did you leave things with the local... deputies or cops?"

"Deputies. Bishop is big enough to have police. But we just have deputies. And I didn't. They asked what happened. I told them I hid the girls in the cold box while watching the shoot-out from the cook's station. And from all the gunplay—they shot each other."

Frank rubbed his chin. "Did they tell you not to leave town?"

Dice shook his head. "The deputy had a hard enough time

trying not to puke again. He's kind of like the kid nephew you keep around out of respect for his mother."

"Who all knows you have a bunny rifle?"

Dice shrugged. "A few people. I don't really socialize much. I work and then study. When I go out shooting, I go alone."

"What did you do in the corps?"

"Sniper."

"How good are you with the bunny rifle?"

The large man adjusted in his chair. They were on safer ground. "At close range, more accurate than my Barrett."

"What's the longest you've shot with the plinker?"

"Occasionally ring the manhole cover a mile up the canyon. But any wind and forget it. Why?"

Frank smiled as he shrugged. "Because she'll never admit it, but the agent investigating the seven is one of us. She wasn't a sniper, but she had a confirmed fifteen-hundred kill. Her sniper was having a serious conversation with the medic, who was his spotter. So she took out their sniper on her own."

"And you know her?"

"We're more than just colleagues, but not quite family—yet. Our connections run deep, like my bonds with my extended family." He held out his hands at the Tinks. "One of our... um... family is on loan to the San Francisco FBI office, keeping watch while the agents are out in the field. Yours is a complicated situation. But when we handle it... and I do mean we. It will be on our terms and with trusted allies by your side."

The big man nodded solemnly. "I'd appreciate that."

14

HOMIES

THE 1960S CHANGED the landscapes of America. Small businesses on Main Street moved into large buildings to attract more walking traffic. Americans could climb into their ubiquitous cars, drive to one parking lot, and enter a single building to walk a mile from one small store to the next. And when they needed a break or nourishment, there was always the food court.

As everything ages, so did the last of the successful malls. Coats of paint, like an older woman's pancake foundation, only attempted to mask the line and damage of time. The hulking edifice provided little more than a landmark and a location for more than the commerce inside. Occasionally, illegal transactions outside attract more money than legitimate businesses that pay taxes.

The two skateboarders rode their boards little or did tricks. They spent their days close to the curb, ready for the cars that pulled out of the stream of traffic.

The exhausted soccer moms got an extra energy boost like the morning's tall quad-shot never did—with or without vanilla, macchiato, and skinny whipped cream.

The frazzled waitress was halfway changed from her day restaurant job and her temporary shift at the Greek-fusion steakhouse.

Needing just enough to clock the extra six hours with hopefully better tips.

And the customers that you could set your watch to. The silver Lexus with the occupied child seat in the backseat. Ninety seconds at the backside of the mall before it opened. Fourteen minutes to the day care. And a third of the bindle to burn the nose at the long stoplight on MacArthur Blvd. Maybe the meth would burn the nose hairs enough to stop growing.

The five-year-old green truck with a lumber rack and large toolbox bolted to the bed eased to the curb. The weathered young man in the torn T-shirt leaned across to the open passenger window. His hand held out the twin twenty-dollar bills.

The skateboarder froze five feet from the truck. His hand was still in his pocket. His eyes were on the large biker who stood beside the driver's open window.

The construction worker looked back and turned a lighter shade than before the sun had permanently tattooed his skin into pre-cancer. He crumpled the forty dollars into his fist.

Rusty leaned forward and looked through the windows at the drug dealer. "It's okay Juan. Give him his meth. He's got the money. I'm only here to talk." He poked the worker where the T-shirt had ridden up short. "Go ahead. Today, you're fine. It's tomorrow where things get sketchy."

The not-so-young skateboarder dropped the small envelope on the seat and grabbed the money. His hand hadn't been in the truck a full second.

Rusty's voice stopped him in his tracks. "Don't run away Juan. We need to talk about the coming war you guys are facing." He patted the worker on the shoulder. "Better for you to get a full night's sleep instead of destroying your nose and mangling your blood pressure. Besides, the Fentanyl that's killing people on the news..." He pointed at the envelope. "Take care of yourself." He stood back as the man used a little more gas than he needed.

Rusty watched as the truck's back tire jumped the curb when

the shaken man cut the corner too tight. He sighed, rolled his eyes, and looked at the drug dealer. "If I walk over there, are you going to run?"

"Maybe?" The young man had already turned his left foot to leave.

Rusty looked at the light up the block, turning. "Well, don't. I don't want to chase you, but I also don't want to get run over. I simply want to sit and talk for a moment. You can go back to work afterward." He stepped small steps to the curb as a car rushed over to where he had been standing. Watching the harried commuter, he stepped onto the sidewalk.

"What do you want?"

Rusty studied the young man. What looked like a young teenager had wrinkles belonging to a thirty-year-old. Rusty figured him for his early twenties who was shaving bits and pieces off the product. The habit was aging him, but he didn't know it. "I'm looking for people dealing for Dorfman."

The dealer waved his hand over his head. "They over on the Bristol Street side. That fuck be malo loco."

"The dealer or Dorfman?"

The dealer twitched as he looked around for his partner. "Both. But Dorfman totally crazy fuck. He thinks you shaving short, he cap yo ass. Muerto. No talk. Just bam, and you be gone. A vato be stupid to work for him."

Rusty pulled his business card out of his pocket. "This is my club card. There's a war coming. And it's aimed at Dorfman. It's time he went away. His drugs are killing people." He pointed at the dealer. "And as you said, he's also killing people. It's going to stop. But it's going to be messy. If you can get out of the business, now is the time. But before you go, we'd appreciate your crew telling us where Dorfman's dealers are. And if you need help to get straight, we can help there too."

The young man studied the card and then tapped it on his thumbnail. "Straight up?"

Rusty pulled his shirt up. The last of the tattoos were dots and faded rubbings. "Straight up. We even have a doctor who is helping take off the gang colors. The Aztecs are here to help, brother."

The man stuffed the card in his back pocket. "I'll put the word out about Dorfman's people. The rest...? I'll think about."

Rusty put his hand out to shake. "It's the best I can ask for. I'm looking forward to hearing from you. Suppose you don't want to come by the clubhouse. We'll come to you. Choose a coffee shop with windows. I'll buy you dinner." They both knew why the windows were essential for meeting someone on neutral turf. Caution always applied.

———

AS THE SUN NEARS THE OCEAN, DAY ACTIVITIES TURN TO night. Most people move slower; some dig in and move more determinedly. The kid at the land end of the pier bounced from a somnambulistic person to other robots walking their dogs. Each time, mumbling about his wares. "Mailbag, elf on the shelf, lazy boy. Mailbag, elf on the shelf, lazy boy." Occasionally, a person would produce a few bills. The kid would nod, take the money, and twitch his head at the guy on the electric bike. As he flashed a hand sign, the bike guy would nod as he reached into the suitable pocket. Concealed in his hand was the correct drug. He made the pass to the customer, and the dance started again.

Chopper watched the dance from down the sidewalk. People walked past. Most never went beyond seeing him enough to not trip over him. A few registered the wheelchair but forgot about it by the fifth step. It was a phenomenon he had been told about, but he didn't believe it until his wheel mentor took him to the middle of a busy street fair on Cinco de Mayo. Chopper had recognized several old friends from the neighborhood. But when he called out, they looked around for the voice and person they knew. But only with the third call did they look down. His mentor referred to the extra call as the two-by-four.

Chopper slowly rolled over to the electric bike. "Hey homes? Looks like business is slow."

The man started and finally saw the man in the chair. "What you need?"

Chopper sleepily closed his eyes as he shook his head. His hands rested in his lap. His eyes opened, and he studied the man. He dressed like a beach hipster, but his face and arms talked more of the previous generation. "How's business with Dorfman these days?"

The man looked around.

Chopper chuckled. He remembered all the street worries. "Nope. Just us talking in the sunset. Two old homies talking about how tough it is to do business these days."

The man squinted south down the long sidewalk along Seal Beach. "Fucking Nazis. We used to work in the north end. Fuckers came at us with heavy artillery in their pants." He looked down at Chopper. "You know what I mean?"

Chopper nodded. He turned his hand over and twisted the business card out of his palm. He held it out. "There's a shitstorm headed their way. Just them. But to make it a tsunami, we need information. If you come to the clubhouse, the beer is on the Aztecs. Call if all you want is to call. We're good there too. We man the phone twenty-four seven. If you want to meet, let's make it Norm's or any other coffee shop with big windows. I get bullet claustrophobia these days." He bounced his hands on the tops of the wheels. "I'm not looking to get shot again."

The man smiled and raised his faded Hawaiian shirt. Chopper recognized the spider scarring of a large caliber bullet wound patched up in the hood. "I heard the Aztecs were out of the business..."

Chopper smiled. "We are. We're in the business of helping others get out as well. I can tell from the lack of tattoos you escaped the gang shit. It makes getting out a little easier, but help makes it work better." He pointed at the card. "Put the word out. We need to know every aspect of Dorfman's operations. Street to the top. Where they are, how they do it, and when. Beyond that... keep the card if you want to talk after the shit storm. But right now, we're focused on shutting his ass down for good."

The man snorted softly. "Prison is too good for the likes of him. I can think of a dozen better remedies. One involves concrete, a lot of chains, and a sunset cruise."

Chopper stuck out his fist. "Keep the faith, brother. One way or another, we'll make this work."

DICE SAT IN THE BOOTH. THE LARGE WINDOWS LET HIM watch the street, but they also reminded him how vulnerable someone was to being exposed to the street. He listened to the guy a couple of years younger than him. But the wear on his face was halfway to his father's age.

Pepper leaned in as the guy pointed at the map. "They don't let their gang sell anywhere in the neighborhood. This house... they never water the lawn, so nothing grows. The lady next door... she's called the cops about the cars night and day... but the cops—they never come. This is vato land. Only the vatos have the bigger guns. And as for paying off the cops..." He leaned back against the booth, shaking his head with disgust. "I wouldn't put it past any of them."

Pepper looked up, studying the young man who had walked in, talking like a homie or vato but was now talking like there was education behind the face. "How heavyweight do you think the house is?"

The man rolled his eyes closed as he breathed through his pursed mouth. "I was sitting with a homie in his yard. We saw a black Sub back in the driveway. We couldn't see much, but more than a few large bags were going in through the side door. They were there for at least ten minutes. The driver never turned the Sub off and sat there the whole time—ready to drive." He shrugged. "There's a carport back there. I've never seen the Jeep move, but the gray car comes and goes. There's a black chick. She drives it. When she shows up with groceries, a couple of guys come out and take them in. She just backs in and sits there with the motor running, and they come out. Other than that, we've never seen a single person mowing the lawn or washing the cars or anything— except for all the people coming and going through the front door. Backpacks go in sagging, puffy, and come out heavy. Motorcycles, low riders, and citizen cars. No trucks. No rednecks or red hats."

Pepper folded the map. "Okay Peaches. We'll keep in touch with you."

The man pointed at Pepper's neck. "The doctor dude? It really works...?"

Pepper stretched his head and neck to one side. His right hand pulled on his T-shirt neck. "This is after only three. I'll get one more, but after that, it will only be little spots here and there. He knocks you out so he can cover sizable areas at a treatment."

"And the social lady?"

Pepper bobbed his head. His smile was a warm smirk. "Just go talk to her. Then decide for yourself."

15

PUSHING THE LIMITS

TINY BENT over the bar and tapped the small, empty pasteboard box on Chopper's head. "Out. Empty. Nada. Go Fish. There ain't no more. Nada mas." He dropped the empty box, once holding five hundred business cards, into Chopper's lap. He pushed back on the bar. "Don't feel bad. I don't think any of us would have ever thought we would run out of cards."

Dice chuckled. "It's the things you never expect. When I bought my first chef knife, I looked at all the steel and thought it would last forever. And then I sharpened and edged the knives five or six times every day I cooked. I bought my new set about two years ago. They should last until I'm old... If I get on with some cops and then the FBI."

Chopper smiled wonky. "Yeah, so you stop cooking." He pointed at his feet. "I've never had a pair of shoes last a year, and now... these are over five, and I'll replace them when I get bored."

Tiny tapped a coke down on the bar and slid it over for Dice. "So... where did we get the cards from before?"

Chopper shrugged, his eyes closed. "Yo, no sé."

"Well, we need more. You guys are throwing them around the

OC, and the phone is blowing up. We need more and probably a second phone line."

Dice rubbed his thumb and fingers together. "Here. Do you have any more? I'll get more made."

Tiny scoffed at Chopper's wagging head. He pulled out his wallet and leaned forward. He'd buried the single card under the flap at the back of the bills' section. Holding it in the air between his index and middle finger. "This comes back to me. You don't call the number written on the back. You don't look at it or even sniff it. To you—it doesn't exist."

"Got it." Dice pecked it out of the fingers as he glanced at the number. "Don't call..." His eyes got enormous as he elongated the name. "Sa... bri... na." He looked up with a low whistle.

Chopper's head snapped up. "Sabrina? Pedro's ex, Sabrina? South Shore Slut Sabrina? South Coast Plaza..."

"Stop!" Tiny grabbed for the card. Dice was faster.

Sticking the card in his pants pocket, he smiled. "Don't worry. I'll keep Amanda our little secret."

Chopper frowned and twitched his head back and forth between the two large men. "Wait. Is it Sabrina or Amanda? A brother needs to know."

Dice squeezed Chopper's shoulder as he walked behind him. "A brother doesn't need to know. They just want to have sexy dreams about what isn't his to know." He bounced his eyebrows at Tiny. "I'll be back in a few hours."

TINK, WITH RED HAIR, LOOKED AT THE CARD. "NICE print job."

Tink, with neon blue hair, leaned over her shoulder. "How many did you bring for us to spread around the Anaheim area?"

Dice fished out a few more cards and held them out.

Red Tink stared at them. "You need to go get more."

Pussy dropped a box on the bar. "There's five hundred... minus a tiny stack in my purse. Make it last."

Neon Green smiled. "We're gonna need a bigger box."

The Latino dressed in a latex LAPD uniform wandered up with an empty glass. "That's what we said." He passed the glass to Pussy and looked at the green Tink. "And we cover all of Orange County." He turned and rested his hand on Dice's prime rib of a shoulder. "Seriously. Us deputies can dump another thousand by next week. And I can always drop one of those small boxes with each of the Riverside and San Bernardino County deputies. They have a Dorfman infestation as well. And, if I know one thing about starting a war, if you're going to stir up the red ant's nest, also whack the hornet's nest and tip over a beehive or six. Use a bigger paddle. Always go grande or stay home."

Dice groaned and pulled out his phone. Looking at the last called numbers, he tapped one. "Hi. I was in this afternoon and ordered some rush business cards..."

The woman's voice oozed out around the side of his head. "Oh yeah. You're the guy as big as Reacher. Three thousand cards for the Aztecs. Custom gold pyramid and black type. Yeah. This is Traci. I did the printing. What's wrong with them?"

He smiled as both Tinks leaned in to listen. "I'm an idiot. I need three thousand more. How long will it take? And can I come pick some up this evening?" He eyed the deputy eyeing his muscles.

"The files and paper are still in the machine. I'll start running them now. Three thousand, was it?"

Green Tink held up her hand with all her fingers and thumb spread. "I'm getting told to stop thinking like a pendejo and make it five thousand."

The voice was a half-tinkling giggle. "They ain't wrong. At five, the price break brings it to cheaper than the three. Give me about an hour or so."

"Thanks. I'll see you after dinner." He looked at the three, paying him attention. The Tinks beat the deputy to the punch. "Where are you taking us to dinner?"

Dice groaned. "How far can I get on twenty-two bucks and some change?"

Green rolled her eyes at the blue. They chorused. "Our treat."

The young deputy sagged. "And the dashing cop loses again."

Dice tapped the fake police officer's chest. "How long are you going to be here?"

The guy smiled. "Paul and Mike are going to get here at about six thirty, and we're going across the street for burgers. We'll be here until about nine. Paul and I both have a shift tomorrow. He can run the cards and information up to the outer counties."

Dice glanced at his watch. "Yeah, that works."

The evening had long gone from the boisterous busy to a relaxed chill. Dice had forgotten how people in Southern California enjoy dining and relaxing outside until it gets below sixty-five. Jackets were something they forced you to wear. Or you put on if you were going up to the mountains. But the concept of wearing a jacket to be warm while you sat around a fire pit? What are you... *nuts?*

The fire pit danced merrily inches from their knees. All three heaters, with their pillars of flame and radiant heat, made the rooftop almost balmy. Only the two Tinks snuggled in their windbreakers. Dice had chuckled at the official three letters stenciled on the back. Pussy rolled her eyes and explained it didn't stand for Federal Law Youth. They only shared the jackets with two other young women trained to make the half-mile dive. The skinny cable from the top of the Matterhorn among the Disney cast creates a rarefied sorority. Each year, they invited back all the past flyers for a special dinner at the residence.

They turned toward the door as it squeaked. A petite Asian woman accompanied Frank. The two Tinks jumped up and hugged her. Dice rose.

Frank pointed at the cluster hug. "The one in the center is as close as it gets to my daughter. Well, Ming is the Asian daughter. Her sister Tree is the blond, white one. But she's in New Orleans figuring out a dredge problem or something." The three separated. "Ming, this is Dice."

Her hand preceded her. "Hi. Pounds told me a lot about you. I figured if we're going to help, I'd better come meet you."

He looked at the tiny hand disappearing into his sizable paw. "Help?"

She held her hand out at his seat. "Please. Don't let the size or age fool you. You picked up five thousand new cards for the rest of the week. You already burned through over two thousand. The cards have kept the phone number backed up. I assume the Aztecs are putting orange highlighter dots on a triple-A street map."

He cleared his throat. "Blue... but go on."

As Frank pulled a chair over, she waved her hand to clear the air. "Point is, the map will be almost all blue by Wednesday and useless."

Dice winced at the honest assessment. He thought about what he saw in the bar when he dropped off the cards that afternoon. "What did you have in mind?"

Ming glanced at Frank. "Um... we took some liberties. The phone stopped ringing at the clubhouse at eight o'clock this evening."

Dice frowned at her and then at Frank. Frank pointed at Ming. She had her phone out. She pushed the green icon and the speaker. The phone rang once.

The voice was female and professional. "Aztec clubhouse connections. This is Bunny. How can I help you?"

Ming smiled at Dice's confused face. "Thanks Bunny. I'm here with Dice. How many are working the phones tonight?"

"Baby, Sweet Thing, and me, Ming. We're trying to train some of the boy crew."

Ming nodded toward Dice. "How many for tomorrow?"

"We'll have five or six. But Mama was looking at the phone logs of the clubhouse and what was getting pushed to the busy signal... We might need to pull in a few more. That's why we're training Slug and his team. Chips is building the input map and database from San Francisco. We should have it all live by the time she goes to work in New Zealand tonight. She's doing the late shift on the dredge."

"Great, Bunny. Who went over to explain things to the Aztecs?"

"Jazz. She took her motorcycle. She figured it would be best to show her credentials up front."

Ming smiled. "Great. We'll talk later when I get back. Thanks for riding herd on this."

"My pleasure, honey." The connection was snipped off.

She slipped her phone into her back pocket and sat back. "Right now, we're plugging all the tips into a basic map system we already had. We put live links to the information as we get it. Later, we'll pour it all into the new map system and a better database. When the sheriff's departments are ready to bring it all down, we can give them maps and data any way they want." She crossed her legs.

Dice knew the little girl had outmaneuvered him. "I'm impressed." He looked over at Frank. "I guess I wasn't listening last night."

The man smirked with a twinkle in his eye. "Oh, you were listening. But I didn't tell you much. Last night, I wasn't sure how deep they wanted to get in. I should have known better. It's not their first rodeo helping Nash fight the bad guys."

Ming blustered a laugh. "Nash? She was easy. You popped our cherry on the drug smuggling." She turned to Dice. "We think this is just a continuation of that previous case." She glared at Frank. "Which lasted until I turned sixteen."

He put up his hands in defense. "Hey. I was kind of tied up."

The Tinks snorted. "Yeah, and laid around the hospital for a year."

"Not my fault."

Ming held up her two hands in the middle. "Hey. Cut him some slack. He saved Danny's life. And I got to learn how to drive, in the Bently—eventually."

Dice sighed as he rolled his head toward Frank. "Looks like you have more baggage than I do."

The man chuckled. "Only when it comes to my women." He flinched and pulled his phone out of his pocket. He stared at the caller's number and name. "Speaking of trouble." He thumbed the green icon. "Good evening, Nash."

He listened for a moment. "Nope. Chips was right. In fact, your cook is sitting about seven feet from me right now."

16

CLOSING DOWN

Nash shoved the phone in her pocket and glared at Muna. "When did Chips tell you the cook was talking to Frank?"

Vern frowned an eye. "Who's Frank?"

Uncle rested his hand on the deputy's arm.

Muna rubbed her face with both hands. "I'm tired. Isn't it bedtime yet?"

Nash growled across the small fire in the short bottom of a fifty-five-gallon drum. "When?"

The small black woman rolled her head as she stretched her neck. She stopped with her head back. She could have been talking to the moon. "This afternoon."

"Afternoon is a large place in time. One o'clock in the afternoon? Three twenty-seven this afternoon? Or did your hot pork rinds turn into four twenty this afternoon?"

Muna chewed on her upper lips as she brought her head forward. "You were busy."

Nash barked a single snap of a laugh. "Hah! Doing what?"

"Turning over the crime scene. The never-ending paperwork. Bureaucratic red tape from the chains of custody. It was all a nightmare..." Her voice trailed off as Felix and Alex doubled over in hysterics while Uncle buried his face in his mug. The laughter in the empty mug echoed like a donkey's braying.

Nash glared at Uncle. "You're not helping, Indian."

He dropped the mug into his lap and held out his hand with the palm up. "It's your powwow, Indian." His giggling got the best of him. He stood. "Your dog needs a walk."

Powder rolled her back to him as she groaned.

Uncle lowered his voice into a growl. "I said. The dog needs to go for a walk."

Powder rolled back over and creakily, inch by inch, ratcheted up onto her legs. She glared back at Nash, who had not come to her aid. The two disappeared into the night.

Nash returned her glare at the junior agent.

"Okay. About two. It slipped my mind. I was busy looking for background on the Reno guys."

Vern held up his hands in the time-out signal. "Who is Frank?"

The four chorused in frustration. "An old detective."

The silence fell and held for a full minute before Felix began snickering. Nash rolled her eyes and looked at Vern. "He was a sheriff's detective in Orange County. It's a long story, but there is as much of a family down there as you're looking at here. We kind of got blended these last couple of years."

The voice came from his deepest well. "But he's not a sworn officer now."

Nash let her eyes slide shut as her head vibrated. "No. And neither are any of his sixty wild children. Nor are any of their computers sanctioned. When they help, my boss gets busy else-where and doesn't want a report."

"They're illegal?"

Muna snorted. "Not illegal... intrinsically. Just not... um... halal."

Vern harrumphed as his eyes twinkled. "Is that right?"

Nash studied Muna.

The junior agent tried to hold the stare but lost. "What?"

"Did Chips fill you in on what they were doing? I mean how random is it that our number one suspect wanders to a city of ten million people and runs into Frank Pounds?"

Muna held out her hands. "He knew someone who knew someone, and they knew Frank. How random do you need it to be?"

Nash was silent. The fire danced in the black of her eyes.

Muna pursed her lips and blew out her breath. Rising on one hip, she pulled out her phone. "Hey. Mama Nash wants to know how they knew each other or how they got together."

She hummed as she nodded her head. "I don't know." She groaned. "Just a minute." Holding her phone to her chest, she looked at Felix. "What's red and goes oh, oh, oh?"

Felix hesitated and then giggled. "Santa walking backward."

Muna scowled at him and pulled the phone back up to her ear. "He guessed or already heard it. Let me know when you have more. Have fun in New Zealand. Bring me back a wallaby."

She slid the phone into her pocket. "She didn't know." Rolling her eyes, she glanced at Felix. "I think Oz and Mike have turned her."

Felix sat up and smiled. "Does that mean we're going to Orange County?"

Alex grumbled. "If we're not shooting anybody, I'm going home. I need to rebuild Uncle's engine."

Nash raised one eyebrow. "What's wrong with his beater truck?"

Alex waved his hand in the air loosely. "He's got a high-speed flutter in his muffler's wobble bearings."

The voice wafted across the night air. "I keep telling you, you just need to flush the elbow grease in the work joints."

Alex laid his hand out as he pointed into the black. "What the ghost said."

Vern eased lower in the chair to get his knees closer to the fire. His head rolled toward Nash. "Often?"

She glowered. "Nonstop."

He rocked his head. "Now I see why you took the case. You just needed a peaceful break from the inanities of the alphabet soup."

"You have no idea how right you are."

Her pocket whistled. She snorted with a warm smile. "And then there is my wife. The gala ran late tonight."

She thumbed her phone and hit the ringing icon. "Good morning, princess. How was the party? Any bodies I need to go hide?"

"A fascinating evening with the deputy director and his wife. We left the party early and went back to their house. They have a litter of little fluffy fur balls." Nash could hear the exhaustion in her wife's voice.

"Are we getting another daughter?" Nash stared into the night—wondering how close Powder was.

Mina's growl was amused. "I said fur balls. Not potential. They might be champion material in someone's eyes, but not mine." She cleared her throat with a husky cough. "No, the evening was getting to see Tony's domestic side. He whipped up snacks that could pass for hors d'oeuvres at some of the best galas. He took six months after college to study cooking in France. Some small school in the south of France. Maybe we need to go there."

Nash snorted. "Who's going to take the classes?"

Mina yawned. "Probably Lele. But if someone is cooking, they need someone to eat it…"

"Goodnight, Mina. You have a doctor in the morning."

"Yes. But I can sleep through the chemo."

Nash knew it was a lie. She had sat holding the vomit bucket. "I need to get back to my meeting. We have a long drive in the morning."

"Are you coming home?"

Nash's head twitched as she watched Uncle and Powder return. "Changing location. Our number one person of interest decamped to Southern California."

"Night." The phone snicked metallically and then muttered the soft horn of a text message. Nash returned a purple heart emoji and shoved the phone in her pocket.

THE WATER WAS BLACK AND CALM AROUND THE LONG white yacht. Discreetly, armed guards patrolled the front and sides. An angry voice emanating from the open doors of the salon was nothing new. They knew how to stay clear of the back lounge area and out of the volcano's way.

The bald man threw the business cards on the table as he screamed. "Who the fuck are these Aztecs? And what happened to four million of my product?"

The slender blond shifted his weight from his left foot to the right. His tan face and arms spoke of days' sailing in the sunshine. "A biker gang up in Fullerton. They've been passing these out for the last several days. And we can't find Manny, Rodolfo, or Freddy. Or the product."

"Fuck Manny and the dope. These fucking Aztecs... Are they moving on my turf? Is that what this is? A turf war?" The bulging vein in his forehead throbbed as his face turned a deep crimson. Despite his efforts to maintain a youthful appearance through expensive facials and skin treatments, his age was catching up with him. But he refused to acknowledge it—no one dared to tell the powerful man he was getting old. Nobody wanted to die.

The bikini-clad young woman, barely out of high school if she had ever gone, squirmed in the overstuffed chair. Her nail file paused as she looked at his face. "Pumpkin, your face is turning purple again. You need to calm down. Nobody is trying to move in on your territory. Nobody is stupid."

He looked at the blonde. The eight thousand stuck in her chest hadn't helped what she lacked in her head. But she calmed him down at night until he slept for a few hours. And then, after he had visited the toilet, he would nudge her awake, and she'd continue with the sucking to put him back to sleep. "Pookie, how about you make one of those little sandwiches for Daddy that you make so well? Go on. Make me a sandwich. And take it to the stateroom. I'll be there soon."

She thought about it and then smiled. "Okay pumpkin. But don't wait too long. You know I might go to sleep."

He waved at her as he sipped on his bourbon. "I'll wake you up." He watched the three strings making her bikini as she walked down the hallway. The short, sheer cover-up hid her body as much as a plate-glass window. He wondered what the surgeon was going to charge him next for her ass. His eyes returned to look at the three men standing in the salon, working hard at looking anywhere but at the girl younger than their daughters or mistresses.

Dorfman rubbed his right eye. The pain had been getting worse. The high blood pressure pills the quack prescribed for him didn't seem to work. "Look, Ivan." He blinked to focus. "Figure out what the hell is happening and shut it down. I won't tolerate this shit on my turf. The goddamn bosses in Mexico will make me their bitch if they think I'm losing control up here. So gather your crew and do whatever it takes. Just get it fucking done."

The man nodded. "Yes, boss. I'm on it." He turned and gave the other two a stern glare. Another night, they didn't get to wrap him in chains and take him for a swim out past the breakwater. Retirement was only possible if you had somewhere safe to go. He knew even returning to Russia wasn't an option. "Another time boys." Ivan slid out the large open door and headed for the dock. He knew the two edifices of muscle were only there in case Dorfman decided he needed to be taught a lesson—or retired with chains.

Looking back at the longest yacht in the marina, he slid into his G Wagon. Somehow, even the feel of the custom leather seats didn't bring him comfort tonight. He thought about the fistful of cards he had thrown away instead of showing them to his boss. They would have pissed him off even more, even to a retirement party. The coming war wasn't turf, and he knew he wouldn't survive if he continued the same as before. They flooded the county with cards, and he knew they were gathering information of the deadliest kind. It was time to visit the old neighborhood.

— — —

THE PRIEST RESTED HIS HANDS ON THE EDGE OF THE altar. Before him were the only sources of light in the small church. He had lit the two candles before kneeling in the sanctuary to recite the midnight prayer quietly. In the old days, at least a few faithful would stand in the nave, or the body of the church. But the elderly could no longer stand on the cold stone of the floor. And the younger ones were too busy elsewhere with their lives. The priest feared the world was neglecting the church, just like he sometimes felt neglected by the church.

The priest flinched at the metallic sound of the front door. The door's weight was more felt than heard as it quietly closed. Even in the nave's magnitude, the closing changed the air pressure. He could sense a presence, but he couldn't hear any footsteps.

"Back when we were young..." The voice was soft and respectful. "I remember the presbyter used to say the mass aloud. Loud enough for the two brothers being held by their ears to hear. Even as their drunk mother leaned against the back pillar."

The priest crossed himself and nodded. "Back in the day, rude boys used to wait until the priest finished the prayer before they interrupted the sanctity of the church." He braced his hands on the edge of the altar and pushed. His weight rocked back onto his feet, and he rose. It was getting harder each day. "We could dispense with the confessional. You'd only lie, anyway. So slip a few pounds of flesh in the box and be done with it."

Ivan pulled a small bottle out of his jacket. "Is it too late for a nightcap?"

The priest moved down the steps with his hands folded in front of the white vestments over his black cassock. "It's already past eight in Petropavlovsk-Kamchatsky. But an acceptable five o'clock in much of Siberia."

Ivan twisted off the top and dropped it to the stone floor. Crushing the thin metal under his shoe, he held out the bottle of vodka. "Here is to our grandparents in Siberia." The priest took the bottle and upended it in his mouth. The bottle bubbled twice before he lowered the bottle and passed it back.

Ivan held up the bottle. The two candles showed the contents half gone. "Not a long party."

The priest turned as he pulled the vestment over his head. "When my brother leaves his mistress's bed to interrupt my Lilio, I don't aspire to be sober when I hear why."

Ivan drained the last of the vodka. Stooping, he picked up the smashed metal cap. Folding it into wings between his fingers, he slid it into the bottle and rattled it all softly. "How do you know I didn't come from my wife's bed?"

The priest leaned his head back at his brother. "Because your wife moved to Alhambra seven months ago. She attends church every other week, so she doesn't meet the wife of the carpet seller she is sharing on Wednesdays."

"This carpet seller doesn't attend church?"

The priest flipped his head toward the door to the back. "Come." As he opened the door and led them back, he continued. "He goes to his synagogue."

"Jesus, Danilo, everything is so matter of fact with you. Is there no shaming anymore?"

The priest pushed open the door and entered the small office. Sitting behind the desk, he pulled out the bottom drawer. He held up the half-full larger bottle.

Ivan shook his head. "I need to drive back to Costa Mesa."

The priest bounced his eyes in a resolved shrug and removed the cap. Two large bubbles later, he replaced the cap and returned the bottle to the drawer. "Shame? For who? Who is to cast the stones, and who is to be stoned?"

Ivan held up his palms. "I never liked stones. So with that, I'm out."

The priest unbuttoned his top button and removed the white collar. "So, what are you doing here?"

Ivan shifted in the seat. "I left a packet with you."

The priest's left eyebrow pushed on his closed eyelid as he thought. "We never talked about what you wanted: casket or cremation?"

The pain around the Russian gangster's eyes darkened. "If it's a casket… it won't be open."

17

HIGH WINDS

CHIPS SAT BACK with the large bowl on her chest. The spoon stood dipped into the cereal and fruit. She had figured out the balance of the chocolate puffy cereal. It tasted better when tempered with the blander oat rings and topped with blueberries, slices of banana, and sprinkled with some raisins. Carbs, fruit, and fructose. Grains, antioxidants, and iron. A computer geek's mystery magic for logging long hours, massaging the monitors.

A small yellow box appeared on the upper right of her middle screen. "Gumz foe."

The square pulsed as a red line slowly drew around the edge— counting down the sixty seconds.

Fuck. She swallowed. "Coms, go."

The square grew to half the monitor.

The petite Asian glanced at the screen as she loosened the top button on her red silk blouse. "Ah. Good, you're there. I just got out of a meeting with De Nel. He's disappointed with the numbers coming out of the ore on the Canary River. But he likes the way you reworked building the step-walls."

Chips set the bowl to one side as she sat up. "It'll save them months down the road as they pull out of there. It also turns his mining into a remediation project for the river. Once the guys got the hang of the new idea, they smoothed it into their practices. It doesn't add a single hour to the day as they dredge, but the real profits will be on the backend." She shrugged. "The ore... is not our problem. If his engineers and geologists say the ore is there, well...?"

Ming absently nodded as she looked at one of her other screens. "Have you started working on the designs they sent for the new deepwater berth?"

"Some. Most of it looked fine. Their redeeming feature is they don't have to worry about basalt. The Remarkable Mountain range is almost entirely granite and shist. But the shist is down the way. So is the granite. They won't like it, but I cracked some numbers and came up with building a cofferdam with the overburden they're pulling up now. Park it there for now, and then when they blow up the new areas, the turbidity won't be in the river's water. It'll just collect in the dam and then settle out."

Ming eased back in her chair. "And they just make it go away when they clean it all up. I like that."

"It also means they can make runs with only two barges instead of using three and driving the dredged overburden nineteen kilometers up the river at this time." She shrugged and shoved a small spoonful of cereal into her mouth. Her left mouse clicked on a flowchart she had worked up. "They'll have to barge it eventually, but they'll be able to take down the cofferdam with a sucker or cutter barge. Cheaper than the dragline or backhoe."

Ming focused on the new chart. "And less turbidity. This looks good. Polish this up, and I'll run it past Nells." She looked back at Chips. "What about the side project?"

Chips pulled her legs up into the chair and sat cross-legged. She reached over with her right mouse and dragged the one form into the chat box. She knew it had filled the box on Ming's computer. Her left mouse moved into the share box to show on Ming's screen. "So the one mook we knew had been a dirty cop."

Ming giggled. "Mook? Do you really use the word *mook*? Is this a gangsta movie with Tommy guns, Roscoes, and dames or dolls?"

Chips chuckled. "If this were Vegas, I'd capitalize the term *mook*. But this is Reno, so maybe it's Mook-lite. But no less gangsta. The other three walked the fine line of getting caught but no less playing on the darker side of casinos, dames, and hotels. I found two of them with connections to a place called the Bunny Ranch. And yes, it was exactly as it sounds. There was another one called the Mustang Ranch. Different animal, but same breeding business."

"But four million isn't like sending your kid to the neighborhood store for milk and bread."

The box cleared from form to Ming. Chips' eyes dipped as she shook her head. "No. No, it's not. Somewhere with these four are some serious connections for *The Biggest Little City in America*. And judging by each of their financials, their connections are more like backers than just associates."

Ming winced. "I enjoy helping Muna and Nash... but it scares me the world they deal with."

"Same world big daddy Frank used to deal with."

The dark head leaned forward into Ming's two spread hands. The long black hair fell onto her fingers as she rocked her head around in the grip. Her voice muffled. "I know. I know. It was a better time when I was happy about dragging Frankie into the dredging world. But now, I worry we got sucked into the darker world, and we're dragging you kids in with us." She looked up as her fingers combed her hair. "But excellent work. Whatever you're happy with, pass it on to Muna. I think they're driving today. Or at least they are supposed to be on their way down here to work with Frank and Dice. But keep me in the loop. And outstanding work on New Zealand." She flashed her index finger for their gang sign of number one, and the box disappeared.

Chips stared at the chart of the Reno men. She weighed diving deeper and wondered whether it mattered. Her left hand reached for the large, insulated mug covered with the women of the Marvel universe. A friend had photoshopped the faces—replacing them with the faces of Team Herrera. Jazz loved the mug and ordered a case of them. The forty-eight mugs would keep the team happy for many years to come.

She pulled the top and growled at the empty bottom. Half standing, she noticed the time and date block on her screens. *Ouch*. The day had gotten away from her.

She stopped at the coffeemaker. "Hey Oz? Mike?" She listened for any grunt of testosterone from the inner laboratories—autopsy or forensics. Turning, she walked to each door. The lights were on, but then, they were never off.

She glanced at the skeleton on the large screen as she walked past the forensic computer station. She leaned in to look at the notation. It read Cornel University Medical School valedictorian and foldout 1968. She frowned and then realized she was looking at a printed page with the recognizable folds in the paper. One has three staples, and the other makes the foldout recognizable to most males in America. The X-ray was of a newborn infant, spread like a frog.

Her eyes rolled and ended, looking at the time and date. Unlike her displays, this one included the day of the week. *Fuck. Sunday*.

She returned to her dark corner and pulled up the FaceTime app. Scrolling down, she clicked.

The screen remained gray. "Go for Muna."

Driving. Chips sunk deeper into her chair. "Hey. I'm going to send you what I have on the Reno crew. When you get a chance, you can see if I need to dredge deeper. Or Nash can look at it."

Nash's voice sounded like Chips had interrupted a nap. "Send it to both of us. Muna's driving. I'll look it over, and we'll get back to you. Why are you at the office this late?"

Muna groaned. "She meant to say, why are you there on a Sunday? But I get it, girlfriend. When ready, grab an Uber to the Mayan Palace for dinner. I forgot to get the menu for you. But trust me. Sunday dinner isn't on the menu."

Chips winced. "A Mexican restaurant that isn't Colorado?"

Muna laughed. "Sorry. It's my accent. It is My Yang, as in the Yin and Yang. The Yang is where you go to cheat on any diet you are on. My favorite on Sunday night is the drunken honey walnut shrimp. They make it with large prawns, and it is heaven on earth. Tell them you work with me. They can put it on my tab."

"Yin yang and drunk shrimp. Got it. Let me know if you need more. I need to go to dinner before I dig up New Zealand. Are you dragging Felix down to bribe Tree with?"

Nash cleared her throat as she glanced at the backseat where the youth was sleeping with a dog's head on his lap. "Is there a reason we need to bribe your bosses?"

Chips winced. "Zipping my lips in three, two, and one." She cut the connection. They'd find out what was going on in the OC soon enough.

Tiny dove through the door to the bathrooms and office at the sound of screeching tires. The first volley of bullets was high as they shattered the windows set high on the walls facing the street. He knew the thickness of the bar would be some protection, along with the bathrooms. But he was about to be a sitting duck.

Chopper had wheeled halfway around the desk as Tiny burst low through the door into the office. Bullet stitched across the top of the wall. The large man kept down as he jumped to his right. He kicked the end of the desk and knocked it out of his way. The floor-to-ceiling bookshelf was next. He grabbed the piston and crank rod resting on the shelf. Using it as a pull, he drew the entire bookshelf into the room. He opened the hidden door and turned on the lights in the narrow hallway.

He glanced at the bullet holes getting lower. More chest high. He waved Chopper into the hallway. As he stepped in, he closed the door and rotated the wide metal plate into the two receiving hands bolted to the wall.

Turning, Tiny rushed after Chopper. The man sat at the other end of the long hallway. Chopper reached up and keyed in the numbers on the pad. The small light turned from red to green. Chopper leaned as best he could out of the giant's way. Tiny scooted along the wall but then stepped over the arms of the chair. They built the hallway before the need to allow a wheelchair.

Tiny turned the knob and leaned against the door. The door was the back wall of a rarely used welding station. The row of heavy oxygen and acetylene tanks, along with the crap piled on the metal table, made it mostly unusable. Or at least a place not subject to random examination. He braced his back against the doorjamb and pushed the back of the table with his feet.

"Yeah, I think I can get through."

Tiny stepped to one side as Chopper scrapped his wheels but squeezed through. The large man stepped over to a rack with many long pieces of metal. He grabbed the one bar and fed it into a pipe running along the back but under the welding table. Pushing on the long pry bar, Tiny closed the door and welding station. He heard the lock reset.

Tiny dashed to catch up with Chopper as the man opened the door to the next street. At the primer-painted van, Chopper stopped and held up his right arm. Tiny grabbed the door handle and heard the click as the van read the fob in his pocket. He pulled open the door and lifted Chopper. Swinging him onto the seat, he turned to the back door and the wheelchair.

As Chopper pulled his legs up, Tiny threw the chair into the cargo van. Rushing around, he climbed into the driver's seat and pushed the large button marked run. His hand dropped to the selector as the bullets shattered the back window. Tiny pushed the lever to drive and stomped on the gas as blood and bullets sprayed the front window.

A man stepped out at the end of the short street, raising a rifle. Without hesitation, Tiny swerved the car, and the attacker's body shattered on impact before bouncing off a nearby Prius. As they sped away, Chopper slumped over in his seat, blood seeping from multiple wounds. Tiny's adrenaline rush couldn't mask the pain and unease spreading through his body. He knew the nearest hospital was ten minutes away.

He pulled the steering wheel and took the right turn. The alternative was only a minute away. He prayed the phone in his pants could hear him. "Hey Siri. Call Rusty."

18

MOVING OBJECTS AND EXCREMENT

NASH SCROLLED THROUGH THE DOCUMENT. Pinching the screen, she made it larger. She held it up and squinted.

Muna glanced over with a smile. "You want to use my tablet so your old eyes can read it?"

Nash didn't twitch, but her growl was visceral. "Drive."

The pad floated forward from the backseat. Felix's hand and a disheveled mop of hair followed. "Are we there yet?" He looked around at the desert. "Hmm. Nowhere to eat either."

Nash looked up at the desert. The roller coaster of a highway rolled out for miles. "You're fast. We can stop while you run a bunny rabbit to the ground. Not much meat, but it would be entertaining." Her smirk was toothy as she glanced back.

His moan was more of a soft whimper.

Nash pointed ahead. "See the dark smudge on the edge of the earth? That's Four Corners. There's a truck stop there. We'll get lunch."

Powder nosed her way into the space between Felix and Nash. She stretched, and the lick on Nash's cheek was as close to a peck as she had gotten.

"Jeez. You too?" Nash clanked down at the naked dog. "You need your harness to go into the restaurant."

Powder turned and wiggled down into the footwell behind Nash's seat. A moment later, she resumed her place as Felix snapped the buckles.

Nash peered at the tablet with the document at full size. Frowning, she glanced at Felix. "Did you hack my phone?"

He rubbed his chin back and forth on his wrist, which hung from Muna's back seat. "It came in on Muna's channel. I only opened it for you."

Muna puffed a small laugh. "Don't you know, girl? Nothing is secure or sacred around this kid. Every passcode is another puzzle to be cracked."

Two cars passed, going the other way. "Oh damn. Congestion."

Nash peeked up. "It's on the right. It might look like it will blow away, but it's looked that way for forty years."

The woman in the store area opened her mouth at the sight of Powder. Muna flashed her ID wallet. "Drug sweep." The woman's mouth closed into a small oh.

Nash glanced back at Felix, slowing by the electronics display. They stacked the overload for his ADHD seven feet high under the hanging T-shirts, drones, and fake leather jackets. Talking fish plaques hung alongside childishly stuffed jackalopes on the walls. "Felix, you have time for food or toys, not both. Food is this way."

"Coming."

The seven people in the small restaurant sat fixated on the television, some with mouths open, others slowly chewing. The scene was from a helicopter. The closed caption scrolled above the yellow band with black letters identifying the news crew as Traffic Two. "…*following a massive shoot-out. The bar was the clubhouse for the local motorcycle gang, the Aztecs…*"

Nash stood while Powder and Felix pushed into the large booth. She glanced at the waitress holding menus. "There's a motorcycle gang around here?"

The woman peeked back at the television. "Nah. Thems down in Orange County. I think it's Fullerton. They've been running the same story for the last few hours. Another gang pulled up on the street. Shot up the building and then threw in some of them Moscow cocktails. The place is burning like one of them oil-making places."

Nash bobbed her head up. "Refinery."

"Yeah, them. Coffees?"

Nash sat and slid in. "Three, please. And four waters, please."

"Your dog want it in a bowl?"

Muna closed her eyes as she nodded. "That would be nice." She laid her tablet on the table and worked her magic to find the news. It was the same helicopter but with sound. Muna kept it low.

Nash pulled out her phone. "If he's down there playing with Frank... Let's find out what is going on."

The ringing sounded funny. "Jazz."

Nash bounced her eyebrows at Muna. "Hey, Jazz. It's Nash. What's with these biker gangs going to war in your backyard?"

There was a rustle on the phone, and then Jazz's voice was quiet. "I'm in Amsterdam at a dredging conference. Whatever is happening in the world is beyond me. I have six hundred engineers looking at me right now. I'm on a panel discussion." The click was a strange metallic thud—like a robot falling over dead.

Nash flattened her lips and rolled her eyes huge. "Wrong number."

Muna harrumphed as she pulled her phone out of her pocket. She found the number and pressed it.

"Hey sis? What are you doing? I thought you'd be here by now. Chef is doing something called Biryani, and I need your guidance."

Muna licked her lips. "If it's goat, go with the red wine. Grab a nice white and go with the flow if it's lamb. What do you know about a biker gang named... wait a minute? I had it here..."

"Aztecs? The one blowing up the news right now?"

"Yeah. That one."

"Long story. But yeah, we're connected."

Muna laughed. "Of course you are. But seriously…?"

Ming coughed. "As serious as a couple of dudes shot to shit along with their clubhouse. You know the drug sellers you just finished with…?"

"The three dead guys who tried to turn a drug sale into a stickup and got whacked for their troubles? Yeah…?"

"I understand you're missing a person of interest. He's down here. And he kind of hooked up with Frankie…"

Muna fluttered her open eye at Nash. "Are you about to tell me how some large fan is involved?"

There was someone else talking, and Ming covered the phone. Muna heard her take her hand off the phone. "Tell them if they're stable, send them to UCI Medical Center. We have an open account there for Frank." She snuggled the phone back into her cheek. "Sorry. We have some logistics to deal with. The two bikers went to the closest medical facility. It was the emergency hospital they use for their dogs."

Muna stared at Powder. "A vet?"

"Not just any vet. It's a full trauma center but for animals. They aren't prepared to manage multiple bullet wounds. So we need to hide them at a people place."

"The term is *stashed*. Ming? How deep in are you with this… um… incident?"

Nash waved off the waitress. She looked at Felix. "What was Alex complaining about?"

Felix shook his head. "No real jurisdiction in a gang war."

Nash lowered her head at him. "No jurisdiction or not enough justification to shoot people?"

He pointed his two fingers at her. "Yeah. Those two."

Nash looked back at Muna.

"Well, do what you can, but stay safe. We're still in the desert, so maybe a couple of hours, depending on the traffic."

"See you then. I'll have more information by then."

DICE AND FRANK STOOD BESIDE RUSTY IN A PAIR OF Frank's board shorts, flip-flops, and a surfer hoodie. The distant smoke from the bar was grayer now than black. The welding shop roof had caught fire, but the fire department had knocked it down fast. Frank explained that the black smoke was the tar and paper on the flat roofs of commercial buildings. The white was when the volatiles had cooked off, and it was down to furniture and studs. With commercial buildings, it was primarily black smoke. Family homes were white and gray. Brown was when nobody was near without a gas mask. Brown was chemicals.

Dice kicked the curb in front of him. He bit his lower lip as he looked at Frank. "Can they do it without drawing attention?"

Frank harrumphed in his closed mouth and looked at Rusty and then Dice. He held his hand out toward the smoke. "Attention from whom?" He pointed behind him at the ubiquitous orange mini-mart. "I think I could not only rob them but pack up and steal every bottle or box in the store, and nobody would notice. Everybody is looking at the pillar of smoke and listening to the radio or television. A gang war in your backyard is the kind of stuff you keep telling family back home to scare them into not visiting."

Dice looked down at the curb and then back up with one eye closed. "Okay. Maybe I should have asked, will they be safe at the hospital?"

Frank nodded his head. "The safer place would be at the children's hospital. But they don't deal with gunshot wounds enough to deal with what the boys have." He winced and looked up at the helicopter overhead. "Look, with shootings, most people think of Santa Ana. If you're near the water, it's Hoag. UCI is where people with insurance go. These are bikers—indigents. They get the dregs of care. One step above the veterinary hospital they first went to. Nobody knows the reality of them and insurance or not. But what people think is what matters. Besides, my girlfriend and their surgical team are the best in the business. Let's just take a breath and see what shakes out."

Rusty rubbed his tummy with his hands in the front pockets. "Do you really think it was Dorfman's guys? A daylight hit is ballsy."

Frank blinked and looked around to see if the three men were drawing any attention. "You stirred up the boiling pot hard with those cards. The girls said they had logged over two thousand calls this morning from San Clemente to Long Beach. They were getting calls from Riverside, San Bernardino, and even some out of the eastern ends of Los Angeles. That's a lot of hits on his turf. He wasn't going to just lay back and see what shook out. My guess is he has overlords down south. Anything making him look weak is cause for them to take over."

Dice rocked his head back and forth. "Sounds like you've dealt with him before."

Frank rolled his lips as he looked over. "I believe he was at the bottom of my retirement and the death of my best friend."

Muna pulled out her phone while Nash paid the bill. "Hey, Chips? I know you're in New Zealand right now, but the guy Ruskin and the other guy are working for the casino. Nash and I think their backgrounds sound too scrubbed clean. Something is missing there or stinks. See what you can dig up. You know how to get into my nasty girl's room, so feel free to use the black web for it. If you hit any roadblocks, call me. We're about two hours from Deep Six."

Felix stepped out into the parking lot. He bounced lightly on his toes. Muna looked down at Powder. Both needed to run. The car ride had only wound up more energy in both.

"Why don't you two go knock off a quick mile or two?"

Felix jumped and looked at Muna. "You sure? I mean, we need to be down the road and all."

She tossed her head to one side. "We also need to gas up. Let's say twenty minutes."

Felix's hand waved until they were thirty yards away and hitting a four-minute mile. Muna chuckled. "Those two would be dangerous at Quantico."

"Who would?"

Muna looked back at Nash. "Both. Felix and Powder. I'd bet he could run a marathon in the morning and still be ready for one of his *fast five* after dinner." She looked Nash up and down. "I don't know about you, but running in leather pants is simply wrong. Besides, we need fuel. I gave the Flash twenty minutes."

"What did Chips say?"

Muna looked across the top of the car. "She's already down in New Zealand. When she does those remote gigs, she puts on those big headphones they like, and the dredge is on all her screens or goes VR with the goggles. Personally, I'd only do screens. I want to see what else is on my screens. And the VR goggles make me queasy."

Nash slid into the car. "And then you can't see the bag of pork rinds."

Muna rubbed the side of her nose with her middle finger.

19

DIGGING DEEPER

THE NURSE'S aide wielded a long-handled squeegee with effortless skill as she glided through the frenzied operating room. She deftly swept away any droppings or debris, constantly moving in a dance with the two surgeons and nurses. A chaotic mix of bloody gauze, surgical mops, and other disposable items—all evidence of the intensive surgery taking place—littered the floor. The aide continued without pause, using a dry mop and removing any trace of wet blood or other slip hazard from underfoot.

The floor would remain untouched in most surgeries, but this was no ordinary procedure. Every second mattered, and every movement trained for maximum efficiency. And amid the high-stakes environment, stress hung heavy in the air like the heavy spring marine fog. But for this team, there was no time for nerves or hesitation. Their focus was laser-sharp, and their goal was clear: to give another chance at life to the patient lying on the table. In this room, it was not about anyone's blood pressure except the person they were fighting to save. The team had long worked together seamlessly, always focused on saving the life in front of them—nothing else mattered.

"How are we doing, Hammer?"

"BP is ninety-four over fifty."

"We're not done yet. How are we doing on whole blood?" The surgeon didn't even look up. His tri-power glasses were focused on the bleeding at his hands.

"Number twelve and thirteen of whole blood just arrived. I have a bag of platelets as well."

The surgeon looked at his partner across the body. The woman closed her eyes and twitched her head up. "Hang twelve. Let's put the platelets on a slow drip, about half of a plasma drip, to match the whole. I want the blood pressure so I can see any ancillary leaks."

The female surgeon kept stitching where she had removed the part of the lung shredded by the bullet. "How are we doing on time, Hammer?"

The anesthesiologist glanced at the screen to his right. "You have an hour twenty-seven left. I'm upping his oxygen pressure now."

"I'm sealed. Pan, can you mop the upper area? I want to watch for any deflection or embolism."

The nurse grabbed more gauze mops off the small pile. "He's been in a wheelchair for the last nine years." Collapse was also a threat because of sedentary atrophy.

"Ah. Thanks. Good catch. I saw it on the chart. Who brought him in?"

The blond nurse snorted softly under her double mask and shield. "Animal control."

The two surgeons paused and looked at her.

She shrugged. "They ran to the closest medical help. It was an emergency veterinarian clinic in Fullerton they use for their dogs. They plugged the holes and got a county control officer to sneak them over here."

The male surgeon twitched his head near his nurse to have his forehead mopped. "Smart move. Was this part of the gang shooting on the news this morning?"

Pan nodded as she moved the suction tube to where he was working. "Yeah. His buddy, the guy who saved him, is next door."

"How bad?"

"I didn't read how many holes. But he drew Carter's team."

The two surgeons echoed. "He'll be fine."

"BP's dropping. Seventy-six over fifty-two."

"Shit. Something is leaking. Open the bags. I need the microphone stethoscope."

The nurse fitted the electronic scope to his ears.

"Is this on?"

She rubbed her thumb lightly across the diaphragm. He nodded, and she rested the diaphragm against the lung.

"Lower."

She moved the end down a couple of inches. The surgeon listened as the lung inflated twice.

"Higher."

She leap-frogged where she had started and moved to the middle of the upper lobe.

"Clear. Other side."

She shifted to the middle of the right lung.

"Upper."

The nurse moved the stethoscope's end as the other surgeon stood with her hands loosely grasped in front of her stomach.

The male surgeon nodded at his partner. "Upper. Not bad, but it's filling. Shrapnel in the back?"

The woman moved and reached her hand into the chest cavity. Gently, she felt along the back of the lung. She paused and then nodded. Something is there. "Pan, I need low suction… better to go down along my pinkie."

The nurse inserted the tube and delicately probed for loose blood. They listened for the gurgling to change tone.

The surgeon sighed as her head turned, and she looked up with closed eyes. "Don't move, Pan. It's stuck in there… Got it." She pulled her right hand out. The chunk of bone was larger than her pinkie nail. She dropped it into the out-held tray. Her hand traced its way back along the lung. She looked at her partner. "It's torn. But I don't think this is our bleeder."

"He's flirting with fifty. I need more pressure."

"How many slugs did we get?"

"Two. The other was a through-and-through."

"And we have only three entries?"

"That's what the vet's report said."

The man looked at Pan. "Did he come in with his pants on or off?"

"Shit." She pulled the sheet up. The pants were still on. Nobody had thought to cut them off and examine them below the waist in the rush. The other nurse slit the scissors from the ankle to the waistband. Squeezing, they sheared their way through the jeans and leather belt.

Pulling the jeans out from under the man, the bullet hole and blood patch lay just below the belt on the left side. Centered over the pocket.

"Femoral artery."

The surgeon started feeling down the left leg. The leg was soft from the lack of muscle control. His fingers probed.

Pan rolled her eyes at the female surgeon. "Men. They can't find the coffee in the cabinet, the clitoris, or their dirty clothes on the floor."

The surgeon's eyes crinkled. "Experience with the dirty clothes?"

Pan shook her head as she leaned over and guided the other surgeon's fingers to the firm, swollen right leg. "No way. If Frank drops a sweaty shirt on the floor or bed of the shack, the coyote gets offended, picks it up, and puts it in the large laundry box. They only had to train Frank twice. He has the toughest skin for humans. But with the dogs… he's well-trained. But we put them to the test with a shirt on the bed or floor every so often. It keeps them and Frank in line."

"And they're wild."

"Nah. Frank likes to think he's wild. But he's domesticated. It's the coyotes who are wild—for now."

They looked over at the blood flooding out of the leg where the surgeon had cut. "I don't get it. The entry is through the left gluteus maximus. The slug should have traced straight down…" He stood and looked over his glasses at Pan. "Okay. You're the bullet queen. What am I missing?"

Pan redirected the nose of the suction tube to clean directly at the incision. "Okay, mister thorax; the bullet enters the back and hits the number seven rib on the right side. Where does the slug end up?" She moved the tube to the bottom of the cut as she palpitated the leg below. The shrill suction turned to a deeper burble.

"If it deflects up, the lung. But if it's to the right of the spine, the pancreas or liver."

Pan smirked. "Why not the kidney?"

"Not low enough…" He reached his finger into the incision. "What have we got here?"

"And as the axiom goes, with the lesser power to the slug, the most likely is the least likely for the ultimate resting place. And for almost all the time, you're right. But this man has one other complication."

The surgeon opened the cut four more inches above and below. "What makes him special?"

Pan raced the suction tube along the incision and then pointed for the other nurse to mop with the gauze sponges. "He's been sitting on his sittin' bones for a decade. The entry was inside the male pelvis wall. The slug or a fragment crossed over and nicked or skidded the femoral. My guess is right above where your finger is now. But on the back side." She nodded her head for the other nurse to mop the area. Fresh blood filled the area right away. But it wasn't pulsing.

"Shit."

Pan turned to the crash cart and the attending nurse. "Tourniquet."

She cinched the strap and then inflated it. The blood stopped. "Time."

The female surgeon turned the artery from her side. "Clamp." The cool, stainless steel slapped into her hand.

She bent into the crotch of the man. "Got it. Glue."

Pan held her hand from the back and placed the surgical syringe of super glue into her fingers. The working end of the tiny-nosed tip pointed into the air. "You're good."

The surgeon ran a small bead down the clamped nick on the artery. She watched as the glue interacted with the blood and solidified and cured. "Patch?"

The other surgeon moved his hands as he brought in the tiny patch of synthetic skin to reinforce the glue. He laid it on the cured glue and held the two ends. "Glue."

The woman bent forward and added the second layer into the porous fake skin. The water-thin glue bonded the two layers and fogged as it cured. "Clamp."

The nurse removed the clamp on the artery. They watched for a few heartbeats.

"Okay, let's try it."

Pan opened the air valve, and the tourniquet deflated. They all watched the patch.

"BP is coming up. Eighty over fifty-two and climbing."

The male surgeon looked back at the open chest. "Open time?"

The anesthesiologist paused. "You have seventeen minutes left."

"Let's get the hole in the back of the right lung. How are we on the whole blood?"

"Twelve is gone. Platelets and plasma are at half."

"Okay, let's give this man some dinner. Hang thirteen. I'm sure a biker or former biker will appreciate the number. Let the other two run, but let's hang some glucose. I want this man fed and healthy when he comes back to fight on his own."

They could hear the stapler in the back of the chest. The surgeon handed off the tool and grabbed her handful of gauze mops. Swabbing the area, she resettled the lung. "Give me a couple of minutes." She stood looking at her partner. Her voice was soft and lacked any of her usual edge of command. "Good call on the extra bullet." They stood looking at each other. No nods. No thanks. Nothing needed. It was only affirmation of the decade of their teamwork.

The voice at the head of the surgery table was soft. "Twelve minutes."

The surgeon pushed a single mop under the lung. It came away half clean. "We are good to close."

"BP is one hundred over fifty-eight and rising. We're at eleven minutes."

"Okay. Let's close him up. Ribs?"

"On your right."

20

WHO IS IN COMMAND

CHIPS GLANCED into her large mug. The coffee was halfway down the deep container. She tasted the liquid. "Blah." It was cold. The glow over the top of her wall of information never changed. The lights on the floor's autopsy and forensic lab side were never off. She considered swapping out the incandescent bulbs and fluorescent tubes for LED to conserve energy and controllability.

Oz had delved into the intricate details of the wiring, tracing it back to a time long before the earthquake. But he wasn't referring to nineteen eighty-nine. No, the only real quake in San Francisco turned everything upside down, causing chaos and mass destruction. Any other tremors were mere inconveniences, not even worth mentioning.

Oz then mentioned that it was simply a metaphor for bureaucracies and making changes. And as he droned about red tape, Chips had resorted to remembering the Fibonacci sequence and started backward from the hundredth decimal.

Grabbing the mug, she headed into the light. As she cleared the nasty side of Muna's wall of information, the figure came out of the breakroom, turned, and walked into the autopsy. Chips froze.

Pulling her phone out of the side pocket of her leggings, she frowned at the time pulsing on the upturned face.

She poured the old coffee into the sink and looked at the pot with a half-inch in the bottom. The red light was off. She touched her knuckle to the glass pot. Cold.

Rinsing the pot out, she started a fresh pot of coffee. As the water heated to drip through the grinds, she tapped the two pink packets back and forth with her middle finger. Tearing them open, she added the powder to the splash of creamer in the mug.

She looked in the general direction of the autopsy. *Why is he here?* She opened the refrigerator and pulled out the silver package.

She leaned against the counter and peeled the aluminum foil off the four-day-old banana. It was still greenish—as Mike promised. She shrugged and smiled as she peeled the snack. *You learn something every day—or die.*

The coffee started pouring into the pot. Chips turned and pulled out the pot and replaced it with her mug. The first twenty ounces of the drip were the strongest.

As the coffee neared the top of her mug, she reversed the process and left the pot to catch the rest. Shoving the last of the banana into her mouth, she wandered into the autopsy.

Oz was sitting at the autopsy table reading a paperback book. Beside his hands lay a bag of pork rinds. Chips stopped and picked up the bag as Oz smiled and laid his thumb in the book. "They're kind of bland, but I like the salt."

Chips took one out and popped it into her mouth. She let her saliva melt the confection and smashed it with her tongue on the roof of her mouth. She pulled out her phone and showed him the time as she cleared her mouth of food.

He dog-eared the page and closed the book. "We have a body arriving at four or five this morning. The medical examiner from Lake Tahoe is driving it down himself. He said there were unusual markings he wanted to discuss with me." He shrugged. "I slept in room four, and now I'm awake. So, I came here to read. Laugh, but I'm at ease in an autopsy. It's like reading in a library for me." He swiveled on the stool and shrugged his eyebrows. "More importantly, I'm more comfortable in this room than at home."

She sipped on her mug. "What about on your boat?"

"The cabin is cramped, and the cockpit is cold this time of year and at this hour."

She pointed the mug at him. "Point taken. By the way, I made a fresh pot."

He stood. "I didn't know if you were here, and Mike won't be in until after eight. But I wouldn't want to be accused of wasting coffee."

Chips followed him out of the autopsy room. "Or worse, wasting water during a drought."

The old man's finger appeared above his shoulder. "You know California dialed down the average height of the waves seven years ago." As he turned into the breakroom, he nodded his head. "Yeah. To save water."

Chips groaned and passed him on her way to the dark office. *Man children.*

Sitting, she texted Muna. *I'm going to kill Oz for his jokes.*

The purple heart and the vomit emojis pinged back before she could turn her phone face down on the desk. She smirked. Good to know she wasn't working whack hours alone.

THE SIZABLE FEMALE'S COMPUTER ROOM WAS A SEA OF red with the battle lighting. The night shift, or anyone with insomnia enough to pull any work in the middle of the night, had asked that the general LED lighting be converted to controllable. A day later, any cell phone in the room could raise or lower the ambient light level. The following day, someone found the red; within the week, red was the standard night lighting.

Muna snickered at Baby's frown of inquiry at the text. "Our sister sends her grumble from San Francisco."

Baby looked up at her upper level of screens. "Yeah, she just released the New Zealand gold dredge. Was she bitching about finding only cold coffee or time for bed?"

Muna shook her head and tossed her braid over her shoulder to hang behind the chair's back. "Neither. Dad joke."

"They have a night shift?"

Muna checked the time block. Frowning, she picked up the phone and typed. *Who is there this early?*

Oz.

She returned the thumbs-up.

She looked over at Baby. "It's Oz. There must be an early morning autopsy."

Baby snickered as she did a lousy vampire voice. "Blah, or maybe he is making somebody…"

In unison, they raised their fists into the air and chorused. "It's alive. It's alive." The giggles were short as they both went back to typing. Nobody wasted insomnia or quiet time in the computer center.

Muna noticed the symbol for biotoxin pop up on her treasure chest icon. Someone in her nasty system had just dumped a file or folder. She watched as her bots tore it apart for anything dangerous. The symbol changed to an animated kitten cleaning its paw.

She opened the icon and looked through the brief list of folders. Opening the most recent, she scanned through the documents. The oldest originated twenty-eight years before, in Miami. The image had the look of a scanned newspaper article. But she knew it was a record generated with an old word processor. There were no photos. That ability would be a few years later.

From the tone of the writing, she guessed the article ran on the second page or in the newspaper's financial section. The prosecution's surprise witness had been the accountant of the Political Action Committee. He had produced the damning set of secret records of the actual contributors. The list had a mix of crimes. The minor was racketeering and election tampering. Drug offenses and aiding Russian oligarchs to gain citizenship rounded out the hardcore.

The following file was a memo noting a transfer of a bank employee to a regional bank in South Dakota. The next was an IRS notice of a lien placed after an audit of the bank.

A public notice followed from Idaho. A new accountant had joined the guidance council at a tribal casino. Muna noted the name. The initials were the same in all the records and newspapers. The man's fatal flaw was his love for using all three names. She was sure he had jokingly referred to his initials as his standing since he was a young Gregory Oliver Denton.

The last was a W-2 form for George Oscar Dumont. The company was another casino in Reno. Seen as each document, they were just more detritus cast every second in America. Taken collectively, Muna knew she was looking at a phone call from the U.S. Marshal's office in D.C. or from her boss. She rolled her eyes. The race to shut down the investigation was on. She smiled and hoped the Marshals would grow a pair big enough to call the Napalm Queen. She had some pork rinds to shove down their craw.

———

As the deputy director walked through his office door, he spotted the pink note on his desk. He paused and hung his overcoat on his new antique coat stand. He liked the reverse snobbery connected to its being a Roycroft instead of a Stickley. Personally, he couldn't tell the two apart, nor did he care. It was easier than dealing with a wire hanger. And the broken wooden hanger had left his heavy wool and Kevlar overcoat unceremoniously on the floor a week before.

He diverted his eyes as he grabbed his large stoneware mug from his desk. Whatever the pink note wanted would wait. He growled about when the *While You Were Out* started. The missed opportunity after something like Pearl Harbor came to mind. He had grown up with it. Mad Magazine had mocked it. And still it persisted.

He pushed in a second container of high-test coffee and pressed the button for strong. He leaned back to the counter and waited for his morning starter. The pink square of paper, he knew, would foul his day beyond redemption. *I need a week in Barbados.*

The mug was half empty when the sun cracked above the rooftops and leaked into the ravine of the street below. Tony turned from the window. He could hear someone else enter the office. The noises of the day had started. His time of solitude was over.

He sat and read the pink note as his mug gently settled on the cork coaster printed with the inner rings of a target. The angle of the two arms of the X hugged the single, large hole. It had been a gift from the range master at Quantico. The shot was from a mile away with a Barrett rifle. The shooter was a fresh recruit from the Marine Corps. It wasn't her farthest confirmed shot but her qualifying shot at Quantico. The deputy director never lifted his mug when she was in his office. It was his private pride point. Not one to be shared.

Call U.S. Marshal Tod Unger. He slid the pink note under the stack of other papers on his desk. Whatever Unger wanted in the middle of the night would wait until the middle of his day.

He looked up at the woman standing in his doorway. His longtime secretary had retired to care for her husband—somewhere warmer. He squinted his eyes shut. The name wasn't coming, and he knew Dorthy would not work. But it started with a D. Or was it an E?

Donna sauntered toward him; her high heels were silent on the carpet. *Deadly.* "It's Donna." Her smile was soft but sly. "You'll get used to me. I have an ear for everything. Even if you close your door, I still know what's being said. Because I'm Donna."

She placed a neon pink note on his desk. "I'm Donna, and this arrived yesterday. He mentioned he gets to work early. In L.A. terms, early could mean eight or even six o'clock." She checked her watch. "Give it an hour before contacting him, or I can handle it for you."

He picked up the note, holding it up to examine the color. "Do these come in any other hue?" His eyebrow stood notched.

Her eyes bore into him, unamused and unimpressed. "I've seen them in baby blue before. But the gist remains." She reached under the stack of papers and retrieved the hidden pink note. "How about I grab a pad of foolscap? The torn edges make it easy to hide on a cluttered desk." She tapped her perfectly manicured nail on the pink paper. "You have an ambitious agent snooping around in some cesspool they shouldn't be. Hold on to this until after your luncheon. Then perhaps steer Mister Marshal toward speaking directly with your wayward agent."

"Who's the agent?" Tony asked.

"How should I know? I'm just Donna." She turned to leave but paused and glanced over her shoulder. "But from what I heard, she's like Raging Bull on the warpath. And no agents in this office are digging deep enough to uncover someone in Witness Protection."

He smiled. "I think that was Sitting Bull."

"Raging, Sitting; it's still all bull. Look after your agent." The blue dress was only a half blur, and the doorway cleared.

Tony let out a soft chuckle as he reclined in his chair. "Thanks, Donna."

21

CHASING PAPER

THE LONG TABLE was warm where the sunshine poured through the large window. Nash ran her hand over the epoxy surface. Buried in the three-dimensional sculpture was the longest surfboard she had ever seen. Other than the matching original hanging over the central part of the restaurant. They made the resin look like the foam of a wave washing over the fourteen-foot board.

Ming giggled at Nash's response to the long table and the few chairs. "This is Frank's private table." She patted the old leather and wood desk chair and pointed at the large floor-to-ceiling window. "From here, he can watch the surf come in along the point. Today, surfers lie on their boards instead of sitting and watching the surf. There are only ripples, or what they call a flat surf. So, it's mostly the old grinders, or older surfers, out there lying in the sunshine—sleeping."

Jazz waved her hand at the framed surf photos and posters jamming the walls. And then spread to wave at the undulating sea of antique surfboards and pieces of chewed boards. Whether they were honestly trophies of past shark attacks or not—nobody cared. The effect was precisely what Hollywood or anyone from anywhere else would expect or want from a restaurant named The Surf Shack.

"While Frankie was cooling his heels in the hospital and getting a new spine, he told Danny and me to make nice-nice and become a family. The gun and sword fight had destroyed enough of the building to justify closing it for extensive renovation. Thanks to our friend Granite, a few extra holes in the ceiling and roof guaranteed the rebuilding of the upper structure. They raised the entire dining room four feet. Then, they hid the new air-conditioning and air filtration system in the attic space over the kitchen. The air here is cleaner than at a surgery center or out there on the picnic benches. Danny kept designing the perfect restaurant, and I kept writing checks from a trust fund Frank had never had a reason to touch."

Ming smirked. "It was the first time Tree and I had designed a mechanical setup. So we hired Slug and the boys from the floor below us in the engineering building. That's when we formed Deep Six, which is how it is now. The boys are mechanical wizards, and we crush the programming and research." She waved her finger around at the ceiling. "This was the test bed for laying out the main gallery and dining hall at Deep Six. They hid all the LED lighting. You don't see the lights—only the result. This entire restaurant burns less than two thousand watts an hour of light. Even if Danny were open at night, it would tick in at less than forty-five cents an hour to light it up like daylight."

Muna pointed at the antique surfboards hanging from the ceiling. "Where do you find these old surfboards?"

The tall, emaciated redhead sauntered up carrying a large tray. Setting it on the table, he answered the question and explained the dishes. "I put the call out to the surfing community. It was for Frankie's place, and I guaranteed no harm would come to the museum quality boards." He started spreading out the food. "And we have four bleeding heart attacks with pigs and a fruit bowl for the halal. My K-9 niece gets the Peeper special. Chopped and seared Porterhouse with a side of rice and quinoa. The posters and photos are duplicates of the ones people wouldn't sell us. There are many people who may owe Frank or just like him. I don't have any idea why. The man is an ass for sleeping out there on his dumb board instead of being up here to entertain. But other people don't hold my opinions of the bastard. So, enjoy." He held his arms outspread. The bleached-blond, older waitress slid her right arm around his waist as she dipped under his arm with two carafes of coffee.

The waffles smothered in a strawberry compote with over-easy eggs on top were down to red stains on the heavy white plates. Nash swirled the last of her coffee in the oversized Navy mug. "You were up early."

Muna looked up through her eyebrows. She glared over at Powder. The dog turned and sat on the chair to look out the window behind her. "I told you if I took you out to pee, you weren't supposed to tell on me."

Ming bashfully raised her eyes. "Baby, let slip she had gotten a message from Chips at three this morning. I... um..."

Nash growled. "Was out of bounds. Muna was supposed to sleep in. She has been doing the driving."

Muna slurped the last peeled kiwifruit into her mouth. Three chews and it was juice. She swallowed. "I got a ping from someone in my nasty room. They were sending an extensive file, so I got up to get it on the isolated network."

"And the file was important enough to get up at three?"

Muna glared at the back of the dog's head. "You're still a snitch." The furry ear twitched as Muna's head ground around to lock eyes with Nash. "One of us will get a phone call sometime today. It'll be good to know, going in."

"And the phone call will be...?"

Muna's mouth drew open to a fence of blinding white teeth. "Your friend, Commander KABAR, or a U.S. Marshal ready to rip us a new one."

Nash snorted. "Nothing new there. They're already oh-for-one on that score. They just never learn. I take it you want the Marshal call when it comes?" She pulled her phone out and found the text message app.

Muna dipped her head with a grin of pure evil. Nash held out her phone, took the smaller agent's photo, and poked in the text. *"The Marshal is to call Muna direct. No intervention or no more scotch."* She showed the text to Muna, Jazz, and Ming.

They laughed. Jazz shook her head. "Will he behave?"

Nash growled. "If he likes his scotch." Her phone pinged, and she showed them the text reply. The animated fist turned into a thumbs-up.

Muna chuckled. "He's getting better at texting."

Ming shied her face. "He has a direct line to his tutor." She looked up and held up her palms. "Oh, no. Not me. Chips."

Nash's eyes smoldered as she turned toward Jazz. "Did you hear anything on the bikers?"

Jazz pulled her phone out of her hip pocket. "That's where Frank actually is. I didn't want to worry Danny. He's a third-degree black belt in three martial arts and a silly Nelly with worrying about Frank."

Ming nodded. "He's with the guy Dice. The dude in the wheelchair was a buddy of Dice's when they were kids."

Nash winced. "So how does Dice know Frank?"

Ming rolled her eyes to make them round-shaped and large. "Jazz?"

Jazz sighed. "If I understand the thread right. Dice's best buddy in the marines was married to the gal who has been working for Pussy at the Mary Bar."

Muna squinted one eye. "She's a prostitute?"

Ming laughed. "The manager... well, the new owner, is named Pussy. As in the Bond girl." She rolled one eye and looked at the ceiling. "It gets more complicated. She's a male-to-female trans... with twin daughters named Tink."

Nash held out her hand. "Wait. Frank's girlfriend is Tink..."

Jazz laughed. "No, *her* name is Pan, as in Peter Pan. Tinkapanika is the name she was born with. But she is Pan, Tinkerbell, or Tink because she brings magic to anyone nearby. To Frank and us, she's

Pan. To the rest of her world, she's Tink or Pan. She was in the surgery with Dice's friend." She licked her lips complacently. "See, nothing is straightforward around here."

Nash barked a laugh as she pointed to the two. "Yeah. A vase and discordant music, who work with a tree and a snail's first cousin."

Ming tinkled a laugh. "Let's not forget the baby in the corner, a sweet thing, everybody's mama, and you even gave us an uncle for everyone."

Jazz wiggled her eyebrows. "Miss conceived in the backseat of a Rambler station wagon."

Nash groaned. "Okay. Okay. So, what were we talking about?"

Ming laughed. "Tricia working for Pussy."

Muna wagged her head. "It still just sounds so wrong."

Jazz raised her eyebrows. "And throwing beers for pussy sounds so much better?"

"No. And neither does the term Mary Bar. In San Francisco, a Mary Bar is a gay bar where drag queens hang out."

Ming and Jazz looked at each other and laughed. "Same, girl. But everyone is welcome."

Muna tapped her finger on the table. "So this Tricia, who was married to a big strapping marine, is a lesbian?"

Jazz twitched her head. "Nope. Straight. And now sober. Pussy is her sponsor."

Nash narrowed her eyes. "The bar owner is a recovering alcoholic?"

Jazz nodded. "And drugs. She holds a couple of meetings in the morning before the bar opens."

Nash wiped her hands across the air. "Okay, back to the surgeries."

Jazz smiled at the change of subject. "Preliminary report says they went well. When Pan wakes up, she can call for an update unless Frank calls."

"I thought you'd have an update for me."

They looked up at the woman with bloodshot eyes and blond bedhead. The T-shirt was pure Frank. The Ramones World Tour at Crystal Cove. Torn and holy in all the right places. The black sports bra held decency in place. Whether there was anything below, she lay covered by the shirt to her mid-thigh. She dragged a chair behind her.

The sparkly pink thermos mug landed in front of her as she sat. Danny shifted his weight to one out-slung hip. "Are we eating today?"

She grimaced. "A simple omelet and raisin toast. Easy on the butter. I need the forty grams of protein but not the fat."

"Chef has brie or provolone."

Tink stretched her neck as she thought. "Brie please."

He rubbed her shoulder and gave her a gentle pat. "You've got it, sweetie. Quatre œuf with bunny drop toast, easy on the lube."

Pan sipped on the thermos mug and looked up at Jazz, staring at her. "What?"

The butch lesbian shook her head. "It just never ceases to amaze me how you tame the beast in him."

Pan growled as she shook her head. "I train by sleeping with wild animals." Her one eye closed as she sighed and reached around to her back. Pulling up the shirt, she withdrew the phone out of her panties. She glanced at the screen and thumbed the green icon. "What? And fair warning, I'm about to have the second sip of coffee now."

She sipped while she listened and hummed. "Thanks. Find Frank. I think he's there, hanging out with a giant Latino named Dice. The guy has tattoos all over his hands and arms. Give them the good news. And if the patients are talking, let Frank and Dice in to see them." She hung up and laid the phone on the table. "They're both awake. My guy isn't out of the woods yet, but they'll watch his temperature and check his surgical sites every hour." She frowned tiredly. "So, why are you here?"

Nash smirked. "So it wouldn't look like we were staging a sit-in at the hospital."

The nurse nodded slowly. "Good thing. Security was twitchy yesterday."

Muna held up her left index finger as she rolled to pull her phone out. She looked at the screen and sneered. "D.C. number." She growled and hacked twice to lower her voice. "Agent al-Faragi."

She listened.

Finally, she winked at Nash. "Did you file an inter-agency seven eighty-three with the deputy director's office?" Her smile grew. "No. It's an ongoing investigation. And under five ninety-four subsection twenty-three bravo, I can't tell you squat until you file the proper paperwork. How the hell do you people get anything done over there? Do you always play everything this Loosey-goosey?" She thumbed the red icon and laid her phone face down. She smiled at Nash. "I'll bet the next phone call is your buddy, but not before tomorrow morning."

Jazz snorted. "You just hung up on a U.S. Marshal?"

Nash laughed. "Sure. And he won't call Agent al-Faragi back directly again. They only lose their balls once."

Ming wrapped her hands around Muna's arm and snuggled her head against it. "You sure you don't want to come work for me? I'll build a shooting range in the basement."

THIS MEANS WAR

ALONG THE MONEYED rim overlooking the small town of Ixtapa, people value haciendas based on who has the most armed guards. The men at the gate are for show. The ones walking in the hot sunshine around the grounds are the guards. But the ones who are near the back doors leading to the pool and the forbidden fruit of young semi-naked women—are the trusted few.

The tall glass and remains of a Bloody Mary shattered against the corner cabinet and out onto the rear deck of the hacienda. The angry man swiveled in his high-backed desk chair. "So, where is my product?" The vein only pulsed at the hairline where the Botox ended and the hair plugs started.

Dorfman's fingers wove into his short hair. His forehead rested against his palm. His elbow was planted on the desk. "We don't know. That's what I've been trying to tell you, Ignacio. The guys took it all to the buy. I have eyewitnesses who saw them load it into the SUV. Then they drove off."

"Where?"

"We don't know. They set up the buy and location. We categorize so we don't have exposure. They called that morning, confirming they were there. But never called again. It should have been a ten-minute exchange. Fifteen tops."

The man in Ixtapa looked out across the expansive deck. The view was of the pool and the ocean. There were six young women on the deck by the pool today. He should have been delighted, but then, there were phone calls. "What kind of pendejo do you hire these days?"

"Memo and Lito work for you. But Stanley has worked for me since we were mules packing weed in the alfalfa. They are our best guys. Something must have happened."

"Don't blame this on my men. I will come up there and slap the tongue out of your liar's mouth." The man at the southern end of the conversation scratched viciously at his hairy, naked chest. Calming. "It has been more than a week..." His threat sounded casual, but Dorfman knew it was anything but.

"We tracked their phones... well, Stanley's phone. It's up in the high desert. But it hasn't moved."

"Did anyone go look?"

Dorfman watched as the young blond rolled over onto her stomach. The tiny string hid between her butt cheeks. He wasn't sure if it was better or worse than her lack of a top. He turned back to his desk and the conversation. "Peter is going up there this morning."

The squeak of the chair in Mexico was small, but Dorfman knew it meant the conversation was ending. "Keep me posted, Dorfman. You already paid me for the product. So, if it is gone, that's on you. But if something else is going on... and you don't tell me..."

"Just a little turf squabble. Nothing we can't handle."

The Mexican's throat clearing sounded more like a rocky avalanche. "What the news showed the other day... didn't look like it was little." He closed the phone.

Dorfman glowered at the dead smartphone in his hand. For a moment, he thought about throwing it. *Motherfucker*. "Peter?" He raised his voice. "Damn it. Peter?"

The thin man stepped in from the back deck of the yacht. "Yeah, boss?"

After realizing what the man had been watching, Dorfman buried his face in his hands with his elbows on the desk. Despite being muffled, his voice remained clear. "I want you to go up to that little fucking town where Stanley's phone is and find out what happened to them."

"Right now?"

Dorfman's face raised high enough for his eye to see over his fingers. The bloodshot nature of his eye only enhanced the anger.

"Going now, boss." The man spun on his heel and was over the gunwale in an instant.

Dorfman couldn't remember if the dock was long enough to be there. But not hearing a splash, he shrugged. He stared at the two perfectly tanned cheeks, smiling at the sunshine. "Peaches, daddy needs some calming down."

Her head rose as she looked over her dark glasses at the reflective glass door. *Damn. Just when the sunshine is at its best.* "Coming, Daddy."

———

THE STEEL BLUE EYES WANDERED FROM WORKMAN TO workman. Only the four who were installing the replacement glass in the large window worked as a team. Vern recognized Vincent. The man who had upholstered every bar seat and restaurant booth north of China Lake to the Nevada border.

Rumor had it he had been doing a color swap in Bridgeport. The Topaz Lodge and Casino owner liked the work and dropped a stack of cash before him to come a half-mile across the border. Vincent had stood to his full six feet and told the man it would take a lot more than the small stack to step a foot out of California. The man filled his lunch bucket with hundreds and asked to bill him for time and materials.

The owner's wife had taken a shine to the man's deaf-mute boy helping him. She showed him the third slot machine along the row, looking out at the lake. She took his hand and slipped a roll of quarters into it. The machine paid out each lunch hour while people were eating. She ensured she was working the cage when the boy brought up the bucket of quarters. Nothing was ever said, but when the kid turned sixteen, he bought the car of his dreams: a thirty-year-old Jeep.

Vern watched as the kid silently rolled into a booth seat unit upholstered in the new yellow. The owner didn't think anyone wanted to see the old bloodred upholstery. The young man silently set the unit where his father could get it next, picked up the furniture dolly, and walked back out to the truck. Everything was silent. You would miss the small hand signs if you didn't know what to watch for.

Vern heard the soft footsteps on the parking lot gravel behind him. "When do you expect to reopen, Tyler?"

The man with thinning brown hair ran his hand over his head —straightening the beginning of a comb-over. His bulbous nose of ruptured blood vessels spoke of decades of alcohol and worry. "I expect Vincent to finish late tomorrow. By Friday, Lumsdon will be down to tape off everything and shoot the fresh paint. I'll clean the cook station this weekend, and we'll be back open on Monday."

Vern nodded slowly. "Just in time for fishing season. You expect Dice to be back?"

The man sighed. He had been in the exact position plenty of times before. "I ran an ad in the Times. Maybe I get someone who wants out of the rat race, and maybe I have to cook a shift or three myself."

Vern looked at the man out of the side of his eye. "But you don't expect him back?"

"He's not the first cook or dishwasher I've had quit. You pay them on Friday, and they quit on Monday. If you can't fill the shift yourself, you'd best not get in the business." The man looked over at the deputy. "Why the interest in my cook?"

Vern stretched his neck as he watched another booth unit slip into the restaurant. "Just had a few more questions I'd like answered." He shrugged his face and one eye as he slipped on his aviator dark glasses. "Nothing really important." He stood and strolled to the driver's door. "I'm tired of eating my cooking. I like the way Dice cooks chicken fried steak. Oh, and his gravy is a hell of a lot better than yours." He tipped his head. "Just sayin'."

He slid in and closed his door. The engine rumbled to life as Tyler rolled away from the hood. Vern put the car in gear and nosed it from the parking lot.

THE LARGE TABLE WAS MADE OF MAKESHIFT construction and hastily assembled by joining three smaller ones. They covered the surface in stacks of meticulously organized paper-work. Lists, maps, and data compiled by the girl team at Deep Six. The folders contained every detail of the Dorfman drug operation. From street corner dealers to drug houses and shooting galleries. They broke the territories up into divisions for maximum efficiency busts. The supply houses, known as *strong houses,* were on their unique list and map because they were heavily armored. Those would be the jobs of SWAT, DEA, and ATF. The two houses believed to be run binationally would also receive special attention from Homeland.

Dice sat with Frank, leaning against the bar, facing the front door. He looked around at the walls of the bar. Photographs and posters of drag queens, gay pride parades, and holiday parties at the bar lined the walls.

Frank looked at the large man. "Still taking it all in?"

His head rolled back and bounced forward. "When I was just a peeper, the only bars I knew were in the local Mexican restaurants in Boyle and Lincoln Heights. The only bar I knew with motorcycles parked out front was over in El Sereno. There was another one in Glassel Park, but it was a different gang. But a gay bar? Heck, I had no idea."

Frank nodded. "It's an eye-opener."

Dice snorted wetly. "Eyes were only the start. After working with Pussy and meeting everyone these last week... It's a whole different world. It's like the shadow of the real world out there. But they all live out there as well."

Frank smirked as his eyelids drooped in understanding. "But then, they come to Eat, Drink, and Be Mary and become who they really are. Or at least who they want to see themselves as."

Dice glanced at his watch and then the door. "Do you think...?"

Pussy walked up behind them and rested her hand on Dice's shoulder. "Relax. They'll show. Besides, six of them are already here."

He looked up with a frown. "Here?"

She nodded. "Their meeting is breaking up. You two need more coffee?" She glanced up at the sound of cars out in the parking lot. "You're about to get busy."

The large man opening the door was only missing a ten-gallon cowboy hat. His uniform was Orange County Sheriff's Office, but the highly polished cowboy boots and the oversized buckle were something else. He nodded as his eyes adjusted to the indoor lighting. "Frank?"

Frank hesitated and then stood. "Sheriff. Thanks for dropping by."

The sheriff glanced at the now-rising large Latino in the stretched T-shirt and tattoos. Frank snorted softly at the sheriff's eyes. "Sheriff, this is Dice Espinoza. This is his idea and war. Dorfman stuck a shiv in his day job, so we felt it was turnabout and all that. Dice, this is the man who has your back. The Sheriff of Orange County."

Dice stuck out his hand. "Sheriff..."

The man smiled. "Mucho gusto, Dice. And I want to thank you for bringing your war to my backyard. We've been trying to clean this scum out of our system for some time now."

The door swung open, and three young people tumbled in, laughing. At the sight of the sheriff, the blonde stood up straighter and smirked. "Well, if it isn't our old friend and peaceful officer. Good to see you, Sheriff. Are you here for the festivities or just a courtesy call?"

The sheriff smiled. "Team Deep Six. Good to see you, Tree. Ming. Who's your friend?"

They looked at Frank and smiled.

Frank drew his face out as he scratched his cheek. "Sheriff, meet Homeland. Agent Felix Farnsworth, this is the sheriff in this county."

Felix stuck his hand out and smiled. "And to answer your next question: twenty, sir."

The man frowned as his hand pumped up and down slowly. "Twenty?"

Tree smiled and hugged Felix's arm. "Yeah, I'm dating a younger man. It used to be salacious, but last month, he turned twenty. So he's not a teenager anymore."

The sheriff closed his eyes as he bit his upper lip and turned back to Frank.

Frank shrugged with a Cheshire grin. "What can I tell you, Sheriff? It's a whole new world."

MAPPING IT OUT

A BLOND DEPUTY opened the door and stuck his head in. "Are we in the right place?"

Ming's chuckle sounded more like a bag of empty beer bottles. "Depends. How many cop cars are in the parking lot?"

The Asian deputy looked around and then turned back as he shoved the blond out of the way. "Fourteen." He waved his finger at the other Asian. "We're from Garden Grove. The surfers are from Huntington Beach." He rolled his eyes with a smirk. "Everything is slower at the beach."

Tree laughed. "I've got Garden Grove here. Are you the Little Saigon squad?"

The deputy shook his head. "Patrol. The undercover is parking his crotch rocket."

"Okay. Here's your packet." She pointed to her right. "You two are in the Carousel Room to your left. Coffee and donuts or bagels are on the bar behind us. There are even cinnamon date sticky buns down near the end. Better grab them before Irvine gets here. We got them at their request."

The two deputies smiled at each other. "The Anteaters lose." He nodded at Tree. "Thanks."

The red and black leather tableau opened the door with the helmet under his arm. Frank chuckled. "I've got this. You're getting slow, Nguyen." He held out the small packet.

The deputy's face lit up. The sun-bleached tips of the brush-cut hair only came from logging long hours of water time on a long surfboard—waiting for large enough waves. "Shit. If I knew they would let the geriatric in here, I would have come the long way."

They slapped their hands together in a thumb clasp shake. Frank snorted softly at the old-age joke. "Are you still trying to get a date with my great-aunt?" They both knew their birthdays were hours apart. Both had seen the other's scared body. But just one had *disability retirement* written up and down his spine.

"Nah. I finally met your mother. Where's the dog and pony show?"

Frank jerked his thumb over his shoulder. "Breakfast wake-up is behind us, and you're in the big room with everybody else. We'll break out all of you undercover after the general meeting. Hug the back wall. It'll be easier to peel you off when we need you." Frank moved his thumb to the end of the bar where Pussy was polishing glasses. "And Pussy has some lox hiding, along with the pineapple cream cheese. It's not Loco Moko, but it be da ono kin."

The man glowed. "Thanks, bro. We missed you at the break over the weekend. The point was on fire."

Frank rocked. "I heard... after. Get some chow. We'll catch up after they finish running the dogs and ponies."

THEY HAD CLEARED THE CAROUSEL ROOM OF THE USUAL small round tables. Only chairs jammed the room. On the wall, the boy team had hung a complement of four oversized monitors and slaved them to Muna's laptop. The darkened screen looked like a short newsreel from World War II. The written sentiment was pure Winston Churchill. *Welcome to the Hell of War. If you thought otherwise, you are in the wrong theater.* Only a couple of younger deputies chuckled. The older ones already knew why they were at such a special meeting.

Muna looked up from her laptop and stood. "Morning. If you are undercover, please move to the back of the room. The general meeting is only seventeen minutes long, and then we will move you to another room. If there is anything we share there, you can coordinate with your uniforms afterward. But most of it will be unnecessary for them to endure." She watched as a few got up and moved to the back row of chairs.

"Thank you. My name is Agent Muna al-Faragi with the FBI. If you think I remind you of your little sister—don't. Your little sister doesn't have to shoot qualifying every ninety days. My last seventeen qualifying cards have been a playful practice of removing the X in the center with my service nine. I also do the same with my personal PPK, World War II Luger, and Desert Eagle Fifty. I am fully combat trained by Quantico and the field. If I rub my jaw from talking too much, it's because this last year, I was pistol-whipped, and he broke my jaw. The man never made it to trial." She watched as the last sobered the remaining smiles.

She grabbed the small clicker and changed the large screen on the wall. Half was a map, and the other was the matching information sheet.

"All of you have a similar map and information sheet in your packet. Please don't wipe your asses with them. Obtaining the information almost cost a couple of great guys their lives. The doctors tell me they hope they will be out of the hospital in a couple of months. Bullets and bombs can do that to you. Trust me. I know. They also lost their clubhouse. Some of you might remember seeing the fire in Fullerton last week on television."

Most nodded.

Nash stood from the back of the room. "My name is Agent Nash Running Bear. I'm the senior agent in this little detail. We are the Special Investigations arm of the national Special Operations. It goes like this for those who know what an Incident Command Structure is. I'm God. On my right hand is Muna. Next to her is the Sheriff of Orange County. On our left are Homeland, ATF, and DEA. Most of you won't interact with them. Your jobs will look like any other day, except they will be a lot busier. We are coordinating with your liaisons. You will follow your department's standard procedures. Your departments will provide backup and a mobile processor to take the prisoners off your hands while on the street. Muna?"

Muna nodded. "Did we lose anybody?"

One of the older deputies waved his finger in the air. "She's god, you're Thor, and the alphabets are the Guardians of the Galaxy or just Avengers?" He smiled at another much younger deputy down the row.

The younger deputy moaned. "Oh marvelous. Now that Hollywood has explained it."

Nash glanced at her cheat sheet and then looked up. "You're Hollywood Hutchins?"

His smile was pure James Coburn. "One and the same."

Her eyes narrowed. "See me after class."

The host of deputies mooed in the same tone as any elementary school class would when someone was in trouble.

Nash cut it short. "You go with the undercover people. You'll be collaborating with Uncle."

The man's eyes brightened. "Yazzie?"

Nash nodded solemnly.

The man's voice was filled with reverence. "Oh, shit guys. This just got real." He looked back at Nash. "How did you drag the bastard out of retirement?"

The small avalanche of stones in the creek rumbled from the doorway at the back. "You know the gods never retire. We just fade into the tree line and wait. Pay attention to the teacher and child, or we'll have to consider detention."

The crowd turned to find the older Indian with the twin gray braids standing next to the one and only Frank Pounds. Frank flicked his finger to point back to the front. There were double takes, but they recognized the point. This was a major multi-county, multi-agency round-up.

Muna tapped a small sheaf of paper on the desk to straighten it. "Thank you. You've now met the ghost of the DEA, and most of you know Frank Pounds—our liaison to Orange County." She held up the small sheaf of papers. "If you would open your folders. Your map should be the first paper."

Nash held a pen to the monitor and circled the various circles. "We printed your maps in color only for the targets. Some of you have red targets. It wasn't clear if the sellers worked a specific corner or the street crossing—so we circled the crossing. You probably already know the activity at those intersections and who the street actors are. But the color is the important criteria here. The first wave will be after the high-value targets—schedule two drugs." She circled the red location. "For some of you in the sketchier areas, those will be heroin, crack, or fentanyl. Some have a mix of all the above. Almost all of you have some kind of fentanyl activity. Over the last ten years, illegally manufactured fentanyl, or IMF, has gone from not on the radar to number one with a bullet. Deaths from IMF have surpassed heroin and even crack, mostly because they are all being mixed with IMF to increase their potency. We aren't fooling ourselves by thinking what we do this week will clear the streets. But if we succeed, it will be one of the largest thorns in your sides for the last decade."

Muna held up the same map in her hand. "Some of you only have red targets. You will collaborate heavily with your undercover crews. Get to know all your undercover. They will collaborate with new partners loaned to us from Los Angeles, San Diego, and a few other counties. In two days, you and the next three classes will spear the spread of five hundred court officers. Along with your department's support staff, there will be everything the federal alphabet can throw our way."

Nash tapped the large screen with her pen and circled an orange marking. "Next down the list are the recreational hitters. Quaaludes are making a party comeback. Shrooms, ecstasy, meth, crack, reds, as well as all the other party crap. These are the second-wave targets. They may not be part of the Dorfman empire, but they'll get caught in the net, and if it leads up the ladder or down the bunny hole, it's so much better. For some, it's a third strike if they don't snitch. So they can be an asset. Just because they might be a junkie working for his next fix doesn't make them a throwaway."

A uniformed deputy in the fourth row raised her hand. "All of our map is orange. Those corner bunnies don't carry. They take the money, and someone else delivers."

Muna smiled and pointed at the woman. "And that is where you will work closely with your undercover, a loaner or three, and one of the alphabet." Her eyes narrowed as she thought about the woman's map. "You're Chico. You have the party town along the south coast. Right?"

"Tourists, tramps, and takeout. Right."

She nodded—ignoring the street talk. Catching the large movement at the doorway, she smiled. She held out her left hand at the door. "Speaking of the unusual... This is Felix. He's your Homeland interface. Don't be confused by his boyish good looks. His experience bills him closer to forty."

Dice, standing behind Felix, leaned close to Frank and whispered. "What did we miss?"

Muna growled. "The hulk trying to cheat on the exam is Dice. Let's just say he's a consultant and the instigator of this party." She squinted at Felix's raised chin, and he looked confused. "You had a question, Felix?"

He waved his finger around at the room in general.

Muna pointed at the female deputy in the middle of the room. "Aren't you riding your little stingray around Laguna?"

His face cleared, and his mouth opened in form. "Ah." He

smiled. "The Stingray is in the garage. I brought an electric mountain bike with fat tires. It looks more like a privileged beach." He pointed at the woman. "I take it you're Ramona Chico?" He raised his thumb at her smile. "I read your file."

Nash rattled her pen against the monitor. "If you look at your information sheets, you'll see they are color-coded to match your map. We didn't assign an order of assault because only you have the street information to assess how to take down your areas. But as someone pointed out, the Street Bunnies don't carry. That's the job of the supplier in the car. You will coordinate with your teams in the next few days to identify those cars and drivers. They almost always have a line of sight on their bunny. So your undercover team needs to pop them right before the uniforms bust the bunny." She looked around. "I know for most of you, this has only been a refresher on the stuff you do daily. But just in case, questions?"

The room was muted with a few shaken heads.

Muna smiled. "Great. Grab your thermoses and help yourselves to some extra chow before you hit the streets. I think most of you will have a meeting tonight or tomorrow morning at your precincts. All four classes will get the same information, but you'll adapt it to your areas. We only care about the results on the streets and the whining from the courts."

The room broke up with smirking chuckles.

UNDERCOVER OR PLAIN SIGHT

"THIS IS A TRACKER." Felix held up the dull black disk the size of a fifty-cent piece. Smiling, he tossed out his other spread hand—palm out. "But wait!" He flipped the disk in the air like a coin.

The group of undercover officers and deputies laughed and chorused. "There's more."

Felix nodded. "It's not just a tracker. It's also a bug tuned to your most common frequencies." Felix flipped it into the air again. "The weighted backing is a thin rare-earth magnet. So, flip it onto the roof of a car or SUV, and it will stick. The outer shell is a rubberized casting, so there is hardly any noise. And it's waterproof in case it rains or the perp goes through a car wash. Once on, the entire roof becomes a microphone." The group mirrored his smile as they realized the implications of a better microphone. A battle they had all fought for. "We only brought two hundred of them, so use them sparingly. And if possible, I'd like them back after you bust the suppliers."

The Latino in a ratty T-shirt, baggy jeans, and boots raised a hand.

"Yes?"

"Why do you want them back if they are throwaways?"

Felix frowned at Frank and Uncle. "Who said they were throwaways?"

The Latino twitched his head to one side. "You said they're cast into the rubber."

Felix's smile slowly grew as he looked around. "What kind of cell phone do you have?"

The man bobbed his head. "Personal or cover?"

Felix grew a picket fence of teeth at Uncle. "Let's piss on the back of the barn and start with your cover. Fish it out."

The man pulled it out and flipped it open.

Felix's head bobbed up as he smiled. "Motorola. Looks like a model ninety-nine or an oh-one. Solid, cheap, and does nothing but make phone calls. Perfect for an illegal wet-back making below minimum wage. The first problem is that the case is too small to shoehorn a tracker or bug. The second is the battery is so small, the bug would kill the battery in an hour." He held up his hand to stop the man's rebuke. "Lastly..." He looked around the room. "Who has hired a day labor in the last couple of years?"

A few of the men and one woman raised their hands.

Felix qualified the question. "Something like weeding. Nothing requiring a license or serious equipment."

The woman's hand was still up.

"Who did you hire?"

She lowered her hand back to her lap. "We just bought an old house out of foreclosure. The yards were five feet deep. We didn't have a weed whacker or mower."

"Where did you find him, and how much?"

The detective smirked. "*She* had posted a card at the Mercado. Her rates were fifteen an hour."

Felix rocked. "In Spanish. What was she driving?"

The woman snorted. "An eighty-one Ford. More rust than paint or primer. She and her teenage daughter cut the weeds with home-made scythes, baled them, and hauled them away."

"Worth every penny."

The woman nodded. "That's what my husband said. So we raised their pay to twenty each. They're just finishing painting the interior. Next week, they'll start fixing the siding and painting it."

Felix held out his hand to the woman as he looked at the original detective. He kept watching the Latino as he asked the punch line. "What kind of phone does she use?"

"She had an eleven, but it died when the scythe hit it. I'm not allowed near the tools anymore. So we bought her a burner thirteen and about two hundred hours."

Felix held up the tracker. "They can recharge wirelessly, even the eleven. The thirteen charges faster. But the battery on these needs about an hour once it dies. Please get them back to me. My partner and I built these by hand. Any other questions?"

The detective looked around.

Felix nodded. "Frank?"

Frank bounced away from leaning against the wall. "Thanks, Felix." He made a wild grab at the tracker as Felix flipped it to him. The tracker bounced several times and then stuck to a metal chair leg.

Frank peeled it off the chair. "As you can see, these little suckers are tough. I was going to tell you about how they survive being shot with a Barrett fifty, and the crash and being burned... but..."

Felix laughed. "No. That was the SUV that didn't survive meeting Nash and Barrett. The tracker you're holding was the one on the top of the van."

Frank tossed the tracker at the metal fire door to the outside. The tracker stuck. "So why are we horsing around with the little dot?" He pointed at the tracker. "Because if you bust the suppliers, what happens?" He pointed his finger around the room.

As he slouched in the easy chair, the older man barked a short laugh. "We get a half pound of street shit and one or two little fish."

Frank wiggled his eyebrows. "Leonard is right. You get shit. But if you spook them after you plant the tracker…?" He looks around. "Where are they going to run to? Mommy?"

The blond sitting in the front row rocked his head. "His supplier."

"Could you all hear in the back? Say it again for the ones sleeping through class."

The blond smirked as he glanced over his shoulder at the detective who had been on the job before he had his first wet dream. "His supplier."

Half the room reared in mock horror. The blond's finger rose to the back of his head.

Frank waved them down with both hands. "Okay. I know you all know that… but I want it to be in the forefront of your minds. When you're out there, I want you to find the supplier and evaluate them. If two are in the car, get the bug on them, back off, and monitor. We can hold off on the bust if they're talking about the business. But get the recordings. But if they sound jumpy, drop the hammer and make it loud. We want the big bunny to run to their den so we can get the big bad wolf."

An older detective with a craggy face raised his hand. "For those of us who don't have so much experience as the kid… How do you suggest we get that sucker onto a supplier's car roof?"

Muna giggled from her corner. "I've got ya, Felix."

Felix stepped out of the way as the large screen lit up.

The street scene was a little grainy. It could have passed from an old spy movie filmed in Europe or an old home movie. It was neither.

In ratty clothes and a battered snap cap, the older man rode his squeaking, rusted bicycle along the street. His hand flipped something in the air as he approached the car with the two men in it. The object landed on the roof and stuck as the man banged his knee against the car door. He then caught himself by slapping his hand on the hood of the parked car. The driver yelled at the man. Frank waved him off with a finger as he rode on. The entire sequence was fifteen seconds long.

The room was laughing at the vaudeville performance.

Frank barked from the door. "Where's the kid now?"

The room full of detectives fell silent and looked around. No Felix.

Nash laughed. "You all thought the guy on the bike was a joke. But check your weapons or your chairs. In the last fifteen seconds, while you watched Frank on the screen, Felix passed out a dozen trackers."

Frank chuckled as most shook their heads. He pointed at the older detectives with gold badges leaning against the back wall. "I think he focused on you unbeatable cowboys in the back row."

They bounced away from leaning against the back wall and stood, grabbing their shirts. To the man, they found their shirts pinned to their concealed weapons. Nothing needed saying. The old man had ridden the bike. And the kid had pegged their weapons. The entire room knew they had just learned the most important reminder. In plain sight was as good as hiding.

Felix stepped out around Dice. He pointed at the now blushing cowboy detectives along the back. "Those are for your teams. They're fully charged. The rest of you…." He pointed at the metal exit door. "You can peel yours off the exit door on your way out. Questions?"

The detectives looked around and then held up their information packets. As each left by their chosen door, there were nods or a thank you. A few cowboys had worked with Frank and didn't resist a friendly jab. "Who knew you could still ride a bike?"

A couple looked at the size of Dice and smirked as they pointed at Frank. "Look after the little guy."

Dice smiled and nodded at Nash and Muna. "He's got the women for that job. I'm just the distraction."

Frank snorted. "He's the arm candy."

Pussy slid up behind the men and slipped her arm around Dice's waist. "Slip some lifts in those heavy boots, and he could almost pass for Mary."

Dice frowned down at Pussy. "How big was Mary?"

Frank barked a laugh. "Seven feet in his surf booties."

Pussy chuckled. "Even on winter days, he surfed barefoot. The man would throw beer in just his jeans and still heat the joint."

Frank nodded. "On the chilly days when the rest of us were in thick skins, he was in a summer weight set of skins, and we could watch the steam boiling off him."

Dice took in the two faces and knew the man was still missed. "Sounds like he was one heck of a guy."

Pussy turned and flipped a towel over her shoulder. "One of the best."

THE HOSPITAL WAS QUIET. DINNER, BATHS, AND sedatives were done. The nurses were catching up on their reports and charts. They glanced at the sound of the elevator at the other end of the long hall. The man exiting wasn't carrying any toys for a patient. No balloons. Just two large arrangements of flowers.

The older nurse rose, muttering, as her eyes narrowed. "Call security."

The taller brunette with a long braid stood and rested her hand on the nurse's shoulder. "It's okay. He's one of mine. Just late."

Nash stepped out of the nurse's station. The dark blue scrub pants swished.

The man laughed at the scrub tops. "I'm shocked. They didn't have any tops with cowboys and horsey motifs? I didn't take you for a Hello Kitty kind of girl."

Nash growled. "I left the cowboys up-country when I went to college. And horses were never my thing. And if I'm buying a top, it better be one I can use in San Francisco. Muna shoots in her full set of pajamas under her tactical vest."

Dice handed Nash one vase of roses. "Here. These are for the nurses and for caring for the bigger kids." He squatted and put his hand out to knead Powder's neck and ears. "How's my girl?"

Nash took the other vase as well. "She could use a walk. Grab some gloves. They work just as good as a plastic bag. I'll have the nurse hold off, knocking the boys out until you get back."

He nodded. "Thanks. Come on, girl, show me where you poop."

Nash watched the two head for the elevator. Powder was not a small dog but was barely taller than the man's knee.

The younger nurse folded her arms as she stopped next to Nash. "Now that is one tall drink of something good. Pity about the tattoos."

Nash snorted softly. "Give him a few months. They are all coming off. He would like to be law enforcement."

"What kind?"

Nash turned back to the desk as she handed one vase to the nurse. "The best kind." She smirked. "FBI. Special Operations, Special Investigations."

The nurse hummed. "Of course."

25

TRADE

MUNA'S GAZE darted around the chamber, taking in the ornate carvings adorning the walls. It was more akin to a lavish museum than a stone church. Each niche, carved into the stone walls, held its own shrine dedicated to a different saint. The flickering yellow candle flames glowed through the crimson glasses. The light cast a golden glow, illuminating the intricate details and vibrant colors. "This feels more like a museum than a church."

Nash hummed in agreement. "For many centuries, churches and cathedrals were the museums. Displaying art for the masses is a newer construct. Art was only for the wealthy. Seeing a painting, especially painted on gold, was mesmerizing for the peasants. It helped sell the whole idea of the church as the conduit to talking to God." She pointed to the front of the cavernous room. "Even the raised stage for the altar is about how you can't go there. Only a priest can. So, if you want to ask God something, you come here, put your money in the box, and ask the man to intercede on your behalf. How does it work in a mosque?"

Muna shrugged and rocked her head from side to side. The long braid swayed across her back. "Pretty much the same. For the men, they can ask questions of the imam. But for the girls... especially once you put on your hijab, you're upstairs with your mother and just praying."

"When's that?"

Muna peeked up at her partner. "The hijab? Basically, when you get your period. In regular public schools, girls stuff their training bras when they notice the older boys and want to attract attention. For the Muslim girls, it's pretty much the opposite. You stop being out there. Field hockey has become a spectator sport. Books and studying in your bedroom replace riding your bike and wishing you had a skateboard. For many of us, it's a time of introspection. Or for some, self-loathing."

Nash glanced back at the man bent close to one shrine. "What about you, Pounds? What did you do when you got your first period?"

His voice sounded distracted. "I swam around the wrong buoy. I was a mile off course when I figured out I was swimming around a sailing course. So, I came in third and still twelve seconds under the qualifying time to go to pain island."

Nash leaned in toward Muna. "There aren't any sailing buoys where the potential SEALS swim. It's just a bullshit story someone made up a long time ago." They walked over. "What's so interesting about this shrine?"

He pointed at the painting. "The writing around the saint is Arabic." He looked at Muna.

She leaned forward. "It's not Dari. Maybe Farsi?" She looked at Nash.

Nash snorted. "I read as much Farsi as I read Athabascan. Powder speaks Athabascan. Maybe she can read the Arabic?" She snapped her fingers to find Powder already beside her leg.

"If your dog can read the glyphs, I'd pay good money to listen."

They turned to find the man standing in a long black cassock. His hands were together in supplication. "I'm Father Danilo. Danny, if you prefer." He shrugged. "Or just Father."

Frank pointed at the shrine. Frank wrinkled his forehead and raised one eyebrow.

The priest's face cleared. "Ah, yes. The patron saint of those who crusade." He shrugged. "They buried the original icon somewhere in Romania or Uzbekistan." His hands moved apart as if he were weighing the answer. "Probably one of the Stans. The Ottoman Empire buried many things. No graven images—only scriptures." He held his hand forward toward Muna. "Writings. Sayings. If I heard you right, you're Muslim?"

"Yes. Sunni. Originally Iranian, but more Pittsburg now. Both of my parents immigrated as small children. My mother was more Ethiopian Afar."

Father Danilo let Powder smell his hand as he approached the shrine. He smiled as the neck and ear were presented to his hand. He gazed at Frank while petting the dog. "To answer your question, the writing is in ancient Persian, probably during the Second or Third Crusade. The saint was a Knight Templar who saved many knights and healed those in the city. Christian and Arab alike."

Muna cocked her head. "So, he's a saint... to the Christians or the Arabs?"

He pointed at the icon. "I can't read the text, but my mentor said the Imams vouched for him during the canon inquiry. As we know, only the Holy Roman Church gives sainthood. Other religions do not share such beliefs."

Frank smiled. "And yet..." He waved his open palm about the church and the many niches.

Father Danilo smiled. "Ah, well... we Russians love our icons. But that's not why you're here."

Nash pulled out her ID wallet and flipped it open. The priest didn't even glance at it. "I noticed the badge on the dog. If she vouches for you... it's good enough for me."

Muna pulled out her phone. "We received a message from the Los Angeles office to come here. We assumed it concerns our ongoing investigation in Orange County."

The priest's smile was soft but small. "Was there a bank robbery?"

Nash's eyes narrowed. "Do you really want to play coy with the FBI?"

The man licked his lips with only the tip of his tongue. He studied Frank.

Frank held up his palms. "Don't look at me. I'm only here to make sure nobody gets killed. They're the ones with guns. I just play with dogs."

The priest took a deep sigh. "Dorfman."

Nash shifted her weight to her left hip. "That covers a lot of territory and nothing at all."

The priest took three slow breaths. "I told him this was a terrible idea." He turned and scooped the air with his left hand. "Come on. It's in my office."

He stopped at the third step when he realized he wasn't being followed. "What?"

Muna raised one eyebrow. "In the movies, if we were just high school kids, it would be the kindly old man in the forest leading us to the abandoned old shack. But a man dressed in a long black dress leading us into a dark church…"

The man stood thinking. He glanced at a few shrines as he unbuttoned the front of his cassock. Pulling the white plastic strip from the collar, he unbuttoned the neck. His eyes narrowed as he bent forward, grabbed the long dress, and lifted the whole over his head. The cassock fell to the floor, leaving the man wearing black boxers and a T-shirt. His black socks ended in black cross-trainers. "Now will you follow?"

Muna looked down at Powder. "Where's he hiding the weapon?"

Powder glanced up at Muna and then at Nash. Neither laughed. She padded forward but stopped halfway and stared back at Muna. Huffing once, she circled the man and sat beside him but scowled at Nash.

Nash held up her palms. "Hey. Don't look at me in that tone of voice. I'm not the one who sent you to do the stupid." She peered at Muna and growled. "Apologize."

Muna sighed. "Sorry. Just needed to check."

Father Danilo shrugged as he bent over to pick up the cassock. "It happens. You would think TSA was used to seeing a man in a cassock. I've never been frisked by a dog before." He smiled as he brushed at a part of the dress. "I kind of liked it. Not even a cold nose that nobody else touches. Now, can you join me in my office?"

The lighting was soft but adequate. He opened a small closet and stared in for a moment. "Black. I think I'll wear the black one tonight." He reached in. Bending, he drew on a pair of black pants and then stepped back into his shoes. He glanced back to check for any response to his old joke. *Nothing.* "Tough crowd."

As they found seats, he bent to the bottom drawer of his desk. The envelope was thick and sealed. "I'm not sure exactly what is in here, but I have a decent idea. Especially if the man is pleading for his life—and to disappear."

Muna pulled out her phone and scrolled through it. She opened a document. "Ivan Petrovich."

The priest dropped exhausted in his chair. "Ivan Gregorio Berengaria Petrovich. Brother of Danilo Alexander Berengaria Petrovich. The right-hand man of Dorfman for over twenty years." He pointed at the large envelope. "I'm assuming this is close to everything you ever wanted to know about the biggest criminal and his organization north of some large cartel in Mexico."

Nash watched Frank and offered her hand out at the tan envelope. "You've dealt with the man a hell of a lot longer than I have. Take the victory lap."

Frank took the envelope and laid it in his lap. He studied the priest, now relaxed in his T-shirt.

Danilo smiled. "You have a question but don't know how to word it. Ask it anyway. It's wrong, but we'll work it out together."

Frank crossed his legs. "One hundred and fifty-six thousand seven hundred eighty-one hours since Dorfman changed my life forever. His people planted a bomb in our engine compartment. The bomb killed my best friend and partner. It landed me in the hospital with seven breaks in my spine and nine broken ribs. I lost three of the ribs and received a titanium articulated spine. I scattered my friend's ashes here and in Hawaii three years later."

The priest stared at Frank. "That's a very large number to know exactly every hour."

"At eleven forty-eight, it will be six thousand, five hundred and thirty-three days. They don't know why, but my mind just knows. How many days since I first jumped into the Pacific Ocean as a Navy SEAL? When I caught my first wave over ten feet as a kid. How many days since I first ditched school to go surfing? How long since the last surgery? It's a blessing and a curse. I don't remember what I ate for dinner last night, but I know it was twenty-three hours and a few minutes ago."

The priest pointed at his desk. "Are you hungry? I have some protein bars."

Frank shook his head as he slid his finger through the envelope's flap. "I'm going to take the girls to my favorite tandoori shack after this."

"Punjab?"

Frank nodded with a knowing smile. "The chicken is amazing."

The priest bent to the desk and grabbed a yellow notepad. "Take them over to Montebello instead. Trust me. The curry will clean the nose hairs from your great-uncle's ears."

The fact the man was writing the information from memory didn't escape Frank's notice. He opened the envelope and pulled out a thick journal, printed sheets, and several photographs. Frank glanced over at Nash. Her eyebrows ticked up. Frank thumbed through the journal—noting the small, marked tabs. The entries were legible and not in code. He passed it over to Nash as he leafed through the printouts. Nash took the printouts and passed the journal on to Muna.

Frank thumbed slowly through the photos. Small strips of white tape had explanations written on them. Frank guessed mailing labels. Some dates predated Frank. He stopped at a picture of what had once been a car crumpled into the side of a freeway overpass pillar. Frank knew exactly how many days, hours, and minutes it had been since. Nash leaned over to look. He nodded gently.

"What does your brother want?" Frank looked up at the priest. "And is he willing to testify against Dorfman?"

"He'll testify, but only on video. He wants Witness Protection—preferably out of the country. Obviously, we can't go back to Russia, but he is also fluent in Spanish, French, and Italian. As kids, he was better at Latin than I was."

Nash cleared her throat. "They can't guarantee work or a living outside the states."

The man nodded. "As long as they don't look at his financials, he can support himself."

Muna stood. "I need to take this call. I'll be right back." She walked out the door as she answered, "This is agent al-Faragi."

Nash smirked at Frank. "The Marshal tried to get between Muna and breakfast when we were at The Surf Shack. She sent him home with a to-go sack with his balls in it. It's a deal they desperately want to make. I'm sure it's a joint effort between more than a few counties."

Frank nudged his chin at the information in her hands. "I noticed he had divided the journal into several counties. I even saw a tab marked Ventura. And with Homeland in on taking Dorfman down, I'm sure they have also been leaning on the Marshals."

Nash held up the documents and frowned at the priest. "Did your brother mention if there were any other copies?"

He shook his head. "No. He just told me to dig this up and have it ready when you came."

Nash narrowed her eyes. "Dig it up?"

The man rolled his eyes to one side. "Maybe dig is the wrong word. It was in a vault at the mausoleum. If anyone peered in the little window, they would just think it was personal documents for our parents. It was as safe as Fort Knox."

She sneered. "Fort Knox is a very secure standard."

Frank and the priest chorused with a laugh, "Until Goldfinger."

Muna stopped in the doorway. "The marshal is onboard—now. Are we ready for dinner?"

26
MOVING IN

THE PRE-MORNING LIGHT lit the wispy clouds, moving lazily over the headlands, heading for the bay. The traffic crossing the bay, across any of the bridges, wouldn't begin piling up for another hour. It was the calm before the storm. A time Chips relished.

She glanced at the small speed clock along the right side of the wing monitor. Forget NASCAR, Indy, or Formula One. This was all about speed—but for a brief time. This was Bonneville. Dipping the spoon into the bowl of berries, bananas, fruity ohs, and chocolate pops, she dug out a huge mouthful.

Her knees were under her armpits, and her bare feet dug into the chair. It was the same form as when she was only six on a Saturday morning. But the cereal had gotten better. Her eyes sparkled as she watched the madcap war raging in the center forty-two inches. The mech warriors were in green armor. The defenders wore yellow. Battle bots were black or red and could be slaved by either team—if they could catch one. The teams had the same strategic potential, aside from obtaining a bot. Lighter weapons had more rounds. Heavier weapons had better penetration but fewer or faulty rounds. Plus, there was always the potential of the carrier being hit and becoming a walking IED. Chips and Slug statically planned everything to assess the teams who were battling for the honor of carrying the Deep Six war banner.

A movement in the deep shadows drew a half smile. Chips recognized Petey's go-to heavy battle avatar. The heavy centipede oozed chunkily out of the shadow and across the debris-strewn field. He had sacrificed speed and heavy weapons for nearly impenetrable armor. He had become the laughingstock just to those who had not faced the tiny nerd in battle before. The green carapace glittered in the artificial sunshine as the avatar paced toward the laughing yellow troll in mostly plate armor.

An enormous troll swung his heavy photon rifle around to dispense the mechanical animal slowly marching toward him. The deadly charges of energy ricocheted off the centipede's back and into the building behind. Significant chunks of buildings and explosions engulfed the background behind the low-to-the-ground avatar as it closed on its target.

The yellow troll holstered his blaster rifle and grabbed the enormous war ax on his back. Double-handed, he held the giant ax aloft. Poised for one crushing blow to the head of the centipede. Petey neared and reared up—offering his head as a sacrifice.

The troll rose on the balls of his feet. His massive arms extended the height of the massive war ax over his head...

The small, fast drone skidded out from behind the building it had been hiding behind. The huge blaster, hanging below the drone, vomited three rapid slugs of pure photon energy—turning the war ax into a stick in the troll's hands.

As he struck with the short stick, the troll screamed upon realizing his deadly mistake. The centipede rose into the strike. The multitude of legs pierced the troll's arms as he crawled to the head and over. As the mass encompassed the body, the tail with its lowest value fixed stinger shaft curled into the crotch of the troll. Sinking the shaft deep into the body, the rest of the muscle-bound avatar encased the troll in a crushing death grip. The yellow blood of the avatar troll gushed from the hole pierced in its nether regions, flooding the raised dais on the battlefield. The small drone, Chips could only guess was Slug, flipped a triple loop of victory overhead.

Chips filled her smile with milky cereal as she watched a large hand creep over the top of the screen and deposited a yellow sticky on the screen. The hand retreated. The sticky stayed. It was definitely not part of the game.

The game flickered once.

She glanced at the speed clock as the arm on the meter retreated from the tiny golden area and gently marched deeper into the usual spread of green. She looked down at the time and date stamp. The morning had started. The early birds were firing up their work machines. People along the West Coast were waking up to alarm clocks and reaching for their cell phones to check for news or messages. Chips's time tapping into the early morning war game raging at Deep Six in real time was over. She would analyze the players later when she woke up in the evening.

She looked up at the yellow sticky.

C Z

B4

ZZZ

She smiled. The senior agent was succinct. She stood as she held the edge of her bowl to her lips. The last of the milk tasted of a blend of fruit and a hint of chocolate. Same as the smoothie she had once made. Great taste but no satisfying crunch or individual flavors of the fresh fruit and berries.

Yawning, she turned the corner into the small kitchen area. Oz leaned back against the counter as he bit into the bagel heaped with cream cheese and sardines. His new passion. She smiled and feinted at a Jaws-sized, toothy, hungry mouth attack at his breakfast.

He bit and then offered the bagel out to her. She shook her head and presented the sticky note stuck to the end of her middle finger.

He tipped his chin up and chewed. As he bounced forward off the edge of the counter, he pointed out toward the office space.

Chips placed the bowl in the sink and ran some water in it. Turning, she caught up with the man. He stood at Muna's giant wall of information—pointing at the pulsing icon in the middle of the screen reserved exclusively for the dark web.

The icon was the usual information triangle with an exclamation point in the center. But someone had placed it over the symbol for toxic biohazard. The information pulsed red; the biohazard pulsed vomit yellow.

Chips whipped out her phone and hit the Hello Kitty icon. The phone rang. And rang. And…

"Hello. You have reached the office of Agent al-Faragi. At the sound of the tone, you know what to do."

Chips didn't wait for the beep.

"What is it?" Oz watched the young woman round the wall of information and stalked into her cave of solitude.

The blonde looked at him over the top of her wall. "Trouble. Big fucking trouble."

The head disappeared.

Chips typed and then sat back. The terminal in the cavernous computer room at Deep Six wasn't being used. She pulled up her inner-office chat box and connected to Baby. The terminal was active.

"Where is Muna?"

"No C 2day."

"Who else active?"

"Most. Game day for boys."

Chips growled and typed. "Not 4 long."

She leaned in and pulled a program out of a lock-box icon. In the dialog box was an icon of an eighteenth-century town crier. She clicked on the icon and typed.

———————

MING SAT SCROLLING THROUGH HER PHONE WHILE TREE found the documentation for the dredging project in the upper Hudson River. Not finding the information, Ming closed her phone and leaned back, wondering why she had gotten up so early. Today was a pajama day. No clients were allowed through the door. And absolutely a sleep-in day.

Tree growled at her screen, "What the ever-loving fuck is this?"

Ming tilted her head forward as she heard the voices out in the larger computer room. Mama pushed her foot against the long shelf desk running the length of the room. Her wheeled chair shot out of the room and onto the mezzanine walkway. Standing, she yelled down into the dining hall, "Who has eyes on Muna?"

Jazz came out of her office holding up her phone next to Slug, doing the same. "We just got it on our phones."

Tree's voice bounced around the building. It was on every speaker. "Muna report to Tree and Ming stat."

Ming stood next to the desk. The two looked at their phones and the computer. Through the glass wall, they could see every computer screen was filled with the same message. Baby and Sweet Thing stood in the middle of the room and showed the same on their phones.

Ming scowled at her phone. "Even the DOD can't hack our system. Who the hell…?"

Ming's phone pinged. "Where the hell are you?"

"Sorry. I was up on the roof at prayers. What's going on?"

Ming's mouth opened and then closed, "Are you dressed?"

Muna giggled. "Of course…"

"Don't use any electronics. Don't take the elevator. Use the stairs and come down here."

"I have a missed call, and there's an emergency notice on—"

Ming cut her off. "We're under attack. Do what you're told. Now."

The click was metallic but final.

Ming looked at Tree with an exasperated look. Tree shrugged. "She's your sister."

Jazz strolled across the computer room and turned into the office. "Who's in control...?" Her finger waved over her shoulder.

They all turned to the sound of a small klaxon horn blowing. Nash and Powder walked into the large room and stopped. Looking at all the monitors, Nash pulled her phone out of her pocket. The alarm horn was louder. She strode to the office, holding her phone out. "Either we are diving, or my phone is going into Def Con three. But I can't shut it up." She held her phone out to Ming.

The small Asian took the phone and pushed the two buttons to force the phone to turn off. She smiled at the silence and handed the phone back. "Muna's on her way down. She was up top doing her morning prayers."

"Holy nightmare, Batman..." Muna stood with her phone out as she looked around the room and found dozens of screens with the same message as her phone. "How...?"

Ming stepped out of the glass office. "The question is more like who..."

Muna chuckled and shook her head. "Oh no. That question the Secret Squirrel Squad has a handle on. I just want to know how." She thumbed an icon on her phone. As she approached the three standing outside the glass office, she thumbed the speaker.

The answering voice was the narrator from the sixties television show, "Buried in the frozen north, the fortress of solitude stood ready."

Muna chuckled. She had heard it before. "Okay, superstar, you got everyone's attention. The question of the day is how you did it. Every screen, and every phone. Even Nash and mine."

The pulsing icon replaced the message on all the screens. Muna recognized it for what it was. "Good night. Sleep tight. Your work here is done."

All the screens were wiped and returned to their previous screens as if nothing had happened. Muna walked to the station she thought of as her remote. Typing in her code, she locked out all other access except to her restricted computer in San Francisco. The screen was black, apart from the pulsing icons.

Ming walked up beside Muna as she sat down. "Oh no. She doesn't get off that easy."

Muna spun around in the chair. Her face was as deadpan as Nash had taught her. "She pulled a full shift yesterday, starting with signing for three dead bodies at six in the morning. If I remember correctly, she gets off the dredge in New Zealand at four in the morning. So either she slept a couple of hours in her chair or an hour upstairs. But after she worked on the load she was so kindly doing for Oz and Mike; she again pulled her shift in New Zealand. If you want, I can pull her key log and see if she worked the last seventy-three straight or got an hour or two of sleep this morning."

"She didn't."

They turned to find Slug standing there with his arms crossed. "I saw her log into Overwatch on the game this morning. There was a twenty-minute gap between New Zealand and Overwatch. She got some breakfast or something. She's been burning too many candles."

Ming slumped. "What was she doing on Overwatch?"

Slug blushed. "I asked her to evaluate the players."

"But the clock speed you guys play at is…"

He nodded. "It glitches and spools except between four thirty and five till six. She calls it her Golden Hour. She gets real-time feed. I don't know how, but she massaged the internet to do her bidding." He held his hand out as he slowly turned around the room. "We all want to know how she did it, but I'd rather have her get some sleep. I already sent her a text. I'm taking her shift on the dredge. She's not allowed to log into anything but email until Friday night at nine. Hopefully, she will find something to do in San Francisco in a few days. Or sleep." He glared at Muna. "I assume you have a way to lock her out of the FBI computers?"

Muna waved over her shoulder distractedly as she focused on a document on her screen. "I'll call our uncles. Maybe Mike can entertain her without letting her go down and take over Google or Apple."

Slug grumped as he turned to leave. "There is that." He looked down at Powder, who was waiting at the door. "Come on, girl. Let's go for a walk."

Muna clicked through a series of grainy photographs, obviously taken at a distance. One was better than the others. "Nash?"

Nash stepped over along with Ming and Tree. "Can you...?"

Muna held down control and pushed forward on the mouse wheel. The photo filled the screen but was too grainy. She backed off slowly and then stopped. Nash nodded. "Romanov. Where is this?"

Muna clicked on the document and pointed it out with her finger. "Syria. He was spotted outside this house seven times in the last two weeks. They think he's moving in."

Nash pointed at the blonde woman without a hijab. "Who is the woman?"

"No mention."

Nash crossed her arms and sighed, "It's a weak link."

Muna typed, "I'll ask."

27
MOVING ON

THE PUPPIES and kittens playing with balls, chews, and each other, painted above the wide rub-rail dividing the wall, lent a cheerful note to the hospital hall. Dice could feel the weight of the building filled with toddlers up to young teenagers. He had talked with parents in the cafeteria who were afraid their child would end their brief lives in the building. Others were thankful for the fresh start with a new leg or arm. He hadn't initially understood why Frank had insisted on hiding Chopper and Tiny at a children's hospital, but he was beginning to. This hospital was quiet compared to the critical one where they had done the surgeries.

He waved at the nurses on the desk. They smiled and waved back. Frank had been right. Some cheerful flowers went a long way. He stopped and looked at the man lying in a bed too short for either of them. Dice didn't know who the small girl was in the pneumatic electric chair, but Tiny smiled as she read to him. She had raised the chair to be the same height as him. Her voice was shy, but he could hear the story over the sound of the oxygen at both of their noses.

She paused to draw a deep breath of oxygen and glanced at the door. Tiny mumbled something, and she smiled and waved her fingers. Dice returned the wave and continued to the next room.

Chopper didn't have the entertainment. But at least he was awake—mostly. He twitched at the man in the door and then smiled. His eyes drooped with drugged exhaustion. His finger pointed up and down at the out-of-place attire. "Did you steal those from Rusty?"

Dice pulled over a chair and dropped. "Nah. Frank's nurse friend Pan told me where to get them. I was lucky. These are the biggest sizes they make with the cowboys on them. Everything larger is just blue." He nodded his chin at his friend. "¿Que pasa?"

Chopper rocked his hand in the air above the blanket. "Estoy bien. Solo cansado."

Dice rocked his understanding. "The bullets beat you up for mere seconds. But the surgeon worked you over for a lot longer."

Chopper smirked. "I've gone three rounds with that guy, and I'm still standing. Well... sitting."

Dice smiled. "Keep breathing, my friend. Can I get you anything?"

Chopper smiled shyly. "Always. If you can't find a machaca burrito with green salsa, I'll take some orange ice cream."

Dice stood and picked up the large water bottle. "And some fresh water. You know you need to keep flushing the kidneys."

Chopper twitched a laugh. "Oh, nurse, can you check my bag? I think it's full."

Dice bounced his eyebrows. "Pendejo." But he glanced at the bag half-full of urine. It wasn't clear, but it wasn't brown either.

Chopper chuckled as Dice ran fresh water into the sink. "What's happening with Dorfman?"

Dice pressed the top back on and set it on the small, elevated table. "The cops are all coordinating today. The grand round-up happens tomorrow. I'll get you some sherbet."

"Thanks."

Dice could hear the exhaustion. He wondered if his friend would be awake when he got back.

THE EXPANSIVE GLASS DOORS SLID OPEN AS NASH, MUNA, and Powder approached. Muna smelled the cigarette-laden air. "I don't think I could ever gamble."

Nash snorted softly. "You already did. Just by getting onto that tiny airplane."

They flopped open their identification wallets as they approached the front desk at the hotel casino. The woman's head dipped slightly as her hand and finger rose. She turned and opened the door to the back office. Seconds later, she was back with a man in a dark gray suit and a yellow tie. The man pointed to his right.

The man raised the walk-through gate at the end of the long series of desks and stepped out. "How may I help you, agents?"

"We're here to see Jack Palande."

"Do you have an appointment?"

Nash deadpanned the man. They both knew why they were there. "I have four million, seven hundred thousand appointments. Now. We can keep doing this dance... while my associate notifies the Nevada Gaming Control Board, we are closing the building down. Then the health department crew standing by can perform their pop health inspection because of reports of bed bugs. Meanwhile, the fire marshal under federal direction will inspect every single fire extinguisher..."

The man glanced at Muna with her phone and finger at the ready. "This way."

They stepped into an elevator requiring a key. The man never touched a floor button.

A man stood by the tall windows in his suit slacks and tailored shirt, looking out at Reno. He sipped on a cup of coffee. "Four point seven million dollars is less than what this city makes in five minutes." He turned to face Nash and Muna. Powder stayed where Nash's finger tapped the leather pants.

"We have four bodies to go with it. You can have the bodies back, but the other is evidence in an open investigation."

The man's one eyebrow twitched. "Four bodies." He waved his hand around in the air. "Just floating out there in the universe. Unattached. So you decided I might be interested... Miss...?"

"It's Agent, Mr. Palande. Agent Nash Running Bear. Special Investigation division of Special Operations. And yes. We, the FBI, felt you might be interested in the death of four men in your employment. Men who hadn't shown up for work for, say... the better part of a month."

"I have people who quit all the time. It's the nature of the business." He stepped to the large glass desk and set his coffee cup down.

"Do they all quit and walk off with millions of your dollars?"

The man hovered his eyelids as he sighed. "This is getting tiresome, Agent. How would you even know it was my money? A dollar bill looks like any other dollar bill."

Muna looked up from her phone. "No dollar bills. There were six straps of fifties, but every other strap was hundreds. Straps from your casino." She ignored his rising hand. "More specifically, the straps are exclusive to your high roller cage."

His hand fell, and he stuffed it in his pocket. "That would be a hard case to prove. Money is very liquid in this business."

Nash grimaced. "Yes. Yes, it is. Just as liquid or mercurial as your lists of high rollers. How many whales do you think will fly in here when word gets out how their names were found along with money to buy a hundred pounds of Mexican sourced, schedule two drugs?"

"What is your point, Agent? I'm a busy man, and this is beyond tiresome."

Nash put her index finger in the air, and her mouth cracked open. She held the moment for four heartbeats and then closed her mouth and dropped her hand, "Actually, this face-to-face was the point. I have everything I came for. Sorry for the intrusion." She turned and looked at Muna.

The man's voice was on the edge of being in control, "What about the money?"

Nash looked over her shoulder. "You already said there was no way to prove it was yours. Therefore, when they release it, I suppose they will burn it." She shrugged her face, and the three strolled for the door.

The muscle didn't know what to do. He looked askance at his boss.

Nash stopped inches from the man's face. They were eye to eye. "Move it or lose it."

The man stepped aside.

As Nash opened the door, she turned, "One more thing."

The man at the windows fumed. "What?"

"The only address of residence we could locate for the four men…? It was downstairs. They'll be releasing and shipping the full body bags this afternoon. If you don't want Greyhound dropping them in your lobby, I suggest you contact the Los Angeles County Coroner's Office and give them addresses to ship to." She turned, winked at the muscle, and they left.

MUNA PUSHED BACK IN THE PLUSH SEAT. THE CORPORATE jet was much roomier than the commuter jet they had taken up. "Nice of him to provide us with a flight back to Orange County."

Nash rolled her head over. "I'm sure there is a whale heading for the airport as we speak. A special phone call to invite the person to play high-stakes poker privately with someone else they respect." She shrugged her head. "Or a celebrity."

"What kind of celebrity?"

Nash looked down at Powder, who was lying on her foot. "Who knows? This is Reno, not Vegas. So a second-string sports semi-star would work. They need to be noticed, and the casino will probably front them with some cash to play with. They get seen as a high roller and the high roller talks. It's a win-win."

Muna jerked her head in understanding. "What do you think will happen to the money?"

Nash breathed out of her nose. "It will be a long time before they even consider releasing the evidence, long after the man has retired. The investigation is bogus. We know what went down. We know they killed each other. And they're all dead... so what are we investigating?"

"What are we doing in Orange County?"

Nash smirked as she rolled her head over. "Pursuing justice."

Muna thought a moment. She studied Nash. "Dorfman or Dice?" She pushed her hand out into the air. "You all but said you saw Dice kill those three men..."

Nash winced. "But what I saw and what we can prove with physical evidence are two vastly different things. This is one of those strange gray areas. We know he did it. Plus, he all but admitted it. But there is nothing there but hearsay.

"Meanwhile, he started the roll on Dorfman. And if we wrap up Dorfman and get some solid leads back across the border, then Dice has his vindication, as well as the gratitude of more than a few sheriffs." Nash closed her eyes as she grimaced. "He wouldn't be the first impure to become a lawman. Don't get me started on Wyatt Earp."

Muna sighed. "Dice is a pretty stand-up guy." She glanced over at Nash. "When he gets smart enough, he's going to see Tricia standing there waiting for him. He just needs to get past her dead husband and move on."

Nash opened her eyes and looked over, frowning. "You think she's..."

Muna barked. "Oh please. That she has the hots for Dice?" She gave a goofy face as she shook it up and down. "I don't think she would ever admit it, but I think she had feelings for him back when her husband and Dice were marines together."

Nash shrugged her lower lip and rolled her head back. "She's a solid catch."

Muna took a deep breath and let it out through her nose. Her voice was to herself. "So is he."

HITTING THE STREETS

THE NEWPORT FREEWAY is nine lanes wide as it runs through the heart of Orange County. If the Golden State and the San Diego freeways are the arterial movers of the daily blood, the Newport freeway is the lifeblood running to the sea—until it stops and becomes a standard four-lane Newport Boulevard. By six in the morning, cars line up around the coffee drive-throughs on the northbound side. The cars with surfboards have mostly passed south to catch the dawn waves.

The two young punks stand twitching a few blocks away. In the early morning, their customers range from construction trucks to white-collar workers in leased electric cars. The mommy-needs-an-edge cars will bump the curb after school drop-off and before yoga.

The homeless push rusted chrome shopping carts stolen from several markets. They had long figured out how to rest the front-end on a skateboard to defeat the automatic wheel lock. Once back to their squat, it's a fast fix with a hammer and chisel. The need to keep valuables hidden and secure calls for wearing most of their wardrobe, even when the sun is shining. A shabby trench coat can cover all the requirements. Add an old ratty T-shirt around the head as a do-rag, and you have a perfect Marvin, the man with a filthy rag who will spit on your windshield and then smear it as he claims to clean the glass—unless you hand him a buck to go away.

"If you spit on my car, Marvin. I will sure as fuck come out there and shoot you."

The bum stumbled the last few feet to the windshield. Slapping his hand with the filthy rag on the top of the car, he catches himself. His face lowers to the glass as his lungs heave noisily, searching for some liquid.

The driver cracks his door on the dark blue Impala. "I'm warning you, Marvin. I will fuck you up until you can't walk."

The dark face contorted as his rubbery lips adjusted the saliva. "I'z needs ta money. I'm sick."

The passenger pushes a bill over to the driver. He passes it to the window. "Here. Lance done gives you a ten. Take it down to the kids. Maybe they'll give you a taste."

The bill disappears into the filthy rag as the man twirls along the clean paint job—hip-checking the door closed. But leaving the dark rubber disk on the roof.

"Hey. Get off my car, Marvin." The driver grumbles and looks out of the window at the side of his still-clean car. "Stupid fucking homeless. They need to find a job or something."

The passenger settled deeper into the seat as he watched the two kids down the street. "Leave him alone, Oscar. Your sister's in the same boat."

The driver glowered at the passenger. "Fuck you. She's in a shelter. She's getting it together. Her baby daddy didn't make rent. She just needs some time."

"Maybe Dorfman can find her some work?"

"What? Walking North Broadway? She ain't no whore."

The passenger sat up and pointed down the street. "Runner's coming."

The pop blast of a siren preceded the nose of the car appearing in the driveway—cutting off the kid on the bicycle. The kid veered and turned into the alley the cop had come out of.

They watched as the other kid hopped around the back of the mommy minivan. As he ran across the street, the mommy burst from the driver's door dressed ready for a marathon. Her legs ate the air twice as fast as the kid. The flying tackle took the kid down as his feet touched the sidewalk. His face smeared green as the two slid on the small grassy knoll separating the sidewalk from the parking lot.

"Fuck." The driver turned the key as they watched the mommy whip out zip ties.

Oscar grabbed his seat belt and buckled in. "Get out of here, man. There be one serious bitch."

The driver peeked in his side mirror and pulled the steering wheel. Resisting the urge to stomp on the gas pedal, he surged the big car around and turned up the side street. Keeping his speed at only ten over the limit, he cruised through the neighborhood. It was the escape route he had used many times, running to go restock in the middle of a busy day.

Marvin listened to the small radio in the Tidy Diaper van and smiled at the other detective. They watched the small red dot moving along the map on the screen. "They weren't kidding. I wish my car radio could pick up the sports channel that clear."

The monitoring detective smiled down at him. "Jeez, Oliver, I keep telling you. Spring for the satellite radio, and you will get everything you want."

He growls at her, "I'm not giving some fat cat corporation two bills a year just for radio."

She snorted as she watched the red dot stop. "But you still pay the big bucks for cable."

"And the internet and a landline. You know as well as I do; if you call nine-one-one, they can't see your location from a cell phone."

She pointed at the screen. She leaned her head toward the microphone clipped to her shoulder, "Seven five three eight Sea Back Drive."

The radio squawked two static clicks.

She tapped the screen. "How long did they say the microphone was good for?"

Marvin peered down the street. "At least a week." He looked up. "They said when the sound became scratchy, it was time to replace or arrest. We can hear the aftermath if they clear the strong house before SWAT shows. Maybe they'll run to higher ground?"

———

THE BENTLY HAD BEEN A HARDTOP COUPE. THE wrecking yard had already destroyed the roof when Frank had offered the owner a few bucks over scrap for it. Smiling, the owner also offered a stroked and bored street-legal engine and transmission to turn it into a unique street rod. Frank's friend Granite had used a blowtorch to remove the damaged roof. With over three hundred days of sunshine, Frank had never gotten around to adding a convertible top.

Frank smiled under the wraparound dark glasses. The parking lot was just distracting enough to allow them to watch the drug bust.

Dice casually held the spotting scope to his right eye. "There's just one guy in the car."

Frank grimaced behind the glasses. "Check the bushes. Maybe the spotter is peeing."

"Nope." Dice's movement was smooth and small as he scanned the area two blocks away. "Wait. There's a shirt in the bushes. It's low." He slowly smiles. "The guy had to crap." He dropped the scope and looked over at Frank. "Ever crap on a stakeout?"

Frank stretched his neck. "Rookie mistake. Plan ahead. Take the crap before you go." He looked at the man filling the passenger seat. "You were a sniper..."

Dice nodded. "Sometimes planning ahead was folding a quarter roll of paper into your back pocket. In the sandbox, I kept paper in my pocket twenty-four seven."

Frank sneers. "You kids. You only worked seven days a week? For us, that was a short shift. But we had to do those uphill…"

Dice laughed at the old joke. "Both ways. In deep snow."

Frank chuckles. "No snow. Just heavy surf."

Dice rocked as he raised the scope. "Did you ever miss being dry?"

Frank grimaced as he rolled his head to watch the woman pushing her shopping cart toward the white SUV with the back door rolling open. "Nah. I hated being dry. It meant we weren't working. Sometimes, we used to sleep in the showers." He rolled his head over to watch the other man eyeing the target. "In fact, I'm too dry now. I might have to pee myself to calm down."

Dice snorted softly. "Chill. There's a kid on a stingray doing wheelies toward the car."

"A curly mop for hair?"

"Yeah. I think he's wearing one of your T-shirts."

"Ramone's playing Crystal Cove? He better not tear it. That's my favorite."

Dice shook his head softly with his eye still in the scope. "Nope. It's a hand flipping the bird. I think it's a Deep Six shirt."

"Yeah. It must be one of Tree's shirts. They wear them at gaming battles. It's their war flag. It's my favorite shirt to watch."

Dice smirked under the scope. "And the eagle has landed. He flipped it on from the center court. Back tire only, all white line, no asphalt. I think he's singing something like a crazy kid."

The old detective chuckled. "One of the older DEA agents he works with told me it's always the same. He sings the song *We Will Rock You*, and it's always off-key." Frank pulled up the walkie-talkie and keyed the button. "Armed and ready. Showtime."

Three sets of double clicks returned like a wave of static.

Dice smiled. "Feel like old times?"

"I loved working with Kalani. The man brought his mālie, Hawaiian calm, to the job. But our Taurus turd always smelled like rotting fish vomit. The day shift had no respect. You tell them never to arrest drunks or anyone near the ocean, and the first thing they do is head for the peninsula trolling for day drinkers."

The black-and-white Shamu was in the center lane, headed north. As it passed the two young punks on the sidewalk, they hit the lights and pulled a noisy U-turn with a squawk of the siren.

The two punks turned to run and were looking at two more police cars, just stopping at the edge of the parking lot. They both squawked their sirens as they turned on their lights. The punks froze. One dropped his skateboard, and the other gently laid his bicycle on its side. Four hands slowly raised.

Frank snorted softly in disgust. "Underage repeats. Dorfman is pure scum." He turned toward Dice.

The smile grew tighter. "And we have two running east for the hills. Go to Mommy, little bunnies. Show us where they live."

Frank glanced down. "What do we have on the map?"

Dice picked up the map. "I think they had circled a few blocks about a quarter mile from here." His eyebrows ticked up. "Did you want to go watch?"

"Nah. We need to keep you fresh for your date."

Dice slumped down in the seat as he put the small scope down. "Tomorrow is a good day to die."

Frank turned the key, and the enormous engine rumbled to life. "You've been hanging out with Nash too much. I'm ready for some oysters." He picked up his phone. "Hey bitch?"

The mechanical English voice oozed from the speakers. "Bitch here. How may I service you, Frankie?"

He pulled on the shifter. "Text Mickey."

"What would you like the text to say?"

"Lunch at Rusty Pelican in thirty. You're buying." He nosed the hulking car out of the parking lot. To say goodbye to the arresting officers and deputies, he goosed the gas. The tires left his signature thirty feet of black on the asphalt.

"You have a return text from Mickey. Would you like me to read it to you?"

Frank laughed as he glanced at Dice. "Yeah. Give me the fucking message."

"Mickey texted, 'Fuck you in forty.' Will there be a reply?"

Frank kept chuckling. "Nah. Go back to sleep."

"Bitch sleeping now."

Dice barked a jerky laugh. "Who do I have to kill to get my phone reprogrammed for that?"

"Play nice with Felix. And promise never to use it in earshot of the girls." He looked over. "It was Tree's voice. She was programming a speech app for one of the dredging companies. I think they're Dutch but do a lot of work down south in Australia and New Zealand."

Dice's face was wide open. "Isn't it kind of naughty language for a business? Or a young woman?"

Frank peeked over. "Did you swear in East Los Angeles?"

"Si."

"The corps?"

"Yeah."

"Well, you're also going to swear when they slap a badge on your ass."

Dice winced. "Yeah..."

"Sailors swear, and dredgers are mostly sailors. The girls... well, not often. Except for Jazz. But she was a deputy and dates a sailor."

Dice laughed. "And rides a kick-ass motorcycle."

"Yeah. Biker, too." He wiggled his eyebrows as he floored the gas, and the demure Bently roared up the on-ramp. "How do you like your oysters?"

"Shucked."

SHAKE THE CHINA

THE DRIVER HUNG his head forward onto the steering wheel. The sunlight streaming through his windows bothered him. His days of doing repo work were in the dead of night. If it was a full moon or close, he was in Mexico fishing. He made more between the hours of midnight and five in the morning than most tow truck drivers made in a week. If the car was impossible to recover, the finance guys called Ace. If the truck was parked with all four wheels locked, you called Ace. When the owner was known to carry a weapon or parked the vehicle in a secure lot, you called Ace.

He slowly raised his head. The piercing blue of his eyes never matched his dark complexion. The early aging he inherited from his mother didn't help but make him look years older than he was.

He raised his spread hands above the steering wheel. Thin white edges showed at the ends of his fingernails. *I'm going to need a manicure after this.*

He listened to the soft rustle of the man walking up along the truck. He stopped and looked up. The neck protector on his body armor kept his head from looking up. His voice was soft. "You good to go, Ace?"

Ace glared down at the man in the same black tactical jumpsuit as him. "You know how much I hate the daytime, Rogers."

The armored suit swallowed the futile shrug. "That call was way above our pay grade, dude. I just get my orders. You just get your payday."

Ace bobbed his head and grimaced. "I go left, and the tank takes out the end of the building right behind me. What the fuck could ever go wrong?" He glared at the man's bald spot. "Are they fired up?"

The sergeant looked back down the block at the large black mass of angular metal. His team had bought copies of a dozen post-apocalyptic movies and cobbled together their own monster. The machine had a design and manufacture focused on doing only one job, from the solid rubber to the top hatch from an Abrams tank. The front nose looked like the railroad snowplow it was designed after. Mounted on the sides were rows of eight-inch well-drilling pipe filled with concrete. The pipes bolted on or off as they needed replacing. An alternative name on the side said it all: Renovator. The powerful engines weren't built for speed but to be unstoppable.

Decades before, there had been adaptations of old military tank bodies fixed with battering rams to destroy the front doors of the strong houses—until someone built a house specifically to counter the ram. Two deputies died when the ram arm was violently forced back through the body of the tank. The team went back to the drawing board until an inmate in Soledad prison asked for a meeting with the commander of the SWAT team.

The inmate had asked for his life sentence to be dropped to only five more years, but at a country club prison where he thought he could learn to play golf. His argument was simple. He asked about the hand-held battering ram the police now used instead of kicking in a door. The answer was the doorways had become armored and pinned to the steel door jambs. He had smiled. "So, why are you going through the door?"

The name of the first building destroying tank was simply

number one. They named the rest of the tanks after the man in Palm Springs who was honing his golf swing—Archie.

The Renovator was the next generation. It squatted low in the middle of the street. The heavily muffled dual engines vibrated the asphalt and the feet of the officers standing next to it. The tactical vans stood ready to follow the tank.

Ace would remove the thirty-year-old Cadillac from in front of the house. This gave the tank a free run at the end of the building facing the side street. The fifteen tons of concrete-filled drilling pipe covering the sides would shear off the side of the building. Once it passed, waves of the SWAT team would step off the tactical assault vans parked in the yard. The SWAT team practiced the entire operation to fit within the time between the occupants' first "Oh" and their final "Shit."

The radio squawked. "Rogers?"

The man looked back down the street. "Go."

The man in the dark slacks and white shirt held the walkie-talkie to his mouth. "We have green light."

Rogers double-clicked his microphone and reached up to pat the door, "It's all your show, Ace."

Ace blipped his engine and stuck the shifter in gear. He glanced in the side mirror and saw the tank roll. He knew in second gear they could outrun him, up to forty miles per hour. But with the turn and short block, neither would get above thirty.

Ace hauled on the steering wheel at the corner. The giant Marmon truck, with its conventional nose, needed all the lanes in the rundown section of residential streets. He straightened out and eased down on the accelerator. He jumped past third into fourth and then reached for the silver lever on the dash.

In the front was a heavy-duty forklift. Ace had lifted diesel trucks out of spots where they sat pinched in to prevent towing. The owners were at least six months behind on their payments. For some, it was a game. For others, the fickle trucking industry wasn't kind to single owner-operators. Either way, when Ace was called, the owner had to pay or lose the truck. And once they lost a truck to repossession, they couldn't get a loan without at least half down.

The forks lowered. By feel, Ace raised the forks to a foot above the ground. The forks were long enough to penetrate the front side, go through the seats, and out the other side. On contact, the forks would tilt back, pinning the car to the front of his truck. Once skewered, he could make the violent jump onto the curb and make a fast left turn in the yard. The heavy car would only bobble but not slide off. The long, heavy towing bed on the truck was more than enough weight to balance even the heaviest of diesel trucks. A Cadillac wouldn't even twitch the scales.

As he neared contact, he downshifted to third and tapped the lift lever as his thumb rested on the tilt. The forks made contact, and the car slid on. Ace bumped the lift and thumbed the tilt. He felt the numb grunt as the car's tires smashed on the top of the curb. His front tires were next.

He held the steering wheel steady until he felt his rear tires make the curb jump. Pulling on the one side, the oversized truck slewed to the left. Out of the side of his eye, he saw a single man behind the house pull up a pistol. Ace chuckled. "Not today, Beelzebub. Say hello to my little friend."

The man fired once before he ran back behind what he thought was protection. The Renovator's front plow couldn't raise or lower, it was welded solid and sheared away the top half of the curb. Chunks of sidewalk flew yards away as the twelve solid rubber tires hit the curb and left their mark on the Southern California gray-brown yard.

The roaring engines spewed a thick cloud of black smoke as the massive plow and side rails hit the building's front corner. With a thunderous crash, the lower seven feet of the wall lay torn away, revealing the illegal operations inside. Amidst scattered bags of drugs being cut and mixed, two people nonchalantly enjoyed their lunch at a nearby table. The sudden impact jolted the man sleeping on the couch to the floor, his slumber violently interrupted. In a frantic state, a bathroom door flung open, revealing a naked woman gasping for air in shock.

The Renovator turned and bounced out onto the side street. Its job was done. The tactical vans parked in the side yard, facing the now-opened building. As the heavily armored SWAT twitched their guns, the occupants carefully stood, raising their hands.

Several miles away, having dumped the first car, Ace turned the corner and slowed. "Really? You had to park in your fat-assed Archie in the middle of the street?"

The officer saw the specialized giant tow truck and smiled. The man had grown up in the hills of Oregon. His father was a logger. The giant Jurassic-looking trucks were a common site. Even stock, their engines were larger and heavier in horsepower than the others. The other truck companies were proud of their new 500-horsepower engines. Marmon quietly phased out their old 900-horsepower engine. Upgrading to the even more impressive 1600-horsepower Desert Eagle.

He turned to a couple of other officers in black tactical suits and helmets. Ace watched as he pointed to the tactical vans parked on the side of the street and pantomimed, pushing them over onto the sidewalk. A woman in a bathrobe with curlers in her hair stood on her front sidewalk. She watched as she slowly smoked a cigarette and drank what, suspiciously, wasn't her morning coffee.

Ace studied one of the tactical vans. The slogan on the door wasn't the same as Orange County. He guessed at the eastern section of Los Angeles County. Today was slated to be a long day with a lot of excitement. They would need every bit of help they could get. He smiled at the size of his specialized payday. Even November and December didn't come close to the twelve hours the sheriff had contracted him for. Then there was the bonus for each car cleared successfully. Even better, they promised to fill his fuel tanks again when it was over.

As the vans eased up onto the sidewalk, Ace glanced over at the printout he had just received on his computer. They had added three more strong houses to his contract. Mama was getting her new shoes.

Ace eased through the now narrowly cleared street. He stopped at the man in the white shirt and slacks. The man handed him the photo taken minutes before. "Can you take out the RV? We don't recognize the white car."

Ace studied the layout. "If I pull it out of there, can I swing left down the street?"

The man reached into his back pocket. Handing up another sheet of paper. "Sorry, here's the map. It's a dead end, but you'd be clear by about a football field. When Archie takes out the wall, he's going to have to punch through the neighbor's fence. He'll then back up and shield you while the team infiltrates. Will it work for you?"

Ace studied the map. "I'd rather not hit the Tesla, but I'm going to punch the RV right and then back down this street. It's going to move the Musk mobile, but getting this done isn't about being delicate. And in this neighborhood, we already know who owns the expensive shit."

The detective smirked as he rolled his eyes. "That's what we have lawyers for. Let them fight out the scratches. But if you're backed into the cul-de-sac, how do you get out?"

Ace pointed at the map. "As soon as they stop shooting, I'm going to fill their driveway and the other side of the front yard. You can call Haul-a-wreck to get it. I don't have anyone who can strip it."

They heard the Archie cough and rumble to life. The tactical vans were never turned off.

Ace leaned his head out the window as he put the truck back in gear. "Tell Archie to give me about a block's time to pull it. I don't want him whining about denting his rig on my back bumper."

The man leaned his head toward his walkie-talkie. He blinked as he nodded and pointed down the street.

Ace smiled as he let out the clutch. *On the road again…*

OVERWATCH

NASH ROLLED her head toward Uncle. "You sure you didn't want to be out there having fun?"

He fiddled with his left braid and grumped as he watched the monitor. "Kicking ass isn't what it used to be." He pointed at the Archie taking the side of a house off. The roof cracked and followed the big black vehicle as the wall disappeared along with the fence. "There used to be finesse about how you kicked a door. Now it's all about not leaving the door standing. You kids are in such a hurry these days."

Laptops filled the extended conference table in the large computer room. Detective staff augmented the Deep Six staff running the active map. Slug and the boys had added a projector screen above the usual two-high monitor stack. Each computer station ran overwatch on their part of Southern California. Any area with an active assault or bunny bust was assigned to one of the crews and their backup detective. The lighting of the day was battle-station red. Even the screens were all dimmed to night vision levels. All the girls wore their own personal headphones and micro-phones, slaved to the earbuds in their detective's ear behind them at the table. The communications were soft and constant.

The ghost of a man dressed in a white coat over purple and white checked pants turned at the door to the glass office. He placed a small platter on the desk in front of Nash and Uncle. "You two need to keep your strength up."

Nash looked at the array of what could be canapes or fusion sushi. She wasn't sure, "What are we looking at, Chef?"

He smiled at the neophyte question. His open palm indicated the end closest to him. "You start here. This is the French end of canapes. We have blends of soft cheeses like brie paired with flora or plant base. You will find fresh fennel, roasted dandelion root, and blends of lavender, rose, and deadly nightshade. As you move down the board, delicate meats will lead you toward heartier cheeses and, finally, roadkill. Nothing has a Scoville rating above a standard salsa cruda or a cilantro salad with arugula."

Uncle leaned forward and picked up a piece at his end. "Road-kill? And you didn't lead with that?"

Chef closed his eyes as he sighed. "One usually starts with the subtler flavors and works up to the stronger so you can appreciate all the work... producing... He rolled his eyes. Oh, who am I kidding?" He glanced back at the war room. "With all these mouths to feed, I ordered it catered. Frank told me who to call, and I wanted someone else to taste test it."

Nash chuckled and studied Uncle's face as the man grabbed at his throat. "How's the heathen food, Indian?"

Uncle gave up the dying gag and leaned forward. Plucking one from the middle, he popped it into his mouth. "White man knows how to disguise the oil and gasoline on the roadkill. I give it two thumbs-up." He smiled at Chef. "Mmm, Costco Provolone. My favorite."

Nash chose one of the brie and lavender. "I'll make sure he gets all the deadly nightshade. We can bury him out in the desert or somewhere."

Chef smirked as his eyes crinkled in happiness. "Always an

auspicious time when you visit. And don't worry about Powder. She's helping me choose the right fish for dinner tonight."

Nash leaned to look around the man. "You're going to cook for all the…"

"Heavens no. The caterers will be back at six. You're going to be eating alfresco on the roof. It will be a small, intimate party of twelve. Dinner is at eight sharp. Rumor has it a certain young lady is going to produce the woman she has been seeing lately." He shivered his arms and fists. "It's extremely exciting. Even Tree hasn't met the mystery woman."

They all turned as Sweet Thing threw her arms and fists in the air as she squealed. "The winner." She spun around and stepped toward the older detective. She held her hand out in the air. The older man looked down the table—unsure how to respond.

A much younger female detective growled at him. "Don't be an ass, Broward. It's only a high-five. It's not like she's your subordinate or your great-granddaughter. She's not looking for a chest bump, just a slap of skin. Take the win, dude, or we're putting you back on the Alzheimer's meds." The line of detectives all held their hands out in the air.

Sweet Thing howled as she started slapping hands. "Ho yeah. Killin' it."

None of the detectives was going to point out that her section only had five locations circled and just one strong house.

Tree pointed Sweet Thing at Darlene's section. "They are getting ready to take down two strong houses simultaneously. Their street sweepers are also still working the spawn. Take your teammate into their field and work the White Mage magic."

The girl smiled. She looked at the man on the verge of retirement. "You ready for more ass-kicking, Bestie?"

He chuckled and held up his palm. She popped him a five and stepped back to her terminal. Hitting the lift on the keyboard desk, she re-engaged standing. "Where do you want us, Darlene? Andy and I are ready for raw meat."

The man behind her blushed. A detective next to him elbowed his arm and smiled.

———————

THE TWO MEN WALKED ALONG THE PIER. FISHERMEN lining the rails, changing their bait from day to night. The sun turned from golden to rusted orange. A dog beside the man sitting on a bench raised its head as the two men passed. Dice smiled at the languid dog and the old man, confused by the bait on his hook.

"Is that you in a few years?"

Frank burped a flutter of his lips. "Hardly. The coyotes kill one of them if it slows down too much. They might sleep sixteen hours a day, but when they're awake, they're working on getting fed."

Dice glanced back out along the pier. "Don't you feed them?"

"Sure." Frank scanned along the sidewalk at the end of the pier. He nudged his finger at the man's elbow and veered toward the northern rail. "When they get lazy, they go scratch at the shack's back door. Danny has a soft spot for them. He still gets a stiffy about hand-feeding a wild animal who lets him pet them and scratch behind their ears."

Dice folded his arms along the railing. "I thought you said he was a germaphobe?"

Frank snorted softly. His face rested in soft amusement, "He is. He just hasn't relaxed enough to realize the dogs have never had a bath, run around in the brush, and don't get shots. The day he does —he'll never touch them again. But it'll be too late."

"How so?" Dice nudged his chin up the beach, where the two kids made a deal.

Frank nodded at the dealers. "It'll break his heart. He'd never even have a goldfish for fear of its dying on him."

"Dogs die."

"And coyotes don't live as long as most dogs. I've already lost a couple. But he just sees the one in front of him. It keeps him going." They watched the sheriff's car come out of the side street, turn, and take aim at the kids. "We have one now. She's a mother twice over. But she still squirms and whimpers like a young pup when he steps out to throw her some steak."

"How old?"

Frank watched the kid on the stingray ride past the bust. The mop of curly hair flopped around as he stood and pedaled harder. "About five. She's got a couple more litters in her. She enjoys being a momma. If she's nursing, Danny feeds her." He rolled to lean sideways against the rail. "She's the one who is going to break Danny's heart. He's thirty-four, but she's everything to him. Her and work."

"He needs to get out more."

Frank looked down at his huaraches and the chipped pink nail polish. "Yeah. Something like." He looked up at Dice. "What about you? When are you going to wake up and kiss Tricia?"

"Hey guys."

They looked back at Felix, riding up to them on a wheelie.

Frank smirked. *Saved by the bell.* "Hey wonder boy. I'm assuming another successful deposit of a tracker?"

"Last one for the night. How has your day been going?"

Dice bounced his eyebrows. "We've watched twelve busts and the take-down of one of those crack houses."

Felix made a sound like a Model T car horn. "Thanks for playing. But they're called strong houses. No crack in this area. Crack is more a Los Angeles problem. The people here just buy their cocaine and roll it into their high-end bud rolls. But I'd still give you a B for effort."

Frank glanced at his dive watch. "Knocking off early?"

"Tree said we need to be home by seven to get cleaned up and ready for dinner on the roof. Chef said dinner would start exactly at eight. Something about a lobster in a thermos waits for no man."

Dice snickered. "Lobster thermos. This I want to see."

Frank groaned. "Thermador. Lobster Thermador."

Dice smirked. "Maybe. But these last few weeks tell me not to jump to conclusions."

——————

CHIPS PADDED HER WAY INTO THE AUTOPSY. HER EYES focused on the sheet of paper in her hand. She didn't look up. "Hey Oz?"

"What can we do for you, Chips?"

She still didn't look up. "What's the difference between a cadaver and a carcass?"

The two men snickered. "This is a carcass. The cadavers are in the cabinet."

The paper twitched. "So if you're working on the body, it's a carcass. But if it's in cold storage, it's a cadaver?"

She heard the whir of Mike's leg. She didn't move. His hand closed over the piece of paper. She finally let go but didn't look up.

"What are you doing with a blank piece of paper?"

She held up a pen. "To write information on."

Oz barked a laugh. "Okay, I'll bite."

"The open shell of a computer tower is a carcass. But today, when I was ordering, I called it a cadaver. The guy laughed and asked if I was an embalmer. I misheard him and thought he called me a bomber. It went downhill from there." She continued to look at her toes.

The large knife stopped an inch away from her chest. It slowly rose to under her chin. As it neared, she looked up at the large man with white hair and a mustache. His voice was not the usual booming instructor. If she had a grandfather, she'd want him to sound the same. "Nothing in here can or will hurt you. I know you are uncomfortable about the dead and bodies. I understand. But today, there is a lesson." He stepped aside to expose the large silverfish on the stainless-steel autopsy table he had been filleting. He used the large knife as a pointer. "The body of a dead animal is a carcass, the same as a dead computer, apparently." He moved the point toward the wall of large square doors. "Behind those doors is where we keep the people. Those are cadavers."

She smiled and moved closer. Placing her hand down flat on the table. She nudged her chin toward the fish. "Are you going to eat all that? Or do you need help?"

The two men had been caught. The chuckling started softly. Chips bounced her eyebrows as she turned and stepped to the door.

Mike turned, holding up the paper. "What about your paper?"

The pen flipped back through the air and landed at his feet. "It's for you to keep score the old-school way. I use computers."

He turned, gawping at Oz. Oz was pointing at the three items Chips had quietly left on the table. Mike leaned over and laughed at a large fishhook tied to a heavy sinker by a small spool of fishing line.

31

MARINA MAYHEM

THE DARK SUV swung heavily into the parking lot. The two inches of armor-plated glass tinted the windows a sallow green. A man in the backseat looked out over his designer dark glasses. They had cost him almost as much as his custom-tailored suit. The shirts he prided himself on ordering from the finest tailor in Hong Kong.

Three other black SUVs parked in a box formation around the man's. The thug with an MK-15 slung under his arm opened the door. His head pointed everywhere but at his boss. The cadre of muscle pouring out of the SUVs was heavily armed but not showing. This was to be discreet. This was the Estados Unidos de América. The most important marketplace in the world.

The man recognized and respected the location. Where the boats floating in the marina may only be worth a few hundred thousand, the people they represented were worth millions or more. The kind of people who have knowledge of people like himself but wish not to see them as a part of their lives.

His shoes were handmade by two brothers in Nuevo Croix. The one was missing his little finger. It didn't affect his skill at choosing or cutting the finest leathers available in the world. The man smiled at the slipper-like feel as the hippopotamus skin shoe over silk stockings touched the asphalt. He loved his petty pleasures—even when he was here on business.

With practiced ease, he smoothed down his hair plugs, adjusted his signature soft white Panama hat on his head, and tugged the front brim. He chose both with precision to conceal any signs of aging or imperfection.

His personal guard nodded at him before closing the heavy door behind him.

Ignacio dipped his head as they started down the walkway to the long dock. Eight other suits swarmed loosely around him.

"Hey. You can't park your cars like..." Two men in suits cut the man off. One shoved cash into his hand as the other man pointed down the parking lot toward the soon-to-open bar and restaurant.

Ignacio waited as two of his men boarded the yacht, one turning forward and the other clearing the way to the back deck.

Dorfman leaned around the corner from the back deck as he waved the half-naked woman to go to her stateroom. "Ignacio. What a pleasant surprise." The lie was as obvious as his orange spray-on tan.

The man drew off his dark glasses and Panama as he rounded the wall into the shade of the back deck. "I was in the neighborhood." His eye drooped as he matched the lie.

Dorfman held out his hand at a seat. "Come. What can I get you to drink?"

The man dropped his Panama on the low table. "I don't suppose you would have any quinine water?"

Dorfman looked at the man in the white ruffled shirt popular south of the border. The man shook his head. "Maybe some soda with a splash of Campari or lime?"

The head of the cartel drooped his eyes with a slight nod and a back wave of his hand. The tedium was exhausting. Even in their business, there were always courtesies of social protocol. One didn't just step into a business associate's house and shoot him. You worked up to it.

The muscles rippled along the back of the man, pouring the tall glass of club soda. His right hand picked up the bottle of Campari, and his left rubbed the lime peel around the rim of the glass. He poured a small circle of the red apéritif, and then, with both hands, he twisted the peel to spray the top of the soda. Turning, he stepped over and set the glass in front of the head of the most powerful drug cartel in Mexico.

The man sipped and nodded. Putting it back on the table, he leaned back and relaxed in the chair. "Tell me, Donald. I am hearing very disturbing reports of the local authorities moving against your distribution network."

"Ignacio. Ignacio. We went over this. They found our guys and the product. The deal went bad, and they're dead. Unfortunately, the product is in the hands of the local authorities, but we know where it is." He smiled. "It's a small town with an even smaller police department. It shouldn't be a problem getting it back." He smirked. "Maybe they also kept the money, and we can retrieve it as well."

The Mexican smiled softly. Naivete was still naivete. "Sometimes small towns can fool you. I would think twice before seriously moving against something appearing so small and simple." He held up his thumb and middle finger a couple of inches apart. "The deadliest scorpion, the Brazilian yellow, is only about this long. It can easily hide in your shoe. Or in your slippers by the bed."

The man sneered, thinking he was far from any scorpion. But then he knew the man in his salon was not the one who talked about death as an abstract. His face sobered. "I'll bear it in mind." Looking about, he cast his hand palm up about him. "But why speak of such dreary subjects? It's a beautiful day, and you have come all this way. To what do I owe this occasion?"

The bartender watched the shadow in the window facing the dock. His face reflected nothing. He had secured his trusted position a decade before.

Ignacio leaned forward. "Donald, the rumors I mentioned before…"

Dorfman hissed through his lips as his body jerked. His hand waved it aside in the air. "Little things happen every day. It is the nature of the business. My men will correct the problems, and then next week, there will be another problem. Some days, it is like herding chickens. Other days it is cats."

The face of the man from south of the border grew dark. He was running out of patience. "These rumors are no rumors. They are facts. Your Federales are taking your house apart, and it is not with a screwdriver or hammer."

Dorfman frowned and slowly rolled forward. "What are you saying?"

"I'm saying they are driving a train through your house. In days, you will have no more house to take care of."

Dorfman's face flushed red. "Bullshit. Where are you listening to such shit?"

The man in a tactical black jumpsuit and body armor stepped into the large doorway. "From us."

Behind him, others were holding shotguns and rifles on Dorfman's men. Another was stripping them of any weapons.

"Who the hell are you? How did you get on my boat?"

Ignacio waved his hand in front of his face. "These would be the Federales I was talking about." He placed his elbows on the back of the chair with his hands above his head. "I have diplomatic immunity. My passport is in my inner coat pocket."

The man in the black suit smirked. "Not today, Ignacio. Your government has disavowed their ties with you. Today, you are a criminal without a country." He chuckled once. "Or, in your case, an illegal alien with ties to massive amounts of Schedule 2 Drugs in a vehicle registered to you." He waved the man up. "Ignacio Ramirez, you are hereby arrested for drug trafficking with intent to distribute and sell. Because of your international status, you are suspected of narco-terrorism and, therefore, to be held in maximum federal custody without a chance of bail. You do not get a lawyer before questioning. You will be questioned under the articles of international terrorism laws. If you have questions, you can shove them up your ass."

As the officer cinched the handcuffs until the prisoner winced, he leaned in close to the man's ear. "Did you think we would let any harm come to our biggest informant?"

Ignacio's eyes ticked to the side. Looking at the officer's toothy smile.

As he pushed the cartel lord toward the door, the officers let him see a confused Dorfman standing there without cuffs. The swarthy face darkened even further, but he knew better than to say anything that might make matters worse.

The parade up the dock was a line of Mexican nationals led by a line of officers in black tactical jumpsuits and armor. Only one line smiled.

The bartender stepped away from the bar. "Finally. After all these years, I get my reward."

Dorfman turned from the deputy, confused. "What reward?"

The man smiled. "Donald Johnson Dorfman, you are under arrest for the trafficking of Schedule 2 and 3 Drugs. Anything you say can and will be held against you in a court of law. You have a right to an attorney. If you cannot afford one, we'll find some sleazy first-year kid to pick his nose in court for you. Do you understand your rights as I have explained them?"

Reality hit the man as his eyes grew large. "You're a cop?"

The man pulled out his badge he hadn't worn in seventeen years of undercover. He hung it in his breast pocket.

The blonde, now dressed in a blouse and slacks and looking ten years older, stepped up beside him. The bartender smiled and winked. They both knew their careers as undercover were over. "And by the way, I'd like you to meet Detective Second Class Tracy Ackerman. You'll get used to her proper voice during your trial. Evidently, she has a lot to say."

She growled, "Boys, let's take out the trash."

32

SHOOT-OUT

THE CENTIPEDE DANCED its staccato across the stone plaza. The surroundings pixelated and broke at the edge of the screen. Only the field of play was important. A manticore appeared at the far end of the courtyard. The yellow lion's body flowed up into the man's upper torso and face. It wore no other armor than a helmet. The arms hung long to the chest of the lion's body. The scorpion's tail curled to strike.

It waited for the centipede.

Chips dug her spoon into the bowl. They had run out of chocolate puffs and bananas. She was down to only fruity-O cereal with cut strawberries, raisins, and fresh blueberries. As she filled her mouth, she wished she had thought about also ordering the large Himalayan blackberries. She lazily chewed as she watched the centipede approach. *Tree should have never given me this power.*

She carefully put the bowl to one side, out of harm's way. Snickering, she took up the controller.

The centipede surged as it rose to enfold the manticore. The manticore froze under the flow of dozens of metal legs. As the head reached the upper body of the man, the arms snapped up and around the centipede. Just behind the head, where the inner workings or muscles were the most fragile.

The hands on the long arms met and locked in a steel clasp. The inner skin of the arms oozed back to expose the small rotating blades as they began eating their way through the steel armor of the centipede. Green ichor oozed from the carapace.

The centipede arched and drew in its fixed spear of a stinger. It jammed against the iron body of the lion's chest. Petey jerked and struck over and over with no penetration. Finally, the lion's rear claw rose, and the stabbing, serrated claws tore at the base of the spear, Shredding the meat until the spear fell away.

As the arms cut through the centipede's neck, Chips waited for the flying death to come around the tall building. *Come on, Slug. Come to mommy.*

The green drone swung around the building and rapidly closed the distance. Under the helmet, the manticore smiled. She had opted for enlarged canine teeth, only for the fun of it, and it cost her nothing in points.

Chips switched her side panel to targeting. She confirmed all the heat, sound, and vibration boxes stayed checked. Bending the manticore forward over the dead centipede, the large tube on its back was where she had spent eighty-seven percent of her armor and weapons credits. Two thousand infinitely splitting flechettes leaped from their home in search of the whining drone. By the first hundred feet, they were four thousand. In the next, they were eight in an ever-expanding cloud of homing death.

Chips glanced over where she had left her headphones. In one ear, she was sure it was Tree calling. In the other, it was the last death scream of Petey and Slug. She reached forward and set down her controller as she hit the enter key on her pink keyboard.

She sat back with her cereal as the two tombstones rose from the battlefield. The banner flapping in the windless air read: Girl Power, on every screen watching the morning game. The small yellow dialog box in the upper corner became a video. She clicked on the box, and it filled the screen. Seven from the girl's team were in the war room. Arms raised and dancing.

Chips chuckled from four hundred miles away. It felt strangely like home, even without the chocolate puffs and large blackberries. Life was good. She had noticed the score sheet posted on the wall over the coffeemaker.

THE ARCHIE PUSHED ASIDE THE COMPACT CAR PARKED IN front of the house. Spewing wads of dirt clods held together by the baked roots of ancient lawn, the Archie veered right and headed for the side of the pink stucco house.

The crash and ripping shattered the morning air. Shards of the desiccated boards, making what looked like a fence, shattered and flew over the black helmets behind the low brick wall. The small swat team was mostly Orange County Sheriff, with a special consultant.

Terracotta roof barrels shattered on the back of the armored machine as it roared into the backyard and flattened the rusted swing set. The backend slithered on the other garbage in the neglected space as the right end of the front blade clipped the small garage. The point of the nose sheared the back fence and tossed it into the air as the machine nosed into the cramped alleyway and the street at the end.

"Move, move, move!" The SWAT team, clad in all-black attire and heavy armor, rose as one and charged over the low wall where they had been taking cover. The living room was a chaotic mess of drugs, remnants of meals, and a few startled individuals.

An older man on the couch sprang up at the sight of the approaching squad. His crazed gaze scanned the group before settling on the largest member at the front. He aimed his rifle from hip level and opened fire, targeting the team member with the obvious white radio unit on his chest.

As bullets ripped through the fabric and armor alike, the large man raised his shotgun and fired back. The blast hit the older man in the chest, sending him flying backward onto the couch.

Amidst all this chaos, the woman let out a bloodcurdling scream as she grabbed a pistol from the table and fired it toward the shotgun-wielding man. The bullet tore through his leg, shredding his pants as it exited. The large man fell to the floor. Grabbing his leg.

But before anyone else could react, a rifle pressed against the woman's head. Her dark wig shifted slightly as the SWAT commander spoke calmly. The woman's hand trembled as she dropped her gun. The other two men were already mimicking a touchdown as they sank to their knees.

One officer leaned toward his microphone clipped to his shoulder. "Dispatch, we need a couple of ambulances at our location. We have two down. One is ours."

"Ten-four. We have two ambulances en route. Be advised ETAs are two and four minutes."

"Shit." He keyed his microphone. "I'm not sure these two have that long."

"Ten-four. Advise as needed."

The team hauled the three walking prisoners out to the waiting command van to be processed. Only the two men were in handcuffs. At the curb, a detective dressed in a white shirt and slacks pointed at the woman. "Take the woman to the other van. Keep her separated. I don't want them talking to each other." He looked back toward the shattered house. "Anybody else?"

The team member with the red Viking beard shook his head. "There was an old guy. But he caught a shotgun blast to his chest. He was probably dead before he hit the couch. Turner is looking at him now."

The lieutenant furled his lower lip and squinted one eye. "Okay. Well, get these two out of here. And keep them separated. No talking."

"Got it, lieutenant." He shoved the one prisoner forward toward the van.

The lieutenant moved toward the ripped-apart building. Two team members were bent over the one on the floor. "How's our guy?"

The blond looked up from the small mountains of bloody gauze and wadding. The lieutenant noted the careful wrap on the leg. "He got a through-and-through in his left thigh. It didn't catch the femoral artery... but the old guy stitched up his chest badly. How long out is the ambulance?"

The lieutenant shook his head. "Soon. But a dust-off would take longer. Even if they had a place to land." He pointed at the overhead power lines. "Just stay with him. He gets the first ride."

He swung toward the other medic on the team. "Turner. How's your guy?"

The young man stood and waved his hand at the man crumpled on the couch. "Check him for yourself, lieutenant. Dice hit him square in the chest with the shell."

They looked at the man's chest and face splattered with blood. "Did we get any photos?"

Turner looked at the detective. "I was just about to. Anything special you want?"

The detective smirked. "Make sure you get plenty in black and white before you move him. They always look good when they flash them on the six o'clock news." He turned. "Get plenty of gritty stills and video of Dice, especially as they load him. The news crews will be screaming for fresh blood. We kept them out of the loop this week, and they want my head."

Turner unstrapped his helmet as he pulled out his phone. "Got it chief. Circles and arrows on the back. With plenty of blood, gore, and veins between my teeth. I'm all over it."

The man on the couch chuckled.

THE BUBBLE-HEADED BLONDE WITH THE ON-FLEEK eyebrows and sparkling eyes looked into camera three. "An early morning raid ended in tragedy for one of Orange County's own. Fair warning, the video provided us is very graphic."

The grainy black-and-white video looked like body-cam footage. It showed two officers rolling over a fellow officer. The blood-soaked wads of gauze and wadding fell away to expose the shot-up chest. Just enough of the bloody wadding stuck to the uniform.

"Special Consulting Officer Diego Espinoza was pronounced dead at the scene. Known to his friends as Dice, he had only served with the Orange County Sheriff's Department for a brief time. But he made friends quickly."

The video changed to the sheriff caught in front of the court-house. "Dice was new to us but rapidly found a place in our department's hearts. Our thoughts and prayers go out to his mother and family in Los Angeles."

The blonde turned toward camera one. "Dice grew up in the East Los Angeles neighborhood of Boyle Heights. He attended Lincoln High and served in the Marine Corps with distinction."

Fast stock photos of the high school and what could pass for his Marine Corps graduation photo followed her quick recap of a man's life.

The cute blonde in a deputy's uniform turned off the television on the wall.

"Jeez. They barely even mentioned me."

Dice looked over at the man in the other bed. "Shut up, Ivan. You're dead."

His eyes lit up over his enormous smile. "Oh, and you are so much less dead?"

The blond narrowed her one eye at the former drug thug and growled, "Cut him some slack, Ivan. I put a hole through his leg. And I'm not beyond doing the same for you for all the shit you guys gave me over the year."

The man recoiled with mock horror and then started coughing. He held his chest.

Dice winced. "Sorry about the beanbag. But they told me you'd be wearing armor."

The blonde turned. "He was. But the light armor cracked because the beanbag was a blood load. They hit harder."

Ivan stopped coughing and groaned. "It still cracked three of my ribs." He looked at the woman. "I still liked you better as a barely legal beach bimbo."

She snorted. "I'll remember that when I spit on your grave." Turning, she rested her hand on Dice's chest. "Sorry about the leg, though. I hear those hurt."

The door cracked open, and Nash slipped into the room. "Getting blown up hurts worse. Shotgun to the face isn't so nice either."

Powder jumped up on the bed at the foot. She sniffed at the left leg.

Dice laughed. "Yeah, I'm hiding drugs in that leg."

The blonde looked at the tactical harness and then at Nash. "She must be yours. I'm Vickie Peterson."

"Nash Running Bear. And that's Powder. I don't know what she's looking for. Drugs, candy, or just another dead body... she does them all." She rested her hand on Dice's shoulder. "How's the dead guy?"

"Doing okay. What happens now?"

She looked over her shoulder at Ivan. "We split you two up. Ivan is ambulatory and, excluding the cracked ribs, can rest in a safe house wherever the Marshals consider safe or convenient. The District Attorney is taking a few days of videoed testimony." She turned back to Dice. "You, on the other hand, have some surgery to take care of first." She pointed at his leg.

Ivan rolled over and sat up. He leaned across with a sober look. His hand came out. "Thanks again. It was nice meeting you. But never shoot me again. Capisce?" They shook.

Dice nudged his chin. "Behave yourself, amigo. And have a nice, happy life."

The man smiled. "May yours be blessed as well." He rested his hand on the deputy's shoulder. "And seriously, I hope your life is long and full of happy babies. You already paid your asshole dues."

She smiled sadly. "Take care of yourself, Ivan. I'm going to miss you. You were one of the nice ones. I'm glad it turned out this way."

Nodding, Ivan looked at Nash. "Ready?"

33

RECOVER

THE LARGE COMPUTER room was back to its usual dimmed lighting. The same nine-thousand-foot pounds of light as in a men's club. Perfect for casual reading, but not strong enough to interfere with the computer screens.

Three of the terminals were in use. Baby's four screens held information on the bottom survey of the Mississippi River south of the Port of New Orleans. The lack of rain in Canada and northern states was affecting the bar separating the freshwater from the saltwater of the Gulf of Mexico. This situation affected shipping and drinking water in New Orleans. The city pulled its water from the Mississippi River itself. There was no escape to groundwater—which was too deep but also contaminated. The city, with one million residents and eighteen million tourists, had limited options to meet their needs, including the use of toilets. Desalination of the Gulf water or purification of wastewater.

One was a forty-one-billion-dollar water plant. The other was too repulsive to consider. The burden of finding an alternative to the city's dilemma fell on the small shoulders of the nineteen-year-old, Baby.

Sweet Thing and Mama were rescheduling the blasting and scraping of the lower Columbia River. The original dredging from Astoria to Portland and Vancouver, Washington, had been to lower the river bottom to forty-nine feet. But nobody had adjusted for the long-term drought affecting the Columbia and Snake Rivers. The effective net bottom was now only forty-six feet. Too shallow for the newer containerships.

<hr>

MING PULLED UP HER HELLO KITTY PAJAMA BOTTOMS over her knees. The cotton rolls were already between her toes. She smirked at the giant man seated in front of her feet. "Get used to it. This is what you'll be doing if you have daughters."

Dice growled. "Don't be so certain."

Ming rolled her head and peeked past Muna and Jazz. "Frankie?"

The man snorted as Tree carefully drew the stroke of pink to the end of his nail, "Yes, dear. Anything you say, dear."

Ming giggled, "Definitive answer?"

Tree hummed, "I have his foot in my hand. It's the only answer he's allowed to make."

Felix glanced up from Nash's nails' clear polish. "Suck it up, cupcake. This is the life you live until you die."

Nash chuckled. "He already died two weeks ago."

Felix pointed his knuckle at her. "Good point." He looked at the large man, now bending to his work. "How are the scabs?"

"They itch. They didn't, but then you had to mention them." He rolled his shoulder under his sweatshirt.

Ming rolled her eyes. "That's the softest sweatshirt we could get. Just don't bleed on it. It's a bitch to get out of the seal's face."

Dice glanced up. "I don't have any tattoos under the seal's nose. I checked. Besides, the scabs oozing are on my back."

Frank grumped, "Oozing is good. It helps draw the ink out of the lower derma. And the sooner you're a blank slate, the sooner we can send you off. How about the new nose and cheeks?"

"I'm getting used to them. It surprised me how the narrowed nose didn't restrict my breathing. It's the hollowed cheeks and Indian cheekbones I'm finding harder to get used to in the mirror." He glanced down the line at Nash.

"How come your nose and cheeks aren't this narrow, Nash?"

Nash rolled her head in the rooftop's sunshine. Her orange-tinted aviators sparkled. "I'm Paiute. It's a plain tribe—mostly the southwest. You should have studied it in the third book. We are softer-featured, with thicker noses and cheeks, except for the Apache. They get more of their features from the Mayan and Aztecs. Hawk noses and more defined features. You'll learn. We don't all look alike. Even Mexico is split. The West Coast got a lot of Chinese features, such as the moon-face and epicanthic fold. But all over the East Coast are the Mayans and Aztecs. Even mixing with the Spaniards didn't change the features. The Iberian Penin-sula has much of the same features as the originals of Latin America."

"But the braids…?"

"It's a personal thing. You don't have to. Many don't. Some of the younger kids think the braids make them look more like a First Nation. Others, like Uncle and me, have a personal connection. For us, we have walked our spirit walk. You? You are living yours. The changes you are making are enormous. In many ways, they are beyond even an arduous spirit journey. You are leaving everything you were—even your culture and identity. You take only the heart inside and become something new."

Jazz glanced up from Muna's feet. "Papillon." She smiled wonky at the man larger than her. "It's French for butterfly. When a cater-pillar goes into a chrysalis, it has one set of organs and a distinct body. When it comes out, the only organs that are the same are the heart and lungs. The transformation even changes the brain. It doesn't remember crawling; it only knows how to fly free."

Ming tapped him on the top of his head. "At times, from here on out, you'll feel like it's only you. But remember, we were privileged enough to be here inside your chrysalis to watch and help in the transformation."

Frank bent forward to look at his fresh paint job. "Just remember, once you're in Witness Protection, none of this is in your life anymore."

Dice peered down at Frank. "That's the part I'm having the most difficulty with. This." He held his hand out at all of them. A drop of pink splattered on Jazz's leather pants.

"Hey. Watch the splatter, rookie."

Dice blushed. "Sorry."

Frank harrumphed. "Not to call you out in front of a bunch of women… but have you thought more about Tricia? You've been dead for more than a week. Oh, and your funeral was pleasant. A lot of tears."

Dice barked a single laugh. "I heard you just walked to the end of the pier and tossed the soup can of ashes into the ocean."

Ming frowned. "Hey. We take ocean pollution seriously around here."

He looked up sheepishly. "No ashes?"

She shook her head.

Tree laughed. "No can. The reflective shine is extremely attractive to large fish. Even a great white can't pass a gallon can."

Ming tapped the top of his head. "Tricia?"

His eyes were damp. "I hadn't asked. And now…? I'm dead."

Muna shifted in her seat. "Men." She raised her phone to her ear. "Oh hi, Tricia. We were wondering about the question of the century. What? What is the question? Well, how would you feel about disappearing with Dice for the rest of your life?" She studied the man's face for horror.

"It's not that simple."

Nash nodded. "No. No, it isn't. But it can be."

He frowned. "¿Que?"

"I know you don't have any family left…"

He nodded.

"How about her? I mean, her husband is dead…"

He slowly shook his head. "I don't know. They never mentioned any."

Muna thumbed through her phone. "Tricia Rhinehart… um… whatever the last name is."

Dice chuckled, "It's Polish Slovak. It means the broken stump in the middle of a frozen river."

Muna snorted wetly. "No, it does not." She turned back to her phone. "Husband died eight years ago. Mother passed… ouch… when she was… um… seventeen. No mention of her father or any siblings." She watched the man studying what appeared to be his inner soul. "From here, it's looking easier and easier." She held her thumb close to her phone—ready to dial.

"But she doesn't know I'm alive."

Frank raised an eyebrow at Dice. "The question is, do you want her to?"

———

THE WALLS OF THE SMALL ROOM WERE UNADORNED steel. Welds ran the length of the corners from the steel ceiling to the steel floor in the unadorned steel walls of the small room. The steel table stood solidly welded to the floor. Only the small glass in the door was a reprieve from the constant flow of raw, gray steel.

The orange jumpsuit contained just enough wool to make the fabric prickly. A trick the Department of Homeland had found helpful in Guantánamo. The tiny pricks combined with the Caribbean heat had created its own torture on a group used to heat. But dry heat.

The two men opened the door. The one in the gray suit, heavy-rimmed glasses, and a floppy head of curly hair lead with the thin folder. A thicker and much older man in a dark suit followed.

"Where the hell is my lawyer?" Dorfman's tongue played at his parched lips.

Felix pulled out the chair and quietly sat. He carefully opened the folder as he watched Dorfman. He waited. The buzz in his ear was not audible to anyone else in the room.

He looked up. "Hal nabda?" His Arabic was as practiced as Nash could prepare him for.

Dorfman frowned at the words. "What?"

"Hal tumaris aljins mae almaeizi?" Felix could hear Nash and Muna snickering in his earwig as he stumbled off the script.

"You just asked him if he fucked goats... or sheep. One of those. Switch to German."

Dorfman leaned back, rattling the chain connecting his handcuffs through the ring welded to the table. "I don't know what the fuck you're saying. I want my lawyer."

"Vielleicht versuchen wir es mit Deutsch."

The man's face turned redder as he searched for help from the man standing in the corner's shadow. "Oh, for fuck's sake. Who the hell are you, and what are you saying?"

Felix leaned forward and looked through the bottom of his glasses while keeping the glasses and the hidden camera pointed at Dorfman. His accent was his worst Hollywood German, stolen from years of watching old black-and-white movies. "It sez here, you are German but prefer to speak Arabic. Zis is not so?"

"No. I'm an American. Who the fuck are you guys?"

"We are viz Interpol. We interview you terrorists."

"I'm not a terrorist. I'm just a drug dealer. How do you get terrorist from drugs?"

Nash clapped her hand once. "Bang. He admits to the drugs, and he has answered twice without asking for his lawyer. Go for the submarines smuggling, Felix."

Felix deadpanned the man as he studied the face. Slowly leaning forward again, he studied the purposely printed tiny typewritten in gibberish. "It says here you have many submarines you used to smuggle terrorists into the United States of America."

"Drugs. Only drugs. No terrorists. I never smuggled terrorists. Only drugs. Do you understand the word drugs? Weed, dope, fentanyl, speed, heroin, drugs...? Do you understand any of this?"

Felix didn't move as his eyes moved from the paper to the man's face.

"Drugs. Nothing more. No people." He ran his dry tongue over his parched lips. "It's all a witch hunt. They want my boss, Ignacio, not me. I'm a nobody." He fell back against the chair. "I am so fucked. Where are we, anyway? Are we even in the United States?"

Felix eased back and finally glanced at the man in the corner. "Genug?"

Nash laughed at the Yiddish word every butcher asked his patron. "Yes, Felix. We got enough. Let the agent from Interpol work him over."

Nodding, the tall blond in the interrogation room flicked his hand toward the door. Felix stood. "Maybe you can talk sense into this one before we send him to Guantánamo. I need a tall glass of water."

Dorfman whined. "Water. Yes. I want some water."

Felix ground his head around to stare at the pleading man in the orange jumpsuit. "Water is only for those who cooperate with what we want to know. Tell us where the bomb is, and maybe I get zom for you."

"Bomb? I don't know shit about any bombs. I'm only a drug dealer."

"Yez. You have zed as much. But how beeg a drug dealer?" Felix held his finger and thumb an inch apart. "A leetle peanut? Or maybe you are..." He held his hand as if he was holding a basketball.

Dorfman sighed with exhaustion. "Bigger. Much bigger." His head fell to the tabletop. "Much fucking bigger."

Felix turned at the door. "Very good, Mister Dorfman. Now we are getting somewhere. Admitting you are the problem is the first step to your recovery."

The man from Washington D.C. sat down and adjusted his thick, black-framed glasses. "Now, Mister Dorfman, let's talk about Ignacio Ramirez's cartel. I believe you stated you have intimate knowledge of his operation..."

GOING HOME

THE BUILDING WAS QUIET. Only the occasional grunt of Pussy wrangling the large kegs of beer into the coolers drifted back to the office. The morning meeting had been small, as many of the deputies were required to attend the arraignments of all the drug dealers they had busted. They all knew most of the young corner bunnies would get their charges tossed, but then what were they going to do? Everyone up their supply line was in the same location they were.

The six cases of long-necked bottles rattled as Pussy tipped the dolly up in the hallway. She slipped off the gloves. They were more for handling all the cold products than protection from blisters. Tricia looked up at the unusual placement of the beer as Pussy eased around the doorjamb and dropped into the seat across from her.

"Don't tell me you're tired. You've barely thrown more than a thousand pounds of beer. Not to speak of every floor out there is glowing like you just waxed it." She waited for the snappy comeback that had become Pussy's response to Tricia's lefthanded compliments on her work.

"Almost done. Pushing fifty is getting harder than pushing beer."

The woman leaned forward with her elbows on her knees. Her head hung, looking at the floor.

Tricia stuck the pencil in the ledger and flipped it closed. "What's really on your mind?"

"Dice."

Tricia swallowed. Opened her mouth and then closed it. She looked at the top of the woman's faux hawk. It needed some touchup tint. Maybe mix some red tips in with the blue. Fourth of July would be upon them before they knew it. She drew in a slow breath through her nose. "I miss him too."

Pussy sat up and leaned back—her head back against the wall. The poster of the enormous wave hung above. The white line carved by the surfer pointed to the left side of her hair. "Where do you call home?"

"San Diego..." Tricia leaned back in the squeaking chair. Her hands rested in her lap. The right thumb picked at the start of a hangnail on the other. "Why?"

The momentary smirk pulled at the left side of Pussy's mouth. "What part?"

"It's called North Park. We lived a couple of blocks from where Pershing Drive came out of the park. It was quiet, and we could walk to the zoo or do any sports at the center."

"Do you go back?"

Tricia turned and hung her right leg on the corner of the desk. She studied her foot. "Shortly after Flaco and I got married. It was supposed to be a Sunday dinner and meeting the family. Mom took one look at Flaco and slammed the door on us. When she was alive, she worked with Mexicans, we shopped at the Mercado, and many of the people at our church were Latino. I never heard her say one nasty thing about them, much less calling my husband that slur. It didn't matter that he wasn't Latino." She winced and looked over. "We never went back."

"Is she still alive?"

Tricia shrugged. "I don't much care." She twisted her shoe to see the side. "Nobody ever came looking for me to tell me she had left me her five left socks and a twenty-nine-year-old car. So, I would guess she's still pissing in her pot. Why?"

"Any other family?"

She slowly wove her head around. "All I ever had was Flaco and Dice. We never even hung out with any of the rest of their team. They weren't like the other guys. Dice would come over, and we would go down to the tide pools off La Jolla. Or we'd go up to the hills and go hiking. There are some areas on Pendleton where they would let the spouses hike. It was like having two great big nine-year-olds or a couple of giant puppies. Those big goofy white ones with all the fur." She held her hand out higher than the desk.

"Huskies?"

Tricia smiled and snorted. "Those would work too. And those big fluffy ones for the snow." She held her hands like claws near her throat. "The ones with the little barrels of rum or something."

Pussy laughed. "Saint Bernard."

Tricia pointed at her. "Yeah. That one. They just bounced from one thing to the next. Always excited. Everything was new and fun for them. With them..." Her voice trailed off. "After Flaco was killed..."

Pussy nodded. "And Dice wasn't around?"

"No. They had split up the teams. I think Dice went to the sandbox. But we lost touch. It felt... Half of my heart was broken."

"And when he showed up here...?"

Pussy could see the wet in the eyes. Tricia wiped them on the back of her hand and passed the heel of her thumb across her nose. "I thought my life was back. I thought the other man I loved... maybe we could make a life together...?"

Pussy gently rocked her head forward. "So you loved him too?"

Tricia licked her lips with just the pink tip of her tongue as she nodded. The tear was silent as it split her cheek. She sniffed.

"Did you ever tell him how you felt?"

Tricia sniffed wetly. "I never got the chance."

"He was sleeping on your couch."

The woman howled like a preteen as she held her hands out. "I know. I was stupid. And now all I've been thinking about is if I had only told him, maybe he wouldn't have gone on that bust." She looked at Pussy. The tears were streaming down both cheeks. "Why did they need him? He's not a cop."

The voice was deep, with a little gravel stuck in the throat, "Because it was the only way I could die publicly."

Tricia's eyes flew open as she looked at Pussy. "Did you hear that?"

Pussy ground her head back and forth as she smirked and stood. "I don't hear a thing. There's beer to throw, and I think I'll just let you make peace with your ghosts." She turned at the door. "But whatever you choose to do, know there are those of us who love you just the way you are. And it's been great having you in the family." She rolled out into the hallway. Grabbing her gloves, she tipped the stack of beer back on the dolly and smiled. "She's all yours."

ALSO BY BAER CHARLTON

The Very Littlest Dragon: NEW Editions
(All-new full-color ebook, a paperback with
coloring pages, and a full-color Collector's Edition hardback)

Stoneheart — Pulitzer Nominee 2015
Angel Flights
What About Marsha?
Pirate's Patch
Flat Surf

I Drink Coffee and Make Shit Up
One Writer's Journey Without Signposts

JOLIE "ROCKET" ROBERTS SERIES
Dry Bridge of Vengeance – Book One
Dry Ridge of Redemption – Book Two

THORNY WALLACE SERIES
Death in the Valley – Book One
Light to Light – Book Two

SOUTHSIDE HOOKER SERIES
Death on a Dime – Book One
Night Vision – Book Two
Unbidden Garden – Book Three
Boomtown – Book Four
One Day Under the Grass – Book Five
Southside Hooker Series: Books 1–5 Box Set
(Collector's Edition hardback & ebook available)

ABOUT THE AUTHOR

Bestselling author Baer Charlton graduated from UC Irvine with a degree in Social Anthropology, monkeyed around for a while, and then proceeded onward with a life of global travel, multi-disciplinary adventure, and meeting the memorable array of characters he would come to describe in his writing. He has ridden things with gears, engines, and sails, and made things with wood, leather, and metal. He has been stitched back together more times than the average hockey team; his long-suffering wife and an assortment of cats and dogs have nursed him back to health after each surgery.

Baer knows a lot about many things in this world. History flows through his veins and pours out of him at the slightest provocation. Do not ask him what you may think is a simple question unless you have the time to hear a fascinating story.

You can find more at
www.mordantmedia.com